DEBIT FUND
A NOVEL BY
DEREK SCHREURS

This book is a work of fiction. The characters, names, incidents, dialogue, and plot are the products of the author's imagination or are used fictitiously. Any resemblance to actual persons or events is purely coincidental.

October 2005

Note for Librarians: A cataloguing record for this book is available from Library and Archives Canada at www.collectionscanada.ca/amicus/index-e.html
ISBN 1-4120-7661-7

Printed in Victoria, BC, Canada. Printed on paper with minimum 30% recycled fibre. Trafford's print shop runs on "green energy" from solar, wind and other environmentally-friendly power sources.

TRAFFORD
PUBLISHING™

Offices in Canada, USA, Ireland and UK
This book was published *on-demand* in cooperation with Trafford Publishing. On-demand publishing is a unique process and service of making a book available for retail sale to the public taking advantage of on-demand manufacturing and Internet marketing. On-demand publishing includes promotions, retail sales, manufacturing, order fulfilment, accounting and collecting royalties on behalf of the author.

Book sales for North America and international:
Trafford Publishing, 6E–2333 Government St.,
Victoria, BC v8t 4p4 CANADA
phone 250 383 6864 (toll-free 1 888 232 4444)
fax 250 383 6804; email to orders@trafford.com
Book sales in Europe:
Trafford Publishing (uk) Limited, 9 Park End Street, 2nd Floor
Oxford, UK ox1 1hh UNITED KINGDOM
phone 44 (0)1865 722 113 (local rate 0845 230 9601)
facsimile 44 (0)1865 722 868; info.uk@trafford.com
Order online at:
trafford.com/05-2556

10 9 8 7 6 5 4

Acknowledgements

This was a project of immense satisfaction to me. I started with the idea that I wanted to write a novel as a challenge. To test my skills: writing, logic, and most of all patience. I ended the journey with what has become a passion. I hope you enjoy reading the story as much as I enjoyed writing it.

I found out early on in the process of planning the book, learning writing techniques, and then eventually the writing that a novel is not as solitary a task as I was led to believe. Although the long hours of writing, re-writing, editing and struggling with the plot were spent in isolation; numerous family, friends, and others provided invaluable input.

Special thanks to Kathy for transcribing the hasty dictation created while I was away on business trips. To Joanne, Agatha, Anne (sisters) and Judy (in-law) who read the rough draft and were kind enough to provide much needed direction. For all of my friends who listened with varying degrees of interest as I progressed though the book to completion. Thanks to Ellen who supplied her significant editing talents.

And especially to my wife Lynn and my children, Matthew and Jennifer, who were with me every step of the way. Thanks for your encouragement and patience.

This edition includes corrections to the glaring typographical errors and logic problems that were so graciously pointed out to me by those first readers of the original run of books. Thanks, I tried to get them all.....

DNS

July 8, 2006

P.S. – (About the author) - Derek Schreurs lives in Kamloops, British Columbia where he works as a Chartered Accountant.

This book is dedicated to the memory of my mother, Maria, and my sister, Agatha. Their strength was beyond words.

Chapter 1

"Greed Kills."

The sign hung above the door of Andrew Dalton's thirtieth floor office at the corner of Union and Pine in downtown San Francisco. It was given to him as a gift, a reminder of what he did for a living. Andrew was taught early on that people make decisions for two reasons—fear or greed. In the end, though, it always came down to greed—the fear was in missing out.

Andrew saw through the façade created by the tall glass spires of the financial district as he watched the white-collar army running the economy. Greed oozed from the interiors of plush offices in edifices dotting the skyline of corporate America where lawyers and bankers hunted for more tricks to turn and executives hid questionable deals from unsuspecting shareholders. Added to this mix were insurance men skimming premiums off the top and stockbrokers peddling their wares.

Scattered throughout this steel and glass labyrinth were the scorekeepers—the accountants—whose gilded reputations had been sullied recently by scandals of complacency and manipulation. Greed had poisoned them, too. Increasing shareholder return meant firm growth, and firm growth meant higher fees. Eventually, the false fronts of these propped-up businesses would come crashing down, taking innocent investors down with them.

Accountants were hearing rumors that they were less trusted than lawyers. That stung. It definitely wasn't a good time to be an accountant. Accounting bodies throughout the world reacted to the slander. A few misguided pirates would not be allowed to damage what was otherwise an honorable profession dedicated to principles of fairness and integrity. Rules were changed and memberships brought in line.

Despite the growing resentment, Andrew Dalton loved the job he knew he was destined to do since that first day his dad let him cash out the family business. He was no run-of-the-mill accountant— he was a numbers detective. His area of expertise was forensic accounting; he was trained to uncover companies' misdeeds. Andrew had a logic-driven mind and he thrived in his world.

Frank Tanner poked his head through the doorway. "Time to quit. The problem will solve itself with fresh eyes in the morning." Andrew's boss was always offering his protégé snippets of advice.

"I know, but I'm almost there and want to keep the trail hot." Andrew knew he would have to work late into the night, despite the advice, and Frank did, too.

"We'll be lucky to recover on this one, so I hate to see my star player wasting hours trying to finish."

"Recovery or not, it has to be done. No sense giving it to a junior who will crank more hours into a losing cause. Why is it so tight, anyway?"

Frank sighed. "Jackson Meats was just hit with the mad-cow scare, so their beef sales have dried up in the past six weeks. If they don't get a strong injection of capital soon, they'll be teats-up, so to speak, and we'll be out our fee."

"Cute." Andrew smiled at his mentor's play on words. He stood up and stretched his Outward Bound physique. His Hong Kong-ordered shirt was wrinkled from the fourteen-hour day spent delving into the file.

"Did you find anything?" Frank asked.

Forensic accounting was like looking for a single blade of grass in a freshly mowed lawn; you scour through tons of paper, looking for unusual patterns and oddities in the accounting, hoping to solve the mystery behind the numbers. Clients paid a fortune for the service, but when successful, the results uncovered illegal schemes, embezzlers, faulty computer systems, and crooked management. Andrew had a few famous wins under his belt, which helped build his reputation.

Andrew rubbed his strained, steel-blue eyes and grinned. An innocent dimple disguised his seriousness.

"It has to be the controller. I'm certain he has a couple of dummy supplier companies set up. I should be able to track it by midnight. But that isn't the issue. I've discovered a pattern of errors that needs to be reviewed. It has nothing to do with the fraud, but something weird is going on."

Frank Tanner was the senior partner at Brooks and Steiner, Andrew's employer for the past four years. His Charles Bronson glare disguised the fact that he was an icon in the field of forensics. He was a no-nonsense leader who ran a tight ship.

"Business is business. Finishing the job is getting it eighty percent right and hammering out a satisfactory conclusion to this file. If it's the controller, wrap up the report and close the file. I need you on more pressing engagements. Jackson will most likely be a bad debt anyway."

After Frank left, Andrew spent the next few hours cleaning up the file and putting together the case to expose the controller. Wrapping up at just after one o'clock in the morning, he was the last to leave. This was not an unusual event. As a rising star at Brooks and Steiner, he was well on his way to becoming the youngest partner ever appointed at the firm.

Andrew had entered the accounting profession knowing he wanted to do something to change the world—not the typical motivation of a bean counter. Formerly known as 'Andy', he officially became 'Andrew' when he turned eighteen and left his island home to attend university. Four years later, with a business degree from Stanford in hand, he began at Brooks and Steiner as a first year grunt. Doing all the difficult jobs, he soon developed a reputation as a problem-solver. Interested in the advisory side of the firm, he was soon enticed by Frank Tanner into forensic accounting. As Frank had promised, the work proved to be challenging and interesting. Working in forensics with his mentor was a feather in Andrew's cap. Long before certain accounting scandals caused massive corporate bankruptcies, Andrew saw firsthand how bad reporting could be used to manipulate events and cause people to make decisions they normally would avoid.

The Daltons owned a small hardware store that served the needs of a local island community on Mercer Island in western Washington State. They supplied the hardware and lumber to the construction industry and brought in pretty much anything that was needed or requested by the locals. James Dalton was a fastidious business owner who accounted for every penny. The daily, monthly, and annual reports were meticulously stored in the back room of the store. When the island became a popular retreat for the rich families of Seattle and the population steadily increased, his business boomed. After a couple of years, James Dalton needed to expand and went to the bank for financing. Although anxious to lend him the money, the banker told James the business didn't have enough equity. Determined, James took in a partner—a summer resident he had come to know, who owned several businesses in Seattle. After the expansion, the partner insisted that Dalton spend more time minding the store and less time number crunching. "Let the bookkeepers do the grunt work," he insisted.

The business was expanded, sales went up and expenses appeared to go down. Despite the apparent boom, however, there never seemed to be enough cash. Before meeting his partner, Frank Dalton had always paid his bills, but he no longer handled the trade creditors who, it seemed, weren't being paid. The business was forced into Chapter Eleven, creditor protection. James Dalton never did get the full story. The monthly reports he received had been manipulated. At the end of each year, the losses were explained away by year-end adjustments and one-time right-offs. The profits evaporated into management fees and administration charges. James Dalton complained to his partner, who assured him that the adjustments saved tax and that the profits were safely set aside, away from the creditors. The money was never forthcoming, however, and after a couple of years, Andrew's dad put the experience behind him and started over.

Driving along Battery Street, Andrew made his way to the apartment he used to share with his ex-girlfriend, Dana, in the renovated area along the Embarcadero of San Francisco's Fisherman's Wharf. The apartment held far too many memories of their three-year relationship, but he had decided to stay there anyway.

He settled himself on the couch with his evening elixir, an ice-cold Corona, and pressed the remote to CNBC. He stared blindly at the screen as the late evening reporter droned on. "…if approved, the recently announced merger between Swiftshop of Belgium and SuperMart will make the latter the world's largest grocery chain in terms of both sales and employees. Despite the Federal government pushing for harsher anti-combine laws, there has been a flurry of major acquisitions by ASC and other conglomerates in the past several months."

Andrew thought about the report he had just wrapped up, wondering if the merger might help Jackson Meats, a major supplier to SuperMart. If vindicated, management would be able to convince the company's bankers to capitalize their losses. With new markets opening up through SuperMart in Europe, they may just survive. It would depend on the controller's reaction.

As the television droned in the background, Andrew thought about the error pattern Frank had told him to forget. It was unusual, he thought, and the company had made no mention of the anomaly in the planning stages of the engagement. Something was wrong. It didn't really matter if it had something to do with the internal theft. They already had enough to convict the controller. The job was done. *It was probably just an accounting error anyway*, he thought, as he drifted off to sleep.

Chapter 2

The bullpen lay in darkness, except for a single light in one of the hundreds of workstations on the twenty-third floor of SuperMart's head office. What was normally a beehive of activity during the day was now eerily quiet, the silence broken only by the soft tapping of computer keys midway down the third row of cubicles. A lone employee, anxiously hunched over her computer screen, looked up every few minutes to glance furtively down the aisle. The incandescent bulb from the banker's light hanging over her station cast a long, dark shadow past her workstation. The woman was not prone to working late hours, but the circumstances demanded her attention.

Muriel Anderson stared intently at her screen, relieved to have only the small bulb from the lamp illuminating her station. The fluorescent lights that beamed down from the ceiling day in and day out gave her headaches. After a third review of the payables summary, she was convinced the problem she had discovered was real. It was the third incident in a week where amounts did not reconcile. Even though she was getting old and couldn't quite keep pace with the rigors of the job, her attention to detail was seldom ill-placed. She had discovered a serious problem and it needed to be addressed.

But after thirty years with the grocery chain and with her retirement only a few months a way, the last thing she wanted to do was jeopardize her anticipated life of relaxation and solitude. While she wanted to forget what was staring back at her on the screen, Muriel had no choice but to report her findings. The activity she was observing could cause serious problems. The new owners of SuperMart might even withhold her pension if it was later determined that she hadn't mentioned the problem. And Muriel needed the security of her pension. She had her mom to take care of at Whispering Pines, a senior's care facility, and she wanted to travel a bit. Scrolling to her internal email, she began to type the memo detailing her findings.

The next day, Bob Craft, Manager of Accounting and Administration at SuperMart, stared at Muriel's email from behind horned-rimmed glasses of questionable vintage. He had assumed his position six months before the company had been gobbled up in the merger, and couldn't wait to leave. And now this. Muriel Anderson had a way of making his life miserable. *What the hell is this?* he thought, as he scrolled down the memo, trying to decipher the lengthy column of numbers. He gave up and reluctantly called Muriel into his office.

"There is a system mistake. If we don't fix it now, who knows what sort of problems we'll have to deal with later," Muriel explained as best as she could. Bob Craft was the last in an endless list of professional accountants she had worked for, each one less competent then the last. She wondered if they had learned anything at all in business school.

Bob sighed. *This woman could find a mistake on a blank piece of paper,* he thought. *Why him?* "I'll get the computer folks to look into the glitch."

"I have three months to go before I retire, Bob, and I don't want to be blamed. This "glitch," as you call it, is not random. Something is going on and I don't want to be held responsible."

"It's not your problem."

Muriel stood up. "Maybe not, but if you don't get it fixed, I'll make it my problem."

After Muriel left his office, Bob sat back in his chair and stared at the screen. *What was going on?* He had been told to expect inconsistencies in the daily reports. "Ignore them," the compliance team of ASC, the new parent company, had directed.

SuperMart used to be a good place to work. When he started with the company it was a regional grocery chain. The founder's grandson, Charles Gates III—Charlie— took control in 1989. Under his guidance, the company had mushroomed into a firm employing 220,000 nationwide and was still growing. Charlie provided what his box store competitors could not do—spectacular customer service. With its great prices and service, the small western chain became the largest grocery chain in the country. The stature and profitability of the company were too good to pass up. Leveraged buy-out hawks circled overhead for years. Eventually, American Services Corp (ASC) swooped down to acquire the business. The ASC offer was the talk of Wall Street, catapulting Charlie into the Fortune 500 top ten richest Americans.

ASC didn't do anything slowly. Within days, the computer systems and internal controls were altered to match the stringent requirements of head office. A legion of computer techies spread across the country to modify and connect the SuperMart mainframes to ASC's central command. Then came the directives—new forms, procedures, demands and controls. The local level accounting departments were relegated to performing the mundane tasks. The planning and strategy sessions dried up. Bob's masterfully designed internal procedures manual became irrelevant—eight years of effort made useless in a day. Then came the strange requests. Unknown head office controllers started asking for insignificant reports about specific stores, regional summaries, and recently, to squelch the 601B reconciliation until further notice. When Bob refused to comply with this request, citing that it destroyed the integrity of the entire department, they threatened to expose his indiscretions.

It wasn't that Bob's trips to Las Vegas weren't for business. He had just padded his expense account to cover some small gambling losses. He knew he would end up giving them what they wanted. He hoped to be gone soon, but a negative reference would destroy his career. Besides, the errors were small.

Bob picked up the phone and dialed. He indicated Muriel as the source of the report and fed it into his shredder.

Muriel set the groceries down and went back and locked her door. It was a decent neighborhood, but you could never be too careful. Leaving out the pot roast for dinner, Muriel put away her groceries and then sat down to peruse the bill. Even though it was a cash register tape from her employer, she always checked to make sure there were no extra charges. She had never found errors. At the checkout, she would look intently while her groceries were scanned. Old habits die hard.

After adding the column of numbers four times, Muriel knew something was wrong. She checked the taxes, the bottle returns and the discounts. They were all correct, but the tape still didn't add up. No doubt the buffoons from ASC had screwed up the retail computer system. She set the till tape aside to bring into work in the morning.

The pot roast looked great when she set it on top of the stove. Her mother would enjoy the leftovers on the weekend. Opening the oven to put in the roast, Muriel lit the burner.

The explosion blew out the windows and walls of the apartment. A small packet of accelerant tucked inside the oven fed the fire as it consumed everything in its path. Within minutes, the apartment complex was fully ablaze, all evidence of the explosion having disappeared in the rubble.

Chapter 3

Andrew paused from working on his file, took off his onyx-framed glasses and stood up and stretched. Walking over to the window, he looked beyond his tired reflection and saw an ambulance race down the street forty-three stories below. *Unlike other professionals such as doctors, firemen and air traffic controllers, accountants never have to rush out and save lives,* he thought. Their job is to pick up the pieces and measure them after the real work gets done. But Andrew knew that if he were inattentive to details, his mistakes could affect people's lives. He could potentially be responsible for lost jobs or people being laid off as faceless corporations downsized and rationalized to improve profits. He knew his work prevented these things from happening. He knew that uncovering corporate scandals saved companies and jobs that could potentially be lost to executive greed.

"We're not white knights," he once told Dana, "but it is satisfying to see the countless hours and effort bear fruit."

He thought of Dana now as he continued to stare at the city lights. She would always reply with some demand for chivalry. "Go forth and save a fair maiden today, but try and make it home for dinner." He had rarely made it home on time, as his career always took precedent, sealing the coffin with one more nail each time. Soon these conversations in his head would stop, but for now it was the closest he came to absolution for losing the love of his life.

The clock on the edge of his desk flashed 2:30 a.m. as Andrew sat down at his desk to shut down his computer and leave for the night. He buzzed Josh Young, his best friend at the firm, a Brigham Young grad. Josh was one of the securities specialists at the firm who worked beyond human hours to help raise funds for corporate America. Or, in his words, "to impress the partners in the irrational drive to the top of the ladder."

"What's keeping you here so late?" Josh asked as they entered the elevator for the two-minute plunge to the bottom of their steel and glass tower.

"Alberton's Produce Corp. Some sort of rush job. Frank was insistent that I drop everything and jump right in. Whatever is happening over there has management completely in a panic. They're being acquired by a large Los Angeles- based grower. The purchaser's internal audit team is coming in to review their books, so their golden parachutes may not open like they planned if they don't look squeaky clean."

"And you're going home this early," Josh teased, as he followed Andrew out of the elevator.

"Man cannot live on coffee and Fig Newton's alone. I'm heading for Mabel's for a power breakfast, and then I'm coming back to wrap up the audit strategy."

Mabel's was a twenty-four-hour-a-day breakfast place down the street from the office—a home-away-from-home for the staff at Brooks and Steiner. Street dwellers came into the greasy spoon with just enough money to buy a cup of coffee and stay warm for a half-hour. Mabel never kicked them out. The homeless who littered Union Street could stay for thirty minutes for the price of a cup of coffee. That was her small token of charity.

Josh loved Mabel's. It was like going home without the hysterics of his overbearing mother.

"I'll join you. My girlfriend will be off nightshift at five o'clock, so I have a few hours to kill. Then I'll head over to Mercy Hospital and surprise her." Josh ran to catch up.

"Hey, Mabel. Two coffees." Josh waved at the friendly proprietor as he swung his lanky frame into the tight Naugahyde booth.

"Sure thing, sweet cheeks," was the reply. "How about a couple pieces of bumble berry pie?"

"No, thanks. I have to meet Grace at five o'clock. But make the coffee strong. I'll need the energy."

Andrew was famished and his blood sugar was low after skipping two meals. "I'll have a piece, Mabel," he yelled as she went into the kitchen.

Mabel was a rough and dirty restaurateur who had become an institution in downtown San Francisco. She had been there as long as anyone could remember. She knew everyone in the business district—and more secrets than anyone should in a lifetime. The food was great and the charity cases had their own section near the front, so it was the place to come to fuel up during an all-nighter at the office.

"So, what do you think the big deal is?"

Andrew had his suspicions, but he wanted to get further into the files before he speculated on the problem. "It's probably a greedy manager wanting to cash in on the pending sale."

"I don't think so. The urgency means something bigger. You'd better get your documentation straight, protect the audit trail. You don't want to be the collateral damage of a takeover gone sour."

Andrew laughed. "Thanks, Josh. I'll make sure the ledgers don't turn on me."

After breakfast, the two associates parted. Andrew went back to the office and worked until six a.m., having settled on a plan of attack for the day at Alberton's.

By noon the next day, Andrew was rested and showered and making his way on I-5 to Alberton's head office in Oakland. Thirty minutes later, he was sitting across from the controller, asking to review the most recent receivables listing and bank deposits. After a brief lecture about confidentiality, he was set up in a windowless room at the end of the warehouse next to the shipping ramp. He didn't know why the in-house bean counters treated him like he worked for the IRS.

Andrew grabbed a coffee and started with a review of the company's internal procedures manual, one of the first steps in a forensic audit. By two o'clock, he was exhausted and thirsty. He had examined six months of transactions but still hadn't found the source of the panic. Packing up the hard copy ledgers, he went to the computer centre and gained access with the keycard provided by the raven-haired receptionist he thought resembled Dana.

After getting a much needed sugar fix from the vending machine, he parked himself in front of the terminal, typed his temporary password on the keyboard and entered the deposits program. Accessing the weekly deposits, he traced the two streams of data for sales and receipts. Within a few minutes, the first anomaly caught his eye. A payment from SuperMart was short by ninety cents.

Then he found several more payments that were short fifty cents each. The errors drew a soft whistle as he found several others shortages before stopping for the day. The discrepancies were familiar, the same problem he had seen at Jackson Meats. Both companies had differences in the payments coming from SuperMart. In total, there were three-dozen anomalies over a forty-eight-hour period.

He packed up his laptop he left the dingy backroom at Alberton's, intent on wrapping up his report at the office. He would follow up directly with SuperMart the next day. Maybe they could shed some light on the problem.

Time to go home for a much needed rest.

Four hours after hitting the pillow, Andrew dragged himself out of bed after a rude awakening from his alarm. A quick shower, followed by a power shake, he then made his way across town to his office. Within minutes of settling into his desk, he checked the Jackson Meats file to confirm his suspicions. Then he made a phone call.

Three hours later, he parked his BMW in a visitor parking space at the offices of SuperMart. Bob Craft, the company's accounting manager, was not very cooperative on the phone but had agreed to see if he could help Andrew unravel the puzzle. Bob, a diminutive, meticulously dressed worm, sat across the desk and stared at Andrew through tiny, wired-rimmed glasses. Andrew sensed that Bob didn't appreciate the intrusion.

Bob stared at the fit, young accountant sitting across from him. *At least he is pleasing to the eye.*

"....just a few days of reports to compare and I will be on my way."

Bob wasn't really listening to what Andrew was saying. "Sure, sure, whatever. As you know, we have thousands of suppliers and pay countless invoices each month. Why are you so worried about a few minor differences?" Bob asked, not really wanting a response. The tragic loss of one of his clerks had left him short, and he certainly didn't need this—what did he say he was?—forensic accountant upsetting his routine.

"It isn't the amount as much as the trend. We really appreciate your help. Alberton's is in the midst of a merger and time is crucial. The same problem occurred at Jackson Meats, my last assignment, although we wrapped that one up before investigating the issue further."

Bob reviewed the list of purchases handed to him and picked up the phone. After speaking for a few minutes, he gently laid the handset into its cradle. The two spoke banally about the Oakland A's game the prior evening as they waited for the reports to arrive. Andrew wasn't a baseball fan, but knew how to bullshit, an art he had perfected while working the charity circuit with Dana. Several minutes later, a clerk arrived with the printout of the payments in question. Bob explained that all payments made by SuperMart were routed through Electronic Data Interchange, or EDI. No check was required; just a bank routing number of the supplier. Once approved, each payment was tagged with an identifying number and disbursed electronically.

Andrew was very familiar with electronic commerce, but let the manager explain the system anyway. He had learned early on in his career that it paid to let an accountant talk. After looking over the report and comparing it to the printout from Alberton's system, it was clear that the payment made through EDI matched the invoice. But the deposit received by Alberton's was different.

"Do you know which system has the correct payment?" Andrew explained his dilemma, hoping for a logical explanation from the SuperMart accountant.

"It seems our numbers agree," Bob Craft replied.

"That's right." Andrew stared at the accountant.

"Maybe you should check with their bank." Bob stood up, signaling an end to the meeting.

The audit trail had just turned cold.

After the auditor left, Bob picked up his phone. The internal security watchdogs from the parent company had demanded his eyes and ears. After Bob described the odd meeting, the voice on the other end of the phone told Bob to inform him immediately if anything else occurred.

Chapter 4

American Services Corp had humble beginnings in the early 1970s. William van Holder, a gangly, pimple-faced computer science grad, designed data tracking software for the airline industry to monitor its passenger lists and flight schedules. The software was complex, and it took all the computing power of the behemoth Cray machines to function.

Van Holder spent three years with Gemini, the world leader of scheduling software, before he and two other programmers left to start their own company. They recognized the enormous potential of data tracking software. It was a time when computer science grads everywhere wanted to control the fruits of their labors. They set up shop in a Bay area industrial park and hung out a sign over the warehouse space they rented, announcing that American Services Corp was open for business. Hundreds of start-ups—all staffed by the bright minds coming out of Berkley, Stanford and UCLA— cropped up everywhere in the area, later dubbed the Silicon Valley.

ASC's big break came when it designed a financial tracking program for Capital West, a regional bank. ASC had anticipated the benefit a bank would have over its competitors if they could provide immediate, real-time acknowledgement of available funds in an account. Thus, VisiTrack was born. Contrary to other software developers of the time, ASC maintained control over the software. Van Holder licensed its use to the bank, thereby retaining ownership of the program and allowing ASC to market the software to the rest of the banking community.

VisiTrack would eventually become the platform that spawned the international tracking software running on virtually all ATMs and debit card machines. ASC servers and databases controlled the transactions, earning a fee from each swipe. Although VisiTrack made the three partners very wealthy, van Holder, who was convinced he was sole reason for its success, wanted complete control of the company. The shareholder agreement guaranteed that all the shares of ASC went to van Holder in the event of his partners' deaths. The power of this control was intoxicating. He forced out Michael Stern, his best friend from college, after it was discovered that he liked having sex with under-aged prostitutes. Shortly afterwards, the exposed Michael Stern jumped off the Golden Gate to his death. Van Holder's other partner, Thomas Frank, died in a boating accident in Mexico.

Over the next twenty years, the company expanded into every facet of the economy. With its enormous wealth, ASC acquired oil wells, refineries, lumber mills, chains of building supply stores, steel producers, and construction companies. It was a feeding frenzy. Van Holder's highly-focused, predatory style became legendary, and he wore his success like a badge, playing host to world leaders and business tycoons at his whim. He controlled lives and destroyed them for his own enjoyment. All facets of his empire were controlled at ASC headquarters in Newark, New Jersey, close to the financing barons of Wall Street and Manhattan. Even when every joker with a software program was becoming a paper billionaire on the stock exchange, ASC remained a private company. With its legitimate presence in the financial markets, the company could raise all the capital it needed. Van Holder was one of the richest men in the world and maintained draconian control over his company.

"I can't believe you let this happen," van Holder growled, unable to control his anger. His steely grey eyes bore a hole in the fidgety man seated across from him.

"We weren't ready to launch yet," the man across the desk replied defensively. "This "test" could raise suspicions that cannot be explained away as a computer malfunction. It wasn't supposed to be networked to our mainframe. The researchers ran the program for 36 hours before we realized it was live."

The researchers worked at the Centre for Strategic Analysis (CSA), an economic think tank financed by van Holder who had immediately recognized the need to develop a private research facility to study globalization. He didn't regret any of the millions he and others had poured into Alex Jacobson's brain trust. The information had helped American industry—and ASC in particular—remain in the forefront, despite the weakening of the U.S. economy.

Van Holder calmed down after his brief tirade. "Thankfully, our man reacted the way he did. These accounting clerks have a way of wanting everything to balance to the penny. The software shouldn't have been run."

"There's another problem," the visitor added. He didn't want to extend this conversation any longer, but suppressing the second problem would only exacerbate the situation.

"What else?" Van Holder stared outside at the heavy rain hitting the canopy covering the entrance to his office. He hated failures.

"The beta test went through the supplier program, extending it outside the SuperMart internal systems. Once it's activated, it can't be stopped." The man proceeded to explain the details of the model and its independence once activated. "It should run its course in ten days, after which it's designed to shut down, having obtained the relevant data from the test."

"Do whatever it takes, but fix it," van Holder ordered before dismissing the man.

Van Holder knew something his visitor did not. Something had to be done fast to protect his plan, the Amsterdam Protocol.

In a server array in the basement of the SuperMart headquarters, the virus waited. Like a soldier in a foxhole, it reacted only when commanded, doing only what it was ordered to do. When the instruction finally came, it wormed its way into the mainstream of Alberton's network. Piggy-backing on top of a utility function, it arrived a nanosecond after being activated. When the time came, the code attacked. When finished, the virus returned again to its dormant state, leaving no trace after it had completed its run.

Chapter 5

Catherine Demitrikov was the head of internal security at ASC. Sitting cross- legged at her desk the silk skirt she wore rode high up her thigh as she leaned across the maple desk to hang up the phone. As she brushed the silky strands of hair away from her face, her slender finger touched the small scar at the side of her temple, a mere inch from her dark Siberian eyes.

Her department was responsible for neutralizing all breaches in corporate privacy. The manipulation of the test model through the SuperMart computer network fell squarely into that category. Like everything else that happened in her life, Catherine took her job very seriously.

Before meeting van Holder, she was the station chief in Mexico for the new Russian Intelligence. She also performed freelance work, if circumstances permitted. The spy game was not like it used to be before the fall of communism. Mexico was far more exotic, more stimulating, and in particular, warmer than her home town 500 kilometers east of Moscow. She had left for Moscow as soon as she could leave the communal farm located near Gorky. Her parents urged her to find a better life than they had endured through decades of Communist rule.

Discovered while illegally selling Levi's, she had fought off three militiamen before being subdued with a stun gun. The commandant of the local police force knew he had found talent when he heard both sides of the story. The bruised militiamen tried their best to downplay the event, but Catherine persisted. The commandant called his cousin at the KGB, and eighteen hours later Catherine found herself on a bus heading east to begin basic training at the KGB training facility at Vologda, Siberia. After a winter and spring at the camp, Catherine had been taught everything there was to know about survival and killing. She was ready to join the ranks of the spy agency.

Her first assignment was to monitor a low-level mole at the Embassy in the American sector of Berlin. Her mission was to find out how the west was reacting to an increasingly popular uprising, which eventually led to the collapse of the wall and defeat of communism. She accomplished her assignment with a mix of creative espionage and spirited sensuality, ensuring the orderly withdrawal of numerous East German Stasi assets before the end. Thanks to her, the mole was never discovered, and Catherine eventually received a more favorable assignment—the embassy in Mexico.

By the time she set up shop in Acapulco, communism in Eastern Europe had all but disintegrated and the KGB had reorganized with less money and fewer demands. To make up for the reduced expense reimbursements, she turned to freelance work to make ends meet. Champagne and caviar didn't come cheap.

As she sat staring out at the open air atrium of the ASC central office, she recalled the assignment that led to her introduction to van Holder. After a year of drug hits and business extortions, her Mexican contact provided the details of an easy mark with an exorbitant fee attached. His name was Thomas Frank, a wealthy American who had come to Acapulco to attend meetings. She would relish the assignment. It was always the same: the stalking, the chance meeting, the intimacy and then the finale. She had followed the routine many times before.

After following her mark the first day, she arranged a meeting at a restaurant near his hotel. Sitting adjacent to him, she struck up a conversation after asking for a match to light her small cigar. Her braless, loose-fitting blouse and short, flowing skirt made it all the easier. By nightfall, they were holding hands and walking along the beach. To ensure Thomas' full attention, she would make it the best night of his life. Giving her target a last night of pleasure gave her more enjoyment for the task at hand. Before they parted company, she arranged to go fishing with him the next day.

To ensure the boat captain would not be making the trip, Catherine left him bound and gagged in his boathouse prior to Thomas' arrival. The thought of spending the whole day alone together made it easy for Catherine to convince the American that the captain had probably slept in. She was an expert seaman, so taking the boat for the day would not pose a problem. Once they were out of sight from land, Catherine approached Thomas from behind and wrapped her arms around his waist before reaching up and breaking his neck. He died instantly, falling to the deck of the boat. Catherine steered the boat up the coastline to a rocky point north of town. Gunning the engine, she jumped from the stern before it crashed into the rocks. Being a strong swimmer, she easily swam away from the treacherous surf.

After a hot shower and a meal, she went to check her Swiss account. Only half the fee she had requested for her services had been deposited. Livid, she tracked down her Mexican contact and threatened to cut off his balls if he didn't tell her who had ordered the hit. When she set out on a mission, Catherine was the most focused KGB agent trained by Moscow. *The bastard who cheated me will soon learn,* she thought as she made her way across the border at El Paso, Texas. She planned her attack during the flight to San Jose, intent on killing the man who had ordered his partner's death.

Arriving at the reception area properly attired in a light blue business suit, her dark hair falling over her shoulders, she asked for van Holder.

"Do you have an appointment?" The receptionist enquired.

Catherine replied in a soft, silky tone, practiced to elicit a caring response. "I'm sorry to arrive like this. I'm with the Mexican government. I'm afraid I have some bad news about Mr. van Holder's partner." She paused for a moment. "He was killed in a boating accident yesterday and because of Mr. van Holder's position, my government insisted that I fly here and tell him in person."

"Oh, my God!" the receptionist exclaimed, holding her hand to her mouth. "I'll get him immediately." In her haste to inform her boss of the sad news, she tripped over the edge of the Persian rug adorning the entrance to his office.

Catherine observed her surroundings with a trained eye; instinctively searching out exit points should anything go wrong. She was impressed with the opulent surroundings and saw that her prey had a taste for the rare and valuable. It would be a shame, but she was not about to be cheated by anyone, especially since it was obvious why her talents had been engaged. She followed the receptionist through the door, not bothering to wait behind in the foyer.

"Ms. Demitrikov, it is indeed a pleasure to meet you." Van Holder dismissed his secretary and stood up, coming around his desk to shake her hand and offer her a drink. "Tequila on the rocks, I believe."

Catherine Demitrikov was stunned. Seldom were her instincts thrown in disarray. "The pleasure may soon be mine," she replied.

"Don't be surprised. Your reaction was predictable. After all, we agreed on a fee."

"Then where is it?" Catherine demanded.

"The rest of the agreed fee has been wired to your account. It was not my intention to screw you, figuratively speaking, but I wanted to ensure we met."

Catherine settled into a chair next to the bar. *Why not hear him out?* she thought. She had her money; the killing would be just for spite. "You have me in a difficult position. You seem to know so much about me, but I know nothing about you."

"We can discuss me later. For now, I have a proposition. My organization needs someone with your particular talents. You come highly recommended, as your actions in Mexico reflect. Pick your own team. The work will be very challenging."

She never looked back.

As Catherine gazed at the African masks adorning her office walls, she formulated a plan. It was necessary to deflect the discrepancies away from the compromised computer program. Their programmer at CSA had done a great job adding the necessary code without the foundation researchers knowing someone had tampered with their program. She had one other loose end to tighten.

Chapter 6

The morning sun was peeking through the clouds as Dana McLeod drove over the Golden Gate Bridge. She blew a strand of hair away from her eyes and chuckled, remembering a comment her goddaughter had made the last time her best friend from back East had visited. "Clouds are just water and fluff, you know, Aunty Dana."

Dampness clung to the hood of her Audi A6, attesting to the dreariness of the day. Arriving at the parking lot, Dana wheeled into a vacant spot and dodged several large puddles on her way to the front door of the sprawling complex.

Dana was an integral part of a team that focused on worldwide competition at the Centre for Strategic Analysis (CSA), a research foundation that delved into all areas deemed essential to the strength of the United States economy. What was deemed essential was determined by a board of directors made up of a who's who of the American corporate and academic elite. The CSA was the pre-eminent think tank in the country and employed the brightest minds in the areas of computing, finance, trade, political science and engineering. The official mission of the CSA was to better America's relations in the international community, to foster free trade and encourage the growth of regional industry and education—in other words, support the global village. Whenever it felt a need—provided American interests were properly compensated—the Foundation would release a sample of its findings, a token to assist the downtrodden of the world (like monsoon stricken rice farmers in Bangladesh; or draught ridden cattle producers in Chile) in improving their yields. This gave the Foundation good press and would ensure their talent pool was well stocked. The vast amount of their research, however, was doled out to a select few who controlled the purse strings.

Dana joined CSA out of Stanford. Although the other two candidates she beat out for the job had published more articles during their post-graduate work, Dana had hit a nerve with her thesis paper entitled 'The Automation of Commerce in the Global Hinterland,' a hard-hitting exposé of America's control over third world commerce. The head of CSA had decided he wanted her, and made sure she was chosen by the selection committee. He was struck by the intensity in Dana's eyes, her air of refined confidence and only marginally by the possible access to her dad's money.

Today she needed to speak with Harry Compton, the Foundation's quintessential computer geek. A genius with an IQ of one-sixty, Harry had started with CSA the same year as Dana. Allergic to hard labor and religion, he rarely left his computer terminal and cared little for the lofty ideals of his current employer. As if summoned by her thoughts, Harry came through the door, a Starbuck's latté in each hand. Dana accepted the latté and raised the cup in a toast before taking a sip from the leak-proof lid.

"How is the food industry integration study coming?" Harry asked.

"The trend analysis is excellent." Dana was happy she had an undergrad degree in computer science. At the time, it had seemed like the wrong direction, but had since proven essential to her research.

"Have you flowed the charts through the mainframe yet?" Harry found any excuse to strike up a conversation with the raven haired beauty.

"I was just about to, but I think I know the answer already. Western Europe, U.S. and South America have all seen a significant increase in corporate merger activity. Five years ago, there were over half a million mid level food suppliers globally. Today that number is below one hundred thousand. Based on my logarithmic study of the industry, there may be as few as thirty thousand a decade from now."

"Interesting," Harry said, not paying much attention. He stared politely at Dana, enjoying the passionate gleam in her eyes as she spoke.

"Hopefully, our study won't fall on deaf ears. The Global Trade Commission (GTC) will be anxious to hear about these stats. The next round of talks in September will be in Amsterdam, right? Governments come and go, philosophies wax and wane, but the pursuit of profit never changes." Dana said.

"Who are *they*? Harry asked.

"The GTC was put into place to allow governments to make decisions that changed long-term corporate strategies, to protect a free trade system they really don't understand."

"All this work is so the Global Trade Commission can make sure big business doesn't take over the world?" Harry queried.

"Exactly." Dana knew her study was iron clad, but realized she would spend the next three months checking and rechecking her assumptions and final results. Alex Jacobson, the founder of CSA, had spent his life building commercial ideals in a world of corporate greed and malfeasance. Sitting alone in her office day after day, Dana reviewed her work, trying to help her mentor meet his impossible goals. She would need to do more and was already getting butterflies about having to present her findings at the upcoming conference.

"Why is Alex is so paranoid about this meeting in Amsterdam?" Harry asked.

"This was the first big test proving the Foundation's theory," she explained. "The database led us to three major companies buying up the producers. By using phony corporate structures and having investment firms front the deals, the food producers still think they are dealing with numerous suppliers for each product. But the same few owners are really the ones pulling the strings."

"So what? Fewer owners, what difference does that make?" Harry spent so much time at his terminal that he often didn't grasp events in the real world.

"Fewer owners mean fewer competitors, and fewer competitors mean higher prices. It's a classic case of an oligopoly, where several companies control an entire market. CSA's mandate is to promote a level playing field in global commerce. The research we do is supposed to go to governments and trade bodies to prevent these things from happening. The isolationists in Congress are bent on tightening the access to the U.S. markets, everything CSA is trying to avoid." Without realizing it, Dana was beginning to sound like her mentor, Alex, as she laid the groundwork for her speech in Amsterdam.

"Review the computer model with me one more time." Dana continued her explanation. "We feed in the names of all the relevant corporate directors, shareholders, managers, plant locations and shipping details that our transport research people provide. By matching names with places and products, we're able to form relationships between the various entities, tying them together either as co-owners or joint suppliers. The computer model uses a correlation test, links each bit of information, and then applies a probability ratio to the relationship; speculating on the possibility of commonly owned business. Using output from the computer model, the field team makes enquires and visits sites to confirm or refute the findings. So far, the model has proven 96 percent accurate."

Dana handed Harry a stack of documents to feed into the computer model. He stole a glance at Dana as he gathered up the information for the final testing. Harry had a crush on her, but who wouldn't? She was smart, rich and good-looking. Her shoulder-length, raven hair was tied back in a ponytail, highlighting her high cheekbones and sensual lips. Her piercing green eyes were the most beautiful he had ever seen.

Dana kept herself in shape by working out at the gym four times a week, despite the rigors of work.

"See me at the end of the day and let me know what happens," Dana called out as Harry disappeared down the corridor."

CSA was abuzz with the initial success of what was becoming known as the McLeod Model. Numerous teams were finding ways to keep on top of the myriad of mergers and acquisitions, but the results from Dana's model were far superior to anything else designed to date. If her model caught the attention of the GTC, it would be used as the platform to study all industry groups, giving the Foundation tremendous influence on Capital Hill to ensure the continuation of global competitiveness.

It took until the end of the next day, but finally Dana and Harry met to review the latest tests. Apparently, their tests had caught the attention of several companies they were researching. That wasn't supposed to happen. The program ran in the background, away from the day-to-day computer functioning of the target companies.

Phone calls were made and Dana was asked to explain her in depth queries to the affected companies. Alex insisted that CSA remain above reproach. If they thought the Foundation was spying to gain market advantage, he would make sure the suspicions were addressed; even if it meant ignoring important information.

"What do you think?" Dana asked.

"It's nothing," Harry assured her. "I'll track the study to the source and rewrite the code."

"I'm still surprised these companies feel they can get away with their subterfuge," Dana mumbled.

She had joined the Centre for Strategic Analysis with strong ideals, but had recently begun to question the integrity of the Foundation and its affiliates. She hoped they weren't also playing these elaborate games to control the markets.

"It doesn't seem right. I plan on doing everything in my power to protect the legitimate, hardworking businessmen who are the real backbone to the global economy. The research being done should surely stop, or at least ensure full disclosure of, the nefarious consolidations now taking place," Dana said emphatically.

"You're a true social warrior," Harry replied, suddenly irritated by Dana's idealistic attitude. "I'll get it fixed."

Harry was a computer geek. The outcome of the research held no interest for him. He had no lofty ideals when he joined CSA. He was just a damn good programmer who appreciated the unlimited resources at his disposal—and the challenge of building smart software. His program was the best. It was the reason the 'McLeod Model', or as he liked to call it, 'The Dana and Harry Show,' worked at all.

Harry smiled at the screen as he made the required changes to ensure the program performed as was expected by *his* employer.

Dana sat across the huge desk from Alex Jacobson. Moisture formed on the nape of her neck as she waited anxiously for her boss to conclude his telephone conversation. When he hung up the phone, Alex stared at his protégé, his hollow eyes giving her his full attention.

"It isn't exactly the model I had hoped for" Dana began. "The field reports didn't come in as expected, and . . ."

"And that can't be good," Alex interrupted calmly. "What happened?" Alex had survived by being able to diffuse panic situations and restore confidence in his harried researchers.

Dana explained the problem with the tests. She was beside herself about the model. "It wasn't supposed to integrate with the individual networks."

"This model will prove extremely useful as the Foundation moves forward...if these problems can be fixed."

Alex considered the impact as he gazed at the mist hanging over the gardens surrounding the campus. He had built this Foundation to meet the needs of its benefactors. It had made him a very powerful man, but he wielded his power cautiously, knowing it would last only as long as his successes. The CSA didn't always have the seemingly unlimited resources presently on display around the complex. It wasn't until 1995, when several key businessmen threw their support in the ring, that Alex had been able to realize his dreams. It didn't come free either, and over the years he had had to compromise many of his objectives to satisfy the whims of his benefactors.

Information was crucial in meeting the global challenges of competition. Looking over the sprawling complex of buildings he had built over the past twenty years, he picked up the phone and dialed his chief benefactor to seek advice about the damage his program may have caused.

Chapter 7

Andrew took the long weekend off, leaving town just after lunch to avoid the brunt of the weekend traffic that would soon clog the exit arteries. Ramping onto the I-5, Andrew floored his BMW, turned up the music and headed north.

He couldn't help remembering the last time he had gone home with Dana. She had finally pried him away from the office for a long weekend and he had spent the entire time on his cell phone, while Dana enjoyed a pleasant time with his parents. On the drive back, they had had one of their many fights about commitment.

His relationship with Dana McLeod had started out strong four years earlier. It had been love at first sight, and they quickly became inseparable. He was completing his CPA designation and she was just starting her Masters in Strategic Studies. She had cast aside her striking looks and privileged life as a third generation member of an East Coast shipping family, opting instead to achieve success using only her raw intelligence. They had met at a student fundraiser for Eastern Europe refugees. Andrew wasn't enthusiastic about attending, but his best friend was a socially conscious art major out to save the world and insisted it was the most important thing in the world to do. So he went along. The McLeod family was hosting the fundraising event. Dana wasn't all that committed to the cause, but since her grandfather had come from Bulgaria and she lived on the West Coast, she had felt obligated to play hostess on behalf of the family.

Watching Andrew as he entered the room, Dana immediately recognized a fellow non-committed attendee. She made her way over to the handsome loner who was nursing a drink, looking totally out of place in the midst of the socially conscious crowd. Sidling next to him, she began talking about something other than the fundraiser cause. They talked well into the night and agreed to continue the conversation over dinner the next evening. Andrew impressed Dana more with his focus and direction than with his wit and sophistication. Within a month, they had moved in together. Both pursued their careers with blind determination, each ready to forego the many sights and activities of the Bay area to improve their employment positions.

The relationship trouble started over an insignificant event—a sailing regatta that Dana had wanted to attend. Andrew needed to work that weekend.

"The Cabot audit came in and I promised Jim I'd have it planned out by Monday." It was Andrew's fourth year at Brooks and Steiner and he didn't want to let anyone down.

"I'm going with or without you," Dana informed him.

"We'll go down to the Wharf for seafood tonight."

"You'll miss a great time." Dana had a miserable time, despite the excitement of the race.

During any typical workweek, they spent a lot of time traveling to and from work, and preparing for their hectic days. (Dana worked in Sausalito, Andrew near Telegraph Hill.) On the weekends and holidays, one or both of them were usually busy working on a project. Dinners were seldom shared on weeknights, and when they were one or both of them would return to their respective offices.

The final Christmas together, traveling east to visit Dana's parents was the beginning of the end. It was supposed to be a great start to a ten-day vacation.

"You'll love my parents," Dana said. "The time away will help us get back to the days when no one else mattered but us."

A usual, she was right. Her parents were wonderful. The Eastern winter co-operated and the two of them had a great time touring the sites of Boston. But on Thursday of the first week, Andrew received an urgent call and flew back to San Francisco, intending to catch a red-eye back the next night. He didn't get back for three days, and missed Christmas dinner. After that, the relationship turned sour. Dana moved into a Milltown apartment vacated by her family's West Coast manager. At first, they agreed to stay in touch, but work consumed the hours, and weeks turned into months.

Andrew shook the thoughts from his mind as he pulled off I-5 at an all-night SuperMart and stocked up on supplies for the weekend. He stopped briefly outside of Eureka and then Portland, arriving at the ferry slip to Whidbey Island just before dawn on

Saturday. He would stop in at his folks' beachfront home in the morning before spending the rest of the weekend at the family cabin. While waiting for the first ferry to arrive, Andrew stole a few hours of sleep. The sound of the ship's horn was deafening, awakening him and everything else sleeping near the pier.

Leaving the ferry, Andrew wound his way through the quiet streets and pulled into the driveway of his boyhood home in time for an early breakfast. He quietly opened the back door. His parents were already in the kitchen, the aroma of coffee strong in the air.

"Hey, sport!" his dad exclaimed as Andrew put down his bag and hugged his mom. Thrilled to see her son, Freda Dalton returned the hug and kissed him on the cheek.

"Hey, sweetie. Here for awhile?" his mom asked.

"Just the weekend. I wanted to get away to the cabin. Work has been crazy and I wanted some peace and quiet. But I have to get back by Tuesday to start a new project, one that has everyone baffled."

"Still on track for Partner?" his father queried.

"They announce in the fall." Andrew saw the pride in his father's eyes and knew now why he had come home. He needed assurance that all the effort was worth it.

"Why don't you stay here? The cabin is drafty. Besides, you can help your father fix the porch."

"Let me see…two days of peace and solitude or 48 hours of back-breaking, gut- wrenching work. How can I refuse?" He feigned agony, but was grateful for the offer. The cabin had seemed like a great escape, but it also held a lot of memories. It was one of his and Dana's getaways, when they used to do that sort of thing. They joked about 'roughing it' at the cabin like pioneers for a few days before heading north to the McLeod family's 10,000-square-foot chalet at Whistler; British Columbia's jet set ski resort.

The SuperMart receipt fell out of the bag into the trunk as he was getting the groceries for his mom. As he went to grab it, the bag of groceries almost dumped, so he left it in the trunk. After the groceries were put away, he grabbed a cup of coffee and headed outside.

Andrew had worked every summer with his dad, even after he lost the business and the family had to start over (except in his senior year, when he spent six weeks with Outward Bound, learning survival skills he never did use.) He had always enjoyed being his dad's assistant. Although he rarely used the skills he had acquired during his summer 'apprenticeships', he could still handle a hammer and crowbar like a pro.

By Sunday night, Andrew and his dad felt like they'd been hit by a truck.

"You can still build them, Dad," Andrew said as they relaxed outside on the porch drinking Coronas and admiring their handiwork.

"Not without my favorite assistant," his dad replied with a grin.

"I'll try not to stay away so long next time," Andrew promised.

On Monday, Andrew wheeled into the parking lot of his apartment building long after the sun had disappeared below the horizon. He grabbed his duffle bag and, seeing the SuperMart receipt, stuffed it in his pocket.

The rains blanketed the city on Tuesday as Andrew made his way home after a game of pick-up basketball with his friends. Already aching from the weekend, the two hours of hoops had stiffened him up completely. The games were becoming more serious with the NBA playoffs in full swing. The Dallas Mavericks were the upstarts, challenging the Lakers for the Western Finals. *June was supposed to be a dry month in Frisco, but so far the weatherman was not cooperating*, Andrew thought, as he gazed through the beating wipers. It was dark when he pulled into the garage underneath his building.

After inserting his key in the lock, the door to his apartment swung open easily. He peered around the open door. His place had been ransacked—furniture was overturned; pillows were ripped open and drawers pulled out, the contents scattered. This was no random act or small-time burglary. He surveyed the room to determine if he should call the cops. His TV and stereo were untouched, as was the Canadian currency he'd left on the top drawer from his last trip to Whistler. It wasn't until he had tidied the living room that he realized his computer was gone. Fortunately, the hard drive was protected by a smart-chip tucked safely away in his wallet, effectively rendering the computer useless. "Why would they do that?" Andrew wondered out loud. He mentally listed the files on the computer: Jackson Meats, Broadstone Cleaners, The City of Sacramento and Alberton's Produce, the last file he had worked on. He had wanted to wrap up his report that night. Now it would have to wait until he had a chance to go back to the office and download the deposit files taken off the Alberton's mainframe.

Not wanting to spend the night in the mess, he headed to a hotel, stopping off at the bank on the way to withdraw some cash. Punching in his PIN, he requested $300. He stashed the bills in his pocket and was crumpling up the ATM receipt when the balance caught his eye. He flattened the crumpled paper and looked again. The account balance was $10,293. Last time he had checked, his current account was into his line of credit and payday wasn't until next week. What was going on?

Andrew made his way back to the office, all thoughts of a hotel room shoved aside. He scanned himself in with his keycard and made his way to the elevators without the usual small talk with the night guard. He rounded the corner to his office and he barely sat down before booting up his desktop computer. Signing onto the Internet, Andrew opened his banking site and downloaded the last four weeks' activity. The balance had grown to $14,000 and change. "What the hell!" He was breathing heavy and beads of sweat had appeared on his hands. All the deposits were small—pennies or dollars. Pages of small entries flashed on the computer screen. Something was going on and he didn't want to wait until his bank opened to find out what it was.

He couldn't dismiss the nagging suspicion that this had something to do with Alberton's. The small transactions were eerily similar to the ones from SuperMart. He had to get to the bottom of it, now.

*Catherine Demitrikov observed Andrew leaving the office tower. She had followed him from his apartment and was waiting patiently outside his office for him to reappear. Settling in behind his BMW, she followed him for an hour before he turned off the highway into a cluster of houses. Her keen intuition, honed from years of counter surveillance, had made Catherine a good judge of character, but Andrew Dalton's move both surprised and impressed her. As the accountant's BMW pulled in front a small house in Sonoma County, Catherine eased her car around the block and entered the alley at the back of the house. She smiled to herself in the rearview mirror. It would have been her next stop anyway.

The rain pelted the sidewalk as Andrew approached the door. He rang the bell twice and then, not waiting for a response, pounded on the door. As he waited, a shadow of doubt made him falter. He wasn't sure why he had come here, but he had to start somewhere.

"What the hell…it's almost ten o'clock!" Bob Craft opened the door slightly, leaving the chain lock intact. He eyed the man standing on the other side of his door, dripping wet, illuminated by the porch light. Not many people knew he was gay. Regardless of the new attitude about an individual's sexual preference, it still affected career advancement and income levels. Guys from the local café knew his home was open and would occasionally crash for the night. It was a way for him to satisfy his needs and remain discrete.

"Who are you?" Bob Craft asked the athletic looking stranger.

"We met today. We need to talk," Andrew began.

Bob opened the door, letting Andrew in out of the rain.

"That problem we discussed regarding the deposits at Alberton's…could it have somehow affected my personal bank account?" Andrew apologized for disturbing him so late at night to discuss the issue, but it seemed odd that the same thing had happened to him right after they had met.

"I don't know. We haven't been able to figure out the problem with our payable system."

Bob knew he wasn't supposed to talk about the system, but to hell with the internal audit watchdogs. This forensic accountant from Brooks and Steiner was pleasing to the eye. Let him ask questions while they enjoyed a glass of wine. He wouldn't talk about anything specific.

"Where are my manners? Would you like a drink? I have an open bottle of Merlot," Bob said, and left the room without waiting for a response.

"Thanks," Andrew called after him, glancing around the room. It was a comfortable, homey living room. Probably his parents home originally. The pictures on the walls and mantle implied Bob was single. The furniture was older and in immaculate condition. He wondered if they were protected by plastic covers most of their life.

Returning from the kitchen with the wine, Bob eased his way past Andrew, who was sitting on the couch. He placed the bottle and glasses on the coffee table, careful to use coasters. "Don't want to stain the furniture," he mumbled as he took a seat next to Andrew.

"Why do you think my account is receiving extra money? Small amounts. There have been hundreds of transactions?"

Bob explained about the discrepancies his clerk had found. Same sort of thing, except SuperMart was getting the extra money. The problem had started a couple of weeks earlier. He was told to report all instances to head office. He did exactly as he was told. Apparently, they were letting some research firm try some new software that was causing mistakes.

"Can I talk to the clerk tomorrow?" Andrew asked.

"She's dead. Killed by a gas explosion in her apartment," Bob replied. "The research firm, the Centre for Strategies—or something like that—a non-profit research foundation, has been running some data accumulation models. Maybe you should talk to them. Did you buy something at a SuperMart recently?"

"Near Seattle, last weekend."

"All the stores are linked centrally. Maybe the computer picked you by accident and somehow it's making mistakes, like at Alberton's. Why don't you meet me at my office first thing tomorrow and we'll straighten this out."

Bob wanted to keep talking, but knew he had already told his visitor more than he should. Andrew listened politely for a few more minutes as the conversation steered to art, then made his excuses, thanked Bob, and agreed to call in the morning to arrange a meeting.

After Andrew left, Bob closed the door and pondered the strange intrusion from the good-looking forensic accountant. He thought he resembled a well-known actor. He contemplated their conversation for a few minutes before settling down in the den to finish his movie and wine.

There was no sound when the front door opened. Catherine walked silently through the kitchen, stopping to grab a knife on her way to the den. The kitchen table was to the left of the cutting block. She grabbed a dishtowel draped neatly over a chair. Catherine moved through the house, noting its orderliness. She particularly admired a set of posters depicting an ad for a Russian Ballet troupe that had performed in San Francisco several years earlier. Everything in the house broadcast the occupant's sexual preference, which left Catherine less enthused about her assignment.

Bob was so engrossed in his movie he didn't see her coming around the couch. Catherine glided along the floor and stood in front of Bob, who stared up at her, perplexed. She liked to confront her prey, see their eyes. Stabbing from behind took all the excitement out of the kill. In one swift motion, she lunged, the knife penetrating Bob's throat, severing his spinal cord on the way out. She stabbed him several more times to make the job look like that of an amateur. This would work out even better than she expected.

Chapter 8

One way or another, ASC always completed its deals. William van Holder was a man at the helm, always with a game plan and would do whatever it took to accomplish the task. He relished being in control.

Catherine had recently completed a research trip with one of ASC's future business partners and was meeting with van Holder to explain the details of the man's transgressions.

"You made copies of the photos?" van Holder enquired.

"As always. You never know when he'll need prodding in the future," Catherine said, "although a second session with him wouldn't bother me."

Van Holder handed Catherine an envelope. "I need you to go to Salzburg."

Catherine glanced at the man she had come to admire, the only man who completely possessed her. "I'll make the arrangements." She rose from the couch and left the room.

As the door slid shut behind Catherine, van Holder depressed a button on the inside of his desk, opening a panel on the wall behind the bar. A large plasma screen displayed the changing landscape of the company's vast holdings. It began with the parent company, and fanned outwards down the screen. Van Holder pointed his laser pen at a section of the screen and pressed the button to expand his selection. Instantly, his construction group chart was detailed. He scrolled down to the spot where Amalga Steel Inc. would be placed the next day. Scrolling back to the main screen, he pointed to the second tier of companies and then to his software group—the backbone of his empire, the genus of his wealth.

He reflected on VisiTrack, the original banking software that had led to his success. It had changed so much with the proliferation of the Internet. The latest version would be the platform to ensure the success of the Amsterdam Protocol. When used in conjunction with credit cards, it would make paper money obsolete.

The earlier versions of VisiTrack had created the debit card explosion. Van Holder realized the banks' competitive nature would prohibit them from sharing their databases. The early versions of account access cards were honored only at the businesses dealing with the card-issuing bank. It was intended to be a "club" system. But the consuming public didn't buy into the concept, so it was replaced with VisiTrack, which was used to bridge the independent banks and businesses with the consumer. ASC set up the virtual clearing house, earning a fee on each transaction. Everyone benefited, especially ASC and its surviving founder. Since its inception, the VisiTrack Clearing System had earned the company billions. All attempts to duplicate the program within the banks and credit card companies were met with van Holder's unique brand of persuasion, leaving no effective competitors. The company's reach didn't extend beyond the U.S., but that was about to change.

Chapter 9

Inside the CSA complex, Dana stared at her latest report. Harry had performed his magic and worked out the bugs. The hum of the building machinery broke the silence of the late night. Dana glanced at the ornate clock hanging in the hall across from her office. It was well past midnight.

Now that the model had been perfected, it was time to do the real work. CSA had been commissioned to do an exhaustive study of numerous industry groups—electronics, food distribution, pharmaceuticals, to name but a few. In addition to the grocery supply chain, the study had been expanded to include the rapid consolidation of companies currently taking place in that industry. It would be a test case for the Amsterdam round of Global Trade Commission talks. The success of the 'McLeod Model' meant that Dana could examine any industry at her whim.

Earlier in the day, Alex had been ecstatic. "The more we hit them with, the better." His mantra was 'something must be done to stop the shrinking base of global commerce.'

The grocery industry analysis began to take shape. Dana stretched, rubbing her eyes and slapping her cheeks to ease the weariness. It was tedious work, not something that should be done in the middle of the night. The intrigue of the search was driving her to continue. She would check for mistakes in the morning.

Common names and locations kept surfacing. Dana concentrated on one group in particular. The Motomito Corporation, for all appearances, was a regional supplier of packaged food products to Southeast Asian countries. On the surface, it appeared to be a public company trading on the Nikkei Index. By tracing stock transactions, Dana was able to track holdings to three Bermuda-based banks. After cross-referencing these banks, she determined that the fund managers who controlled all three banks together owned a majority of the voting stock of Motomito. The connection came when she traced the mailing addresses for the directors of all three funds managers to a single office. A further search uncovered that the office was a drop site where mail was sent to its rightful owner in Japan.

Motomito's reach extended even further. Hidden in its balance sheet was a series of joint ventures and partnerships, which gave the company a controlling interest in a multitude of processing and packaging companies worldwide. At every juncture of Motomito's complex corporate chart existed a partnership, each one controlled by a nominee director. The model was designed to match similarities between companies from a collection of information stored electronically in the U.S. and abroad. The CSA computer system scanned thousands of databases, both public and private, to create its result. It wasn't perfect, but by asking the right questions, the connections were made and common ownership traits surfaced.

Dana was exhausted. She rubbed her eyes again to help her focus. She knew her model was accurate, but never expected it would reveal such a blatant array of duplicity. High-speed internet providers made access to information from around the global almost instant—a cornucopia of data waiting to be discovered. Companies, governments, sports teams, and even weekly neighborhood cookie clubs had a place on the world-wide web. Freedom of information was no longer an issue, she mused; it was a terrifying reality.

CSA had taken full advantage of the mania that was sweeping the globe. With relentless pursuit, it had hired the best computer minds and built one of the largest private computer networks in the world. Programs had been written to create mindless drones reaching out through the web to build the database of worldwide commerce. When institutions felt the need for privacy, CSA's programmers created solutions impervious to any attempts at security. Firewalls were torn down at their whim to complete any data-gathering project initiated at Alex's whim.

Like the programmers at CSA (except for their mission), hackers were the mainstay of CSA's information trough. Their domain began to shrink, however, as governments convened to create privacy laws. Hackers who preyed on unsuspecting visitors to the web were relentlessly pursued. Forced to find new ways to gain access to the private data of individuals and companies, CSA began offering certain pieces of information to select institutions and governments in exchange for access. It was at that point that Harry and Dana joined the foundation. Harry was a graffiti hacker who was picked up after gaining access to CSA's computers, installing a virus that shut the foundation down for a week. Instead of prosecuting, Alex hired the young upstart. Harry's first task was to create a program that would accompany the "friendly" software provided to CSA's information clients. Once installed on a client's network, Harry's program went to work ensuring a constant and unseen stream of information into the CSA private database. Unbeknownst to Dana, this information had been used to create her statistical model and gather connections that nobody else could.

Dana stared at her screen, scrutinizing the data as it streamed out of the database. The nominee partnerships used by Motomito were the key to the globalization of business that CSA hoped to expose. Setting aside her findings, she drafted a short email arranging a meeting with the CEO. She packed up to go, unaware that her findings had already been relayed outside of CSA's ultra-secure network, a firewall system more secure than the Pentagon. The backdoor access had been installed from the beginning, hiding the true purpose of CSA from everyone but a select few. The information traveled a half a dozen states away via satellite link rerouted to its final destination. Even before Dana had left her office, the results were being analyzed with expert eyes.

Chapter 10

Cradling the phone on his neck, Andrew dialed the number scrawled on the scrap of paper from his office. The ransacked apartment looked like his old college dorm during finals. A breeze from the open balcony door scattered the torn pages of his phone book around the room.

The events of the past few days made no sense. The partners of Brooks and Steiner insisted the firm maintain a cool distance to guarantee their clients' reputations. This was the first time an investigation had affected him directly. Andrew rubbed his temples, wracking his brain to find a thread of logic.

His thoughts were interrupted by a voice on the other end of the line.

"I'm sorry, sir, but Mr. Craft has not arrived at the office this morning. Would you like to leave a message on his voicemail?"

Andrew declined, but asked the woman to give Bob his contact information as soon as he arrived. Andrew speculated that Bob had gone to Alberton's Produce to trace the items affecting his bank. He thought about calling Alberton's, but decided to drive there instead.

The black sedan sat unnoticed as Andrew exited the parking garage. His BMW skidded onto the street as he punched a key on his cell phone to dial into his voice mail. Halfway down the block, he spun a U-turn and headed in the opposite direction. Too many messages forced him to change plans and head for the office. As he wheeled around, he swerved to miss the two seriously attired and resolute men emerging from their car across from his apartment building. He didn't see them re-enter their car after speeding past.

Mission Street was bustling with traffic. Cars honked, couriers careened through the idle commuters and a tour bus blocked the lane to Andrew's parking lot. Two street people bundled in rags, dirty and desperate, squeezed past the car and the bus, knocking on the window to ask for change. Raising his hands to feign temporary poverty; Andrew was thankful when the bus moved, freeing him from his guilty conscience.

The understated elegance of the Brooks and Steiner offices was in stark contrast to the street below. A wave of comfort enveloped Andrew as the elevator opened on his floor. He walked past the bronze bust of the firm's founder, his feet sinking into the plush Persian rug adorning the entranceway. Accounting firms weren't known for their opulent surroundings, but this firm was different. Brooks and Steiner oozed success.

As he approached the reception desk, Gloria, the blond beauty who coordinated the office with casual efficiency, shifted her gaze from the computer screen to look directly at Andrew. Her intense, inviting stare challenged people to declare their intentions for entering her arena.

"Is everything okay?" Andrew asked, walking toward his office.

"Yes, sir…well, no, sir. Two gentlemen are looking for you. Not your typical clients. They seemed anxious that you weren't here."

Andrew returned to the desk. "Do you know what they want?" he asked, wondering what other surprises the day would bring.

"No, sir, but they were quite insistent that they find you soon. Mr. Tanner is currently speaking with them."

"Thanks. Don't tell them I'm here." Andrew had decided to ignore the intrusion for the time being.

Once settled in the office, he sat back in his chair and began clearing his messages. The fourth message made him sit up. The muscles in his back tensed. He exhaled slowly as he replayed the message. The surprises kept on coming. It was from his bank.

"There are some issues concerning the activity in your account," the banker intoned. "The balance exceeds a hundred thousand… we should meet."

Bankers seldom called with good news, preferring to remain in the background like the grim reaper, rising up only when necessary. Andrew didn't have many personal dealings with his banker. Several student loans, his car lease and credit cards—that was it. Not even a mortgage, due to the exorbitant housing prices in the Bay area. Andrew called the manager to explain what he could about the current situation, hoping to satisfy him until he could discover the cause of the glitch.

The manager sounded anxious as he responded to Andrew's greeting. "Mr. Dalton, we have been advised to freeze your account immediately. Please come down to the branch."

Andrew declined, but promised to keep the manager informed. "We need to fix this right away, Mr. Dalton. A form is required with these sorts of accounts, and we insist it be signed immediately."

Andrew was familiar with the rules. Recent federal money laundering regulations required disclosure. Many of his own clients had been asked to sign an affidavit stating there were no underhanded dealings going on through their accounts.

After assuring the banker he would be down later, he hung up and decided to try Bob Craft at SuperMart again. The phone was not answered in typical corporate fashion. It was apparent the SuperMart operator was upset.

"Hello, may I please speak to Mr. Craft," Andrew asked.

"I'm s-s-sorry, sir, but haven't you heard? Mr. Craft is dead. He was murdered last night."

Andrew's heart skipped a beat. He stopped listening after the distraught woman relayed the details of Bob's death, a gruesome affair that had left everyone shocked.

"The world is just not safe anymore," she stated flatly.

Andrew felt a bead of sweat trickle underneath his chin. He rubbed his shoulder against his face to clear the moisture. Something was wrong, terribly wrong, and he was being dragged into it. Information about the SuperMart accountant was vital, so he pressed the receptionist for details.

"He was found sitting in front of his TV stabbed to death. Bob was such a great guy. Why would somebody do this?" she wailed into the phone.

Apparently he had had a late night visitor. An eyewitness—a nosy neighbor who called the police—reported a man leaving Bob's house around ten-thirty. Andrew's thoughts reverted back to that evening…what time did he leave? The police had found fingerprints and had been to the SuperMart headquarters to search Bob's office and question the staff. Apparently, another employee had died a few days earlier.

"What happened? Andrew probed.

"One of the accounting clerks was killed by a gas explosion in her apartment. I'm sure you read about it in the paper. It destroyed half an apartment block on the east side of town."

Andrew recalled his discussion with Bob Craft. An elderly lady near retirement had left behind an aging mother. *Were the deaths related?* he wondered. Andrew hung up the phone. Had he been the last person to see Bob alive before he was killed? Contemplating this, he was interrupted by the intercom. It was Frank.

"Andrew, could you come down?"

"Yeah, sure." Andrew wasn't all that sure, but made his way back through reception. The partners had vied for the prime real estate, and Frank's corner office facing the Golden Gate Bridge was the premier spot. Andrew liked meeting in the large space, envisioning when he would take it over. Halfway down the corridor, two men intercepted him. *Must be the visitors Gloria had mentioned,* Andrew thought as they approached him. They were walking quickly, hands tucked inside their suit jackets. They stopped at the elevators and waited for Andrew.

"Mr. Dalton," the first man said. "We are from SuperMart. We would like to discuss a mutual problem we are having."

"That would be great. Come on back to my office. I'll get my bank…"

"That won't be necessary. We would like you to accompany us to SuperMart. We need you to sign a statement." The men cornered Andrew on both sides.

Andrew didn't believe the lie and turned on his heels. The second man wrapped an arm of steel around his neck. Reaching forward, Andrew grabbed the bronze bust beside the elevator and lifted it up over his head, making solid contact with his captor's forehead. Using the man's ankle as a pivot, he twisted around and raced back down the hall to the fire escape. Not wanting to stick around to find out who they really were, he bolted through the door and bounded down the stairs three at a time. Six floors later, he paused briefly but continued his descent when the sound of pounding feet made him realize that whoever these men were, they were serious.

By the time Andrew reached the lobby, his pursuer had caught up with him. The man grabbed his shirt, forcing both of them backwards. Losing his balance, Andrew crashed against the railing and fell hard on the landing between floors heading to the parking garage. When he hit the floor, Andrew kicked upwards and caught the man below the knee, thankful for his high school wrestling letter. The unknown aggressor's cartilage gave way, popping his knee out. A swishing sound was followed by an agonizing scream as his assailant collapsed in a heap sliding down the half-flight of stairs. Pushing against the offending wall, Andrew moved away, but he was too slow. The injured man grabbed his leg and held on tight to prevent escape. The grip caused Andrew to fall forward over the man and down the next set of stairs. He screamed in pain as the stairs assailed his knees. He collapsed on the next landing, crashing into the corner.

A half-dozen stairs away, a sight movement caught Andrew's eye. He crawled around the corner just as a gun went off. The bullet spun past his left leg at a thousand miles an hour and embedded itself in the wall behind his torso. Overcome with fear, Andrew lunged forward to escape what had become a deadly situation. Cascading down further flights of stairs, Andrew flew past the sub-terrain levels on his way to his car. He paused inside the stairwell on his parking level to rest, breathing in short gasps. Nothing he did at the gym equaled the strain of the past few minutes.

Andrew headed for his car, unaware that the second SuperMart man, who had anticipated Andrew's decision not to flee on foot, was waiting for him. Leaving his gun holstered, the second man crouched behind the BMW. He timed his move with trained precision. His orders were not to kill, which made the task infinitely more difficult. As his target keyed the car lock, he grabbed him from behind and they both spun backwards, crashing into a pillar. The man pinned his body tightly against Andrew, leaving little room for movement. The first punch went to the stomach, followed by several more boxer-like jabs to the kidneys. Andrew felt like throwing up as he struggled to breathe. The man's huge hands tightened around him.

"What do you want from me?" Andrew asked meekly.

Instead of an answer, the grip around his neck tightened. Starting to lose consciousness, Andrew managed to wriggle his left arm free, sending a clenched fist up into the man's groin. The hold loosened as Andrew fell backwards against the pillar, this time free to escape. He felt a surge of satisfaction as he delivered a second blow to the man, who was now doubled over and writhing in pain on the floor of the garage. Andrew's foot connected with the man's jaw, knocking him out.

Pain crept through his whole body as Andrew sank into his car and draped his hands limply over the steering wheel. *The last few days didn't really happen*, he thought. Surely a simple phone call would straighten out the confusion. But even before he had finished dialing, Andrew knew he would be wasting his time. Somebody had set a carefully planned trap, and for some reason he was the target.

In a cavernous building three stories below the Montana landscape, several men gathered in a conference room separated from the main complex by thick, glass walls. They weren't happy, as evidenced by the dour expressions on their dimly lit faces. The information they had just received did little to ease their minds. It was purely a coincidence, but even so, they would leave nothing to chance. The report they were discussing, emailed to their notebooks only moments before and filtered for relevancy, contained a short analysis of Dana's findings on Motomito.

The man in charge of the complex and responsible to its owner knew that the study they had secretly funded would cause more harm than good. How was it that CSA had access to their most private data and secret archives? Had they created a Frankenstein?

"Tell our contact to eliminate the data. And find out which network provided the information that made the link to Bermuda," the man said to the person on his left. "We still need the McLeod Model, but she's supposed to find us new data, not spew out stuff we already know."

The third man had waited his turn. He was aware that the temporary solution caused by the SuperMart debacle had failed to produce the desired results. "We were unable to eliminate the accountant."

"Yes, I know. Tell me again how the money ended up in his account."

The third man, a project coordinator in the 'bunker,' as it was known, explained that their mole had taken it upon himself to divert the funds from SuperMart to the Brooks and Steiner accountant. They all knew what had started this chain of events, but since none of them would accept responsibility for the problem, they focused on the contact.

The project coordinator anticipated the leader's line of questioning. "Why not deflect attention away from CSA and our mandate, and solve our elimination problem?" he suggested.

"How?" the leader asked.

"Frame the accountant," the project man said.

"And what about the girl? We can't afford to have her work tied into the setup. Can we run the model without her?"

"No, she'll be needed to generate the information for the remaining industries."

"Then get her and finish the project."

Chapter 11

The sun streaming through the narrow opening in the curtain shone on Andrew's face, rousing him from a deep sleep. Despite the hot shower and handful of painkillers he had taken the previous night, his body continued to ache. Dragging his sore body out of bed, he washed down a few more pills with the tepid water at his bedside and scanned the hotel room. The triple locks on the door made him feel safe and secure after yesterday's encounter. He had chosen this hotel because it had outside access through a fire escape. Although unsure if it would be needed, he felt it was a necessary precaution. The comfortable hotel catered to an exclusive club, many members of which were Brooks and Steiner clients. It was also downtown, near his bank and the office, his two required stops for the day.

Lying back, Andrew massaged the shoulder that had been used as a battering ram. No matter how hard he tried, he couldn't come up with an explanation for the events of the past few days. His review of the Alberton's payable transactions with SuperMart had clearly touched a nerve...but whose? And hadn't the SuperMart accountant mentioned CSA, Dana's employer? What did CSA have to do with the beefy twins who had tried to eliminate him? Frustrated, Andrew got up to have another shower, hoping the steam would clear his head. After his shower, Andrew ordered breakfast and turned on the TV to watch the local news. Nothing special was happening, and there was no mention of the grisly murder of the SuperMart manager.

The bank answered on the second ring and directed Andrew's call to his account manager. After the usual pleasantries, he arranged to meet the banker an hour later. Before leaving the hotel, Andrew bought some new clothes, including a rainproof jacket and a baseball cap. He said a silent prayer as the clerk processed the credit card. Thankfully, it still worked. He cursed himself for being so scared. *But who wouldn't be, considering the newspaper article about the explosion and his deadly encounter*, he thought. It wasn't exactly part of his daily routine. Hopefully, the baseball cap would allow him to blend in like a tourist.

It was a breezy day. The sun shone brightly in the sky, bouncing off the office tower windows to create a colorful kaleidoscope. It was a good day for San Francisco. As he walked the few blocks to his bank, Andrew tried to relax and enjoy the familiar street sounds, the warm temperature and the fragrant air. *Surely this thing would be cleared up*, he thought. As he approached the bank, his apprehension increased. Whoever was targeting him knew where he worked, where he lived and probably everything about his life. A wave of paranoia coursed through him. They clearly knew where he did his banking. He glanced around the concourse of the Union Street branch of the California First Bank. It was steel and modern, in sharp contrast to the hotel he had just left. Nobody appeared to be paying any attention to him.

The account manager's desk was in an open area half a floor up from the tellers. Chin-high, burgundy dividers on three sides of the desk provided a small amount of privacy. Convinced he was being watched, Andrew felt uneasy. Stretching his arms behind his neck, he casually looked around the bank. Nobody. Turning back to the manager's computer screen, which was angled so they could both see the transactions, they surveyed the hundreds of deposits entering his account.

"Do you know where the deposits came from?" Andrew asked, unconsciously looking over his shoulder at the entrance doors to the bank, half expecting the death squad to burst through at any time.

"Are we waiting for someone else?" the banker queried, following Andrew's gaze to the doors.

"No, I'm sorry. Any idea where the deposits came from? Who deposited them?" Andrew turned around to face the desk.

"We were hoping maybe you could tell us," the account manager replied, placing some forms in front of Andrew. "Please sign the highlighted lines."

Andrew ignored the papers as they slid across the desk. "Let's review the account activity first. For all you know it could be the bank's mistake."

The account manager selected one of the recent deposits—a large amount just over nine dollars. "It appears to be coming out of a financial clearing house on the East Coast." After continuing to query his computer for a few minutes, he eventually looked up. "It's a dead end. The deposit originates directly from the clearing house."

Strange. Normally, financial clearing houses are paid to match transactions between banks—either physical checks or electronic transfers. They don't generate their own transactions.

"Who owns the clearinghouse?" Andrew asked.

"A Bermuda based bank—Island Capital Services," the account manager replied after a few more minutes of searching.

"Can you put a trace on the items?" Andrew asked.

"Sure." The account manager looked down at the papers.

Oh, what the hell, Andrew thought, as he picked up the pen and signed the forms. The manager agreed to call him as soon as the trace was complete.

Andrew left the bank and hiked up Mission Street past the panhandlers and gawking tourists on his way to the Brooks and Steiner offices. Upon his arrival, he ducked behind the building to the underground parking lot. Using his key, he entered the stairwell he had so hastily left the night before, climbed up three floors and entered the lobby. Exiting the elevator one floor below the office, Andrew made it to his office without being seen. The space felt foreign to him. His paintings were still hanging on the wall, including the replica of Salvador Dali's 'melting clocks' above his credenza. The neatness was uncomfortable. Someone had searched his desk and files, cleaning up after themselves like a teenager hiding a house party from suspicious parents. He knew which files were missing.

Anxious to clear up the misunderstanding, he decided the firm's lawyers might be able to help. Making his way to Frank's office, he knocked on the door. His mentor looked up and gestured for him to enter.

"There you are! What the hell is going on? I've spent the morning on the phone dealing with this thing." Frank Tanner was unusually tense.

"What thing?" Suddenly very tired, Andrew slumped into one of the chairs surrounding the small conference table.

"SuperMart. Their CEO called to warn me that they're going to the district attorney to file charges of embezzlement...against you."

Andrew, who had been staring out over the Bay, turned around abruptly, dumbfounded. The entire experience was becoming unreal, a trip to the twilight zone.

"Frank, that's crazy! Why would I do that?"

"That's exactly what I said, but they say there's irrefutable proof, money into your account, transactions traced to their bank…something about hacking into their system."

"Oh, yeah, and pigs can fly. Jesus, Frank, why would I do that?"

And be dumb enough to deposit the funds directly into a local account, they both thought to themselves.

"It's a setup. I don't know why or how, but for some reason they need a fall guy and I happened to be at the wrong place at the right time."

Andrew explained the events of the past few days, including what he and his bankers had discovered. Afterwards, the two friends looked at each other. At Brooks and Steiner, the first rule of business was trust—your instincts, your co-workers and yourself.

"I'll call SuperMart. Our legal department can make less public arrangements to investigate this problem."

"Thanks, Frank." It felt good to have an ally.

Frank Tanner looked at his protégé. He trusted him, but the firm came first. The attack at the office the previous day had spooked the partners. Reputation was everything in their business. At the end of the day, the firm had to be the focus; he would hate to lose such a valuable employee.

Andrew left the room and went to his office. Flopping into his chair, he grabbed the phone and dialed the number he knew off by heart, but hung up before the first ring. The SuperMart accountant had mentioned CSA, Dana's employer. He knew his best option was to find out the connection between its research and his sudden unwanted wealth. Hesitating, he stared out the window and gazed over the San Francisco Bay to Sausalito. He remembered when Dana had been hired by the think tank. She had been so excited and proud. She made him drive past the complex three times on the weekend before she started her job. Finally, she would have her chance to change the world. It certainly changed *their* world. He picked up the phone again and pressed redial. This time he let it ring. She answered on the second ring. The sound of her voice sent a small vibration through his body.

Five miles away, across the Bay, Dana could feel herself tense up. Looking at her reflection in the window, she was suddenly unsure of what to say. An awkward silence filled the void.

Afraid of what he needed, finally Andrew spoke. "Dana, I'm in trouble." He explained everything that had happened, except the encounter with the gun-wielding goons. The whole thing seemed so farfetched that he repeated it several times so she wouldn't think he was lying.

"Andrew, I believe you. What can I do?"

He hesitated. Why was he bringing Dana into this? It was crazy, but he had nowhere else to go. "Can we meet?"

"Of course." Dana felt her heart speed up. *It'll be good to see him again*, she thought.

"We might be able to track the problem with the deposits if we can review how CSA's mainframe interacted with the payable system at Alberton's. Somebody must have initiated the deposits going into my account. Maybe others are affected as well." Andrew explained.

"Meet me at my office in an hour." Dana was looking forward to the unexpected reunion.

"Thanks." Andrew felt a pang of regret. Should he involve her? Was it too late to back out now?

"Email your bank activity and I'll start looking at it right away." Dana's response made him realize why he had called. Her quick mind and tenacity, her need to fix things, were exactly what he needed.

After sending Dana the statements, Andrew spent a few minutes surveying his office. Nothing was missing, but somebody had thoroughly searched his office. He knew his suspicions were correct. There must be a link between Jackson Meats and Alberton's— a link someone wanted to hide.

The drive over the Golden Gate Bridge was stunning. Even with the events of the past week, Andrew couldn't help but enjoy the scenery—sailboats slicing calmly through the Bay, ferries loaded with tourists disembarking at Alcatraz and floatplanes gliding noisily overhead. They were all reminders of why he loved the city, despite the daily gridlock. He knew the trip would take over an hour, so he sat back and tried to relax. After ninety minutes, the sprawling CSA complex came into view. Several minutes later, after parking at the far end of the lot, Andrew made his way to the entranceway.

Walking through the large etched-glass doors was like entering a museum. Dozens of original works of art and sculpture tastefully decorated the lobby. The CEO of the foundation took great pride in his success. Andrew approached the receptionist—another beautiful new addition to the lobby since he had last visited—and asked for Dana.

"I'm sorry, sir. Ms. McLeod has left for the day. Is there anyone else who can help you?"

Asking the same question three different ways didn't change her answer. No, she didn't know where Dana went. No, he couldn't go to her office. No, she didn't have a message for him. Why would Dana leave early when she was expecting him? Maybe she had second thoughts about seeing him. What if she was part of the unraveling conspiracy and needed his bank information to secure the trumped-up charges. *Now that was just crazy*, he thought.

After getting no help from the receptionist, Andrew left the main building. Maybe something in Dana's office would provide a clue as to why she left. Veering off the path leading back to the parking lot, he entered the CSA campus, a myriad of circular huts surrounded by lush gardens. He hoped she hadn't moved since his last visit. As he walked towards her office he was glad for his casual dress, the attire helped him blend into the collegiate atmosphere of the foundation. Andrew knew the campus appearance was part of a façade that hid CSA's 'big brother' security system. He knew he wouldn't gain access without proper identification, and as he suspected, the door to her building was locked. A slot device to read a small plastic card, carried by all employees, was affixed to the frame in place of the doorknob. *Damn.*

As luck would have it, just as he turned to leave, the door opened and a group of employees emerged. Andrew approached the door, feigning a lost ID badge. The last person held the door open for him. A forgotten badge was not unusual. *So much for big brother*, Andrew thought as he ducked into the building.

Once inside, he made his way through the narrow corridor to Dana's office, which was in a state of disarray. Files and papers were strewn everywhere. It was not Dana's style to leave her office in such a mess. Amidst the disarray the tacky dolphin penholder he had bought her on their first date at Sea World. He smiled, touched that she still kept it on her desk.

Sitting down behind the desk, Andrew nudged the keyboard and the computer screen came to life. Drawn to the report on the screen, he read the last entry. ".... What do you men want? Why are you here?"

Panic set in as the words registered. *What had he done?* By calling her, had he somehow implicated her in his nightmare? He had to find her. Racing from her office, he searched the other offices. Somebody must have seen her leave. After several frantic minutes, he located one of her interns. Had he seen Dana leave?

"Yes, she was with two men. When I asked where she was going, she mentioned a meeting downtown. It did seem strange. The men appeared to be escorting her. Is she in any trouble?"

"Let's hope not," Andrew said ruefully, leaving a bewildered intern as he sprinted down the corridor and out of the building. He wasn't sure where to go; only that he had to move.

Dana sat in the back of the sedan, hands tied behind her back. She was surprised they hadn't put her in the trunk. *Isn't that what you do when you kidnap somebody?* she thought. She was scared. How did these two men get into her office, and where were they taking her? She could see outside, but the dark, tinted glass made it impossible for anyone to look inside the car. Could this be some sort of attempt to extort money from her parents? Her dad had told her when she was fifteen that she was never to be kidnapped, as he would not pay a ransom. "Look what happened to the brewery family in the seventies," he had said. "They paid, and their son was killed anyway."

Before leaving her office, she had grabbed her purse. "Woman things," she had said. As they pulled out of the parking lot, she had seen Andrew walking towards the main building, but had been powerless to signal him. Sitting in the back of the car, she realized her only hope was to try and reach him. Moving carefully so as to not attract attention, she opened the clasp of her purse and found her cell phone. Andrew's number was still on the speed dial. She wondered why she had never erased it. Dana hoped the men would not notice.

"So, where are we going? I hope you don't think my family will pay the ransom. They won't, you know." Babbling on to distract her captors, she depressed the number one on the keypad, hoping Andrew hadn't changed his number. She prayed the ring wouldn't be heard over her banter.

"Listen, lady, shut up," the man in the passenger seat snapped, turning his head around. "We were hired to pick you up and deliver you, that's it."

Dana froze. She slid her cell phone underneath her thigh hoped that her conversation could still be heard. "It sure was a nice drive over the bridge. No matter how many times I take the drive, the beauty still amazes me. Traffic sure is slow. I hope you aren't taking me to the airport. I don't have my passport."

"Lady, like I said, shut up."

Andrew was running across the manicured lawn, his feet leaving deep depressions in the freshly cut grass, when the "William Tell Overture" began to play on his phone. After several hellos, he was about to hang up when he heard Dana's voice. "…. drive over the bridge….." Listening to the one-sided conversation, he bolted for the parking lot, racing like a maniac to his car. He careened out of the CSA complex and made his way to the freeway entrance, ignoring the waving fists and blasting car horns as he weaved in and out of traffic, steering with one hand, the phone glued to his ear with the other.

He could hear Dana. "I don't like small planes. We're not going to be flying anywhere, are we? I don't like small planes. I throw up."

"We won't be flying in a small plane. In fact, you'll be flying in a private jet. Satisfied?"

"This sure is a nice car. What is it…a Cadillac?"

"Lady, please shut up. And no, it's not a Cadillac; it's a Lincoln Town Car."

"Black, very nice." Afraid her captors might discover the reasoning behind the questioning, Dana made no other comments.

She only hoped Andrew had been listening, and that her cell phone battery was charged.

Andrew wracked his brain. Which airports catered to private jets? The only airport he knew was south of the city, near San Jose. He had flown out of there once to meet with some oil clients from Texas. They had sent their private jet to pick him up for a meeting in Houston. Since they were going over the Golden Gate Bridge, it was his only hope, so he gunned the BMW, thinking maybe he could catch up. They couldn't be more that thirty minutes ahead of him, judging from the time of the last entry on Dana's computer. Flying over the bridge, Andrew was oblivious to the havoc he was creating in his wake. Several cars had spun out of control, creating a pile-up and shutting down access to the city. Sirens wailed in the distance.

Leaving the east side of the bridge, Andrew exited onto Van Ness heading south to 101. The traffic through town would be slow. Hopefully, his good local knowledge would make his trip shorter than that of the Lincoln. Hopefully, he had guessed right as to their destination.

After fifteen minutes on 101 at near insane speeds, Andrew spotted a black Lincoln. He was thankful Dana had tricked that information out of her captors. She would never have known the type of car. She still thought he drove an Audi. The adrenaline was pumping in his veins. He was lucky to find her so quickly. Andrew sped past the car and glanced over at the driver; a sixty-year-old man with his wife. This wasn't going to be as easy as he thought. Of course, it wasn't—only on half-hour TV shows are chases resolved so quickly.

Speeding up again, Andrew realized that if he had guessed the right airport, he stood a good chance of getting there first. He pushed the car to the red line and exited the freeway a few miles from the airport. A few minutes later, he arrived at the small terminal. There was no Lincoln to be seen, but a private jet was parked on the tarmac, ready to board passengers. Ten minutes later, the Lincoln rounded the corner into the airport and headed straight for a private entrance near the plane.

Shit! Andrew said to himself. Of course they wouldn't need to clear security! Pulling his BMW around, he headed straight for the car. The entrance to the tarmac was blocked. Andrew jumped out of his car and ran to the Lincoln. The driver emerged with a bemused look on his face. Andrew recognized him as one of the men from his encounter at the office, and noted he had a new sidekick in the passenger seat. At least he had put one of the goons out of commission.

The man approached him. "Mr. Dalton, what a surprise. I didn't expect to see you here."

The second man was holding Dana. Her eyes pleaded with Andrew as she struggled to get free.

"Let her go." Andrew moved towards Dana and the second man.

"Not this time, Mr. Dalton. But why don't you accompany us? That way we can finish the job we started the other day."

Before Andrew could react, he was kicked in the back of the legs. He tripped and fell face first into the pavement. The pain in his already bruised body intensified. Minutes after being constrained, he and Dana were dragged onto the plane and were airborne.

Chapter 12

It had been years since Catherine had been to Salzburg. She spent several days touring the city and planning her approach to the assignment. She found the city much like it was during her stint with the KGB—except then she had no entertainment budget and wasn't able to enjoy all its offerings. Now she was staying at the Residenz Hotel, a five-star, quaint establishment offering discreet service. It was perfect for her needs.

Wandering through the city centre, Catherine tailed her mark for two days to find out his habits…and vices. While taking pictures of him and his family, a plan soon emerged. It was time to put it into action. Hans Mueller was the CEO of Dextall, a pharmaceutical giant with controlling interests in drug stores and hospitals, and Chairman of the ad hoc Corporate Liaison Committee to the Global Trade Commission. He directed policy affecting ASC's current expansion into Europe. Van Holder wanted him compromised.

Mueller spent half his time with the GTC, aware that global conglomerates were more important than the politicians who purported to run the world. The work was not easy. Even when the GTC ruled against one country's attempt to protect one of its industries, the adjudication process took so long that most of the damage was done to the 'offending' foreign industry by the time the dispute was settled. Both the EU and the U.S.A. were infamous for their protectionist attitudes toward foreign industry. What made it even more complicated was that global conglomerates such as Dextall often benefited from these fights through their direct and indirect interests in the targeted countries. The global profit picture—not how an individual country preformed, was what mattered. By joining the liaison committee, Mueller was able to reduce the disintegration of local companies when it didn't adversely affect multinationals like his own company.

Other than the excitement of this recent position, Mueller led a dull life. Working sixty hours a week left little time for other pursuits. Each morning and afternoon, he walked the short distance from his residence to the small executive office of the company his father started almost fifty years earlier. The main offices were 200 miles away in the cosmopolitan city of Vienna, but Mueller preferred the quiet tranquility of Salzburg. When his father retired, Hans took over the executive offices and moved them back to the site of the company's birthplace. The building had been restored to its seventeenth century opulence. The office had a commanding view of the Festung Hohensalsburg, the medieval fortress dominating the city's skyline. He would often sit at his desk and stare at the colossal structure or occasionally wander through the grounds when time permitted.

It was there that he met Catherine. The young Russian tourist had accosted him at the entrance to the fortress gardens, asking for directions.

"Excuse me," she said hesitantly in German. "Could you direct me to Mozart's Geburthaus?"

The famous tourist attraction was next to his office. As a gracious ambassador of his city, he agreed to show her the way.

"I will give you a personal tour of the city on the way."

"Do you live here?" Catherine asked haltingly. "It is such a beautiful city. Everything in Russia, where I live, is old and broken. Our town has only recently been restored."

Mueller was in his element. He loved the history of this once independent city-state. "My office was the home to the business managers of the Archbishops. They ruled this city as a separate country for almost 1200 years until the Hapsburgs took it over in the early seventeenth century." Mueller babbled on nonstop during the thirty-minute walk.

As they approached their destination, Catherine insisted on buying her guide an espresso. "It's the least I can do to thank you for the private tour."

What could it hurt? He had enjoyed acting as tour guide for this enchanting young lady. He felt guilty, though, as he rarely made time for such activities with his wife and daughter. But he felt obligated; it would have been rude to refuse.

"Tell me more about your home," Catherine prodded. She suffered through the next hour until she knew he was hooked, then she glanced at her watch.

"I must leave now."

Mueller was disappointed. He was enjoying himself. "How long are you in Salzburg?"

"I am studying music here for two more weeks. Hopefully, I will see you again." Standing, she bent over the table and provided Mueller a tantalizing view of her ample breasts. Kissing him on the cheek, she walked away, turning around once to wave good-bye.

Mueller sat quietly for a few moments, allowing her lingering, arousing scent to invade his senses.

Catherine toured with him three more lunch hours before they ended up in her hotel for an afternoon. It would be a tryst he would not soon forget.

Mueller's daughter, Anna, studied music in the city. She was twenty-five and single, a predicament brought on by extreme shyness and an overbearing mother. Quietly attractive, she often hid behind her floppy hat and glasses to avoid attracting attention.

It was late afternoon between classes. She was sitting on a campus bench, her instrument abandoned on the lawn. Catherine followed the girl and sat beside her on the bench.

"It was a good lesson today," she said casually. "We play the same instrument." She pointed to the cello on the lawn.

"It's very heavy," was all Anna could muster, turning her face away.

"You play very well. I am just a beginner. Perhaps you could give me some lessons." Catherine slid closer to Anna on the bench.

"No...oh, no, I couldn't," Anna stammered. "I'm not really very good."

"You're better than the teachers," Catherine replied. Anna blushed but said nothing.

They talked for hours. The orange glow of the setting sun silhouetted the centuries-old architecture. It was beautiful and romantic. As evening fell, they walked hand in hand toward the centre of town, continuing their conversation over dinner.

Two days later, Catherine was on a plane back to the States, both films she had created during the previous evenings safely stowed in her baggage. By the time the films were edited, the Mueller family would be seen as a lot closer than they ever thought possible.

The conference in Amsterdam was in ten weeks' time. With so much at stake, van Holder had to be ready. ASC was his baby. That was why Amsterdam was so important. His vision would soon be realized.

He contemplated the events of the past few days. The forensic accountant was becoming a nuisance. Van Holder was convinced that he had somehow stumbled onto his financial plans, even though the coincidences created by CSA could be easily explained. Then there were the stupid actions of his computer genius. Why did he think redirecting money to the accountant's bank would make him go away? Van Holder couldn't tolerate the incompetence. The bodies were piling up. Now was not the time to attract attention.

The CSA programmer in question sauntered into his office and slid into a chair across the massive desk.

"What were you thinking, Harry?" Van Holder's eyes bored into his covert subordinate.

Harry had been moonlighting for van Holder for the past two years. He had been approached at a foundation fundraiser and was made an offer that was too compelling to turn down. The cash was great, but better still was the unlimited resources and mandate to create havoc. "I was just having a little fun. You know, they used to date—McLeod and Dalton."

"Well, now we have a real mess to clean up. Apparently our forensic accountant has become reacquainted with her. Somehow he learned about the CSA study at SuperMart and contacted her."

"You've got to be kidding! Never saw that coming," Harry replied, chuckling.

"This isn't funny." Van Holder spat. "We've taken the girl, but unfortunately she comes with some baggage. Dalton tried to play the hero, so now he's along for the ride."

"What do you want me to do? As usual, you seem to have everything under control." Harry stifled his smile.

"It's time to end our relationship with the Centre for Strategic Analysis." Van Holder glared at the reprobate.

Harry had ensured the data CSA accumulated over the last two years had been routed to ASC servers deep underground in the Montana bunker. He had overseen the building of the complex during his 'holidays.' It was an immense network that dwarfed the already substantial systems used by CSA. The prospect of destroying a beautiful computer system so nobody could detect the sabotage made Harry smile. He was already thinking about his approach.

"Once you're done," van Holder continued, "I want you to disappear...to Montana. Keep McLeod interested and feeling secure. With the recent events, the timetable has been moved up. Your program will be implemented nation-wide in three weeks."

"Two months early...why the rush?"

"The program is ready, and I don't want to play host to our two new guests any longer than I have to."

"What then?"

Van Holder glared at the computer genius as he stood up. "That is none of your concern," he said, abruptly terminating the conversation.

After leaving the meeting, Harry went home to the confines of his personal computer domain. Amongst the countless hardware cases, switching routers and monitors was the command centre for a genius. During his years before CSA, Harry had created some of the best hacker programs ever invented. Now, years after he had pioneered the techniques, most of the base code was still being used by novice and veterans alike. He was legendary in the underground hacker community, even if he had eventually gone 'legit.'

"Okay, Hal, let's see what you can do for me today." Harry addressed his mainframe by name, stealing the moniker from Stanley Kubrick's "2001 – A Space Odyssey."

"Yes, Hal, I know it's important to misguide the signal from the CSA mainframe's anti-virus program to another server." Harry spoke out loud to his mainframe as he planned the illicit attack on the CSA network. A few moments later, "We're in. And Hal, if anyone asks it was the geeks at West Cal University who purged the data."

Harry was pleased as he entered his commands to destroy the CSA network, making it look as though they had come directly from somewhere within the WCU Administration (in the unlikely event that someone could trace his code.) The virus entered the CSA mainframe innocuously as a data download from the admissions department of the University as a routine data dump. Milliseconds after the CSA server had accepted the command it latched onto the first bit of information in the database. Each field in every one of the millions of files was renamed.

"HALWASHERE" would be the only detail left in each entry. As the virus invaded the system, it also attacked the secure backup server 1500 miles away in Tennessee, which he had compromised several months earlier. Harry liked to plan ahead.

"Thank you, Hal. Your work is spectacular, as usual." Harry sat back with his hands clasped behind his neck, watching the spectacle unfold. Twenty years of data accumulation and methodical study would be wiped out in the time it took someone to play a game of checkers. He was content. A hacker's dream assignment two years in the making was now complete.

Harry removed the hard drive from the server—a little insurance, should future meetings with van Holder not go as planned. Before leaving, Harry removed any identifying traces of his minimal existence in the apartment, grabbed his laptop and left.

Chapter 13

The jet dipped below the horizon as it left the Bay area, banking north-east towards the Canadian border. The corporate plane was spacious, allowing the captives to talk privately at the back of the cabin. Andrew and Dana were seated together, their wrists painfully bound by plastic riot restraints. Uncertain of their fate, the two prisoners were still thankful for their unorthodox reunion.

"You came after me," Dana whispered as she moved closer to Andrew. It felt comfortable having him next to her.

"This is all my fault," Andrew replied remorsefully. He was sure his call had triggered the abduction.

"It wasn't you. I must have discovered something in my research."

Andrew started to protest but was cut short as one of the kidnappers approached. "No sense planning your escape. It's a long way down."

"And you have the only parachutes, right?" Andrew quipped.

"By the time we're done, you'll wish jumping from the plane had been an option."

"How's your friend?" Andrew asked, the fear hidden by the distain in his voice.

"He'll probably walk with a limp. He'll be happy to see you."

The man walked away before Andrew could reply. That was one reunion he wanted to avoid. Instead he yelled up the aisle, "Hey, cut us free. It's not as if we're going anywhere."

The man returned, taking a jackknife out of his pocket.

"Thanks," they replied together, rubbing their bruised, stiff arms.

"Might as well be comfortable on your last flight," the man smirked as he walked to the front of the plane.

A chill ran down Dana's spine. She moved closer to Andrew, grabbing his hand and squeezing.

"Don't worry, Dana. We'll be okay." Andrew knew they had the upper hand— desperation was a potent weapon. The kidnapper's fear tactic had convinced him they would have to act as soon as possible after they landed. In a way, he was thankful for the situation; he was with Dana.

Squeezing her hand in return, Andrew leaned forward and kissed her on the cheek. She smelled of lavender. "Like spring rain," he used to tell her. Despite the ordeal, her hair was surprisingly neat and her dress only slightly wrinkled. Outwardly, she was composed, the true confident spirit. But Andrew knew that inside she was a frightened little puppy. They continued to talk in muted tones about the past seven months they had spent apart, both sorry the relationship had ended.

"Andrew, what do you think is going on? Who would abduct us? Do you think they know we used to live together?"

Wrapped up in their conversation, they didn't see the kidnapper approach. "That's enough talk." He pointed to Dana. "Move to the front of the plane."

Andrew reluctantly let her go. He wanted to ease her fear but was resigned to watching her from the back of the plane. He needed to plan their escape. Hopefully, she would be ready when the time came.

The kidnapper settled into the seat next to Andrew and pulled out a cigarette from a sterling silver case with the initials BAC written in stylized letters on the front.

"Smoke?" he asked. He saw Andrew staring at the case. "A gift from a friend," he said, smiling. "She found it at work last week."

Andrew was about to ask what he meant when the comment sunk in. "You bastard."

"He was fine until you came along and poked your nose in our business." The killer replied.

"And what sort of business is that—murder and theft?" Andrew snarled.

The man ignored the question. "Once we land, you and your friend will be going separate ways."

"What are you going to do with her?" Andrew grabbed the man by the arm, anger overtaking him.

"Do you want your wrists tied again?" The man shook his arm free and stood up to leave. He leaned in close to Andrew's face. "I'd be more concerned with what we're going to do with you."

The night sky was darkening as the jet banked down toward its destination. As Andrew stared out the porthole, he wondered how so much could have happened to him so quickly...and why.

The plane taxied to the end of the lonely runway on the outskirts of a small Montana town close to the Canadian border. Dana was escorted out of the plane, leaving Andrew alone with the newer, tougher recruit from the San Jose airport. Now was his chance to escape.

"Stop!" Andrew yelled to distract the attacker.

"Or what?" The man ignored him and continued down the aisle.

Andrew held the plastic restraining band in the palm of his right hand with an inch of the sharp end sticking out. Feigning a trip, Andrew stumbled down the aisle between the seats. Once he was within striking distance, he thrust the weapon upward. His alert captor moved stealthily out of the way, lashing out with his left foot, catching Andrew in the ribs.

"Nice try."

Andrew coughed, holding his side in agony. "In what branch of the military did you get your training?" he wheezed. *This was going to be difficult*, he thought. He was up against a skilled fighter.

"Navy Seals, if you must know. Dishonorable discharge. Beat up my commanding officer."

"No doubt," Andrew replied as he stood up. He still had one more chance. With lightning speed, he lunged forward, using the leg of the seat as a pivot. Before his attacker could shift position, he punched downward toward the man's groin. When the counter-attack came, he thrust upwards with the makeshift weapon, puncturing the skin and severing an artery at the base of the neck. The man clutched his neck as blood stained the leather seats of the private jet. Leaping over the plush seat, Andrew didn't bother to turn around to assess the damage before heading for the door. He cautiously peaked around the corner. All clear.

The two pilots were busy charting a return flight, unaware of the carnage behind the cockpit door. Andrew made his way down the gangway, dragging the bleeding man off the plane. Hopefully, whoever discovered the mess would think it was his blood and not raise the alarm. He moved quickly toward a small shack that looked like it was the makeshift terminal for the airstrip. The rear lights of two vehicles were visible in the distance. They heading west on what looked like the only traversable road, he noted. Andrew dragged the weak, dying man behind the shack. He ducked down briefly when he saw the pilot's head emerge to look around. A few seconds later, the stairs were raised and the door closed.

"Where are they taking her?" Andrew drew the injured man closer to him. He grabbed his jacket and lifted him into a sitting position.

"I don't know. You figure it out." The captor spat out some blood.

"Do you want me to help you or not?"

"There's nothing you can do for me." The man knew the lucky jab had severed his jugular. Death would come soon.

"If you know you're going to die, why not help me?" Andrew implored.

"Shit happens." The man coughed, blood filling his lungs. A moment later he hunched forward, limp.

Andrew covered the former Navy Seal with debris. A short survey of the building and area confirmed the field was abandoned. As he looked around, the sound of the jet taking off broke the eerie silence, leaving him alone.

Andrew pilfered the meager supplies inside the shack—two granola bars of questionable vintage, a bottle of water and a map. By the looks of the various clippings and route markers on the bulletin board on the wall behind the dusty desk, he was in Montana, one hundred and fifty miles south of the Alberta border, northwest of Great Falls. He was in the middle of nowhere.

Why would they bring Dana here? Obviously, they still needed her. Otherwise, why bother to kidnap her from CSA? He needed to find her before she finished whatever it was they were forcing her to do.

A coyote howled in the distance. A symphony of howls responded. Andrew had spent his childhood summers in the wilderness of the Pacific Northwest, so he was no stranger to the sounds of the night. The ebony landscape extended past the airstrip.

The sliver of the new moon in the cool evening sky illuminated the road ahead with its dim light. Before leaving the shack, Andrew removed the useful items from the dead mercenary and stuffed the map and rations he found in the shack into his pockets. Wiping the blood from the man's windbreaker, he put it on over his own coat, zipped it up and started down the road, uncertain of where he was headed.

Eight miles away, two black Chevy Suburbans turned off the main road. They had just passed a faded wooden sign held up by two massive logs displaying "Fifty-Point-One Ranch." Three hundred yards further, the vehicles turned onto a narrow path and drove past an a-frame ranch house perched on the rolling Montana hills towards an old barn. Two hydraulic levers—incongruous on such a dilapidated structure—opened the barn doors, allowing the vehicles to enter. The doors closed silently behind the vehicles that were now locked in place by the giant arms. The driver of the lead car stepped up to a console and positioned one eye in front of a retina scanner. The floor immediately began to drop. It took less than a minute for the vehicles to descend three stories to the complex below.

Dana was numb with fear. Since her near rescue at the airport, she had clung to the hope that Andrew would find a way out. Now she was alone and terrified. She felt like she was in the middle of a spy novel, not her favorite genre. *Andrew loved those types of books*, she thought. Hopefully, he'd figure out the plot before it was too late.

Once the platform had reached its destination, the two SUVs were driven off into an underground garage. Dana was deposited next to a sealed door, accompanied by an escort; the man Andrew had called 'goon number two.'

"Nice place you have here," Dana said sarcastically.

Before the man could respond, the doors opened from the inside. Unbeknownst to Dana, they were being observed from a security room deep inside the complex. The operators of the Bunker were careful to ensure their security. The stakes were high. The possibility of imposters was not dismissed.

As the door opened, Dana was greeted by a bear of a man. Helmut Gundst was a six-foot-five, 250-pound frame oddly out of place in the underground cavern. He was in charge of the subterranean complex and answered to only one man. He ran the Bunker like a military camp and demanded respect from his people. Everyone did what he commanded. The consequences of not doing so were severe.

"Once I have deposited Ms. McLeod, I'll see you in my office," Helmut ordered Dana's escort. "I want a full report."

Smith, the escort, was resigned to the tongue lashing he would receive. "Have you heard from Antoine?"

Helmut gestured toward the man. "Just get me your report."

"Yes, sir," Smith replied.

As her escort departed, Dana started to speak, but Helmut held up his hand.

"All in good time, Ms McLeod. Come with me. There's a lot to do. My name is Helmut Gundst and this is my show. You will be told what you need to know in good time."

"Time for what?" Dana asked, not entirely sure she wanted to know.

Helmut walked down the corridor, expecting her to follow. They entered the main computer room where people were milling about. The underground chamber resembled a white-collar anthill. Curiosity forced Dana to ask the obvious.

"Ms. McLeod, we are about to change the world. The research you have done for the past four years has greatly assisted us in realizing our goals."

"What do you know about my research?"

Helmut yelled at one of the analysts hard at work across the room. A kid, barely out of college, wearing a white lab coat and carrying a notebook, rushed towards them. A large plasma screen lit up on the far wall. Dana's picture and vitals were displayed for everyone in the huge room to see. Nobody paid attention.

"Please relay to Ms. McLeod her background," Helmut said to the assistant.

"Born Boston, the second daughter to Arthur and Wilma McLeod of McLeod Shipping fame, 31 years old, auburn hair, brown eyes, graduated Harvard third in her class with Bachelor of Science degree, moved to California to obtain Masters, majored statistical analysis, joined CSA four years ago, created what has become known there as the 'McLeod Model', out to save the world."

"Why do you know so much about me?" Dana demanded. "And take that picture off the wall."

"It is our business to know the people who work for us," Helmut replied matter-of-factly.

"I work for Alex Jacobson at CSA."

"CSA no longer exists. Look around you—this is CSA."

The enormous room contained more computer equipment than Dana had ever seen. The CSA network was a toy next to the computing power that faced her. Her mind raced. What was he talking about? She had been at her desk working only twelve hours earlier.

"CSA was formed by Alex years ago, a pipedream for a zealot. It became a perfect tool, and thanks to you, we are almost ready."

"Ready for what," Dana stated dryly. She had no intention of furthering their devious plans, whatever they were.

"Your model is only useful to us with your analysis of the results, something a computer cannot do. We need your intuition, if you will."

"And if I refuse?" Dana felt strangely defiant. Her life was in their hands, but she didn't care.

"Your boyfriend will be killed," Helmut stated dryly.

"How do I know you haven't already killed him?"

"Ms. McLeod, please. You and Andrew Dalton lived together for four years. You know each other very well. I'm sure you don't want him to die." Helmut gestured towards the room in front of her.

Having no options, she nodded her head as they strode to her computer station— identical to her workstation at CSA, right down to the personalized, voice-activated greeting. Dana was back at work, a thousand miles away and three stories below the rolling hills of Montana.

Helmut handed her a list. "You have one month to run the applications of your model for these industries. Call me when you've completed each one." He handed her a card with access information, including his number. He walked away.

Dana looked around. A guard stood near the entrance to the room, watching her settle in. Men and women busied themselves in the myriad of cubicles scattered throughout the room. Whatever was going on required a serious amount of labor. Thinking about Andrew, she sucked in her breath and booted her computer. Just as she was about to start working, she saw a familiar face.

"Harry!" Dana yelled, rising from her chair and running over to hug her friend who had just entered the room. The guard started to move towards her, but recognized Harry and returned to his post.

"Dana, what are you doing here?" Harry asked, returning Dana's hug.

"They kidnapped you, too?" Dana whispered.

"Yeah," Harry lied. "They said they'd kill me if I didn't help them."

"What are we going to do?" Dana murmured, afraid to be overheard.

"Whatever they want. The sooner we're done, the quicker we can leave this hellhole." After assuring her they would be fine if they cooperated, Harry made up an excuse to leave. He hated manipulating her, but it was the only way he could try and ensure her safety.

Andrew had walked for almost an hour when the rain began. The clouds had rolled in, darkening the night sky and obscuring the new moon. Soon the sky opened up, drenching the parched prairie. Flashes of forked lightening interrupted the darkness, providing brief glimpses of the surrounding countryside. Groves of poplar and birch hung in quiet silhouette against the momentary brightness. Andrew trudged through the muck, lifting the windbreaker over his head to stay dry. One of the lightning strikes displayed an abandoned range hut in the distance. The hut was weathered and rustic, but would keep him dry until morning. He rummaged through a dusty wooden trunk and found several moth-eaten blankets. After finding a dry corner under a small section of the decaying roof, he lay down to sleep.

Rays from the rising sun in the clear, blue Montana sky burst into the hut. Andrew glanced at his Timex Ironman—it was five-thirty in the morning. From inside the hut, he could see the desolate grass fields stretching to the end of the horizon. Andrew left the building and continued west down the dirt road. After what seemed like hours, a cluster of buildings came into view. As he made his way to the main building, a black SUV emerged from the barn. Andrew dove behind a small hill, hoping he hadn't been spotted. The passenger in the SUV scanned the horizon. His rifle rested on his lap, its barrel poking out the open window. *For me*, Andrew thought.

Andrew headed towards the barn from which the SUV had emerged. As he made his way around the main building, he paused briefly to look inside. Suddenly he froze. Gazing out the window, barely twenty feet from where he stumbled, was Senator Nathan McDaniel, a veteran politician from California. *What was he doing here?* McDaniel was a no-nonsense republican in the pocket of big business. Although the Senator's name had shown up on several files he had worked on and he was mentioned in several forensic audit reports Andrew had seen, he had never been implicated.

Crouching below the window, Andrew listened in on the heated discussion taking place.

"It doesn't matter now. The damage has been done." The commanding voice was coming from the far side of the room.

"This can't go off the rails. Too much is riding on the outcome," another person responded, most likely the Senator.

"It has been contained," intoned the first person. "And don't lecture me about the outcome. I have far more to lose than you do."

"I've got twenty years on the Hill...and I want 1600 Pennsylvania." Inside the room the Senator paced anxiously.

"Nathan, you'll be scamming deals for the next twenty years, so cut the crap. What's important is that you get back to Washington and finish your part of the deal. I've given you the research...now go and use it." Van Holder was impatient and didn't appreciate the hollow challenge from the Californian Senator, a man whose entire career he had crafted.

"My subcommittee is relying on that report," McDaniel replied.

A third voice entered the conversation. "They'll be ready."

"Just make sure I get what I need." McDaniel said with finality.

The Senator moved away from the window. A few seconds later a door closed and the conversation continued. Andrew hoisted himself up to peer through the window. He recognized the first man's face but couldn't put a name to it. He was about to leave when he heard his own name mentioned.

"...and what about Dalton?"

"Somehow he escaped. Killed a security man, an ex-Navy Seal. A team just left to hunt for him. He won't get far."

The third man had a slight foreign accent. *Possibly German*, Andrew thought. The tone of the conversation became more sinister.

"Does he know anything?" Gundst asked.

"We thought he knew more than he did. Somehow he contacted the McLeod girl. My operations director thinks the SuperMart accountant gave away the connection."

Andrew crouched down again. *What did this mean? What had Bob Croft told him that was so crucial?*

"The program shouldn't have been run. It wasn't ready," Gundst replied.

"And who's to blame for that?" van Holder sneered, glaring at his subordinate. "We're only weeks away from a complete launch."

"McLeod is working in the Bunker as we speak. She was given a little incentive."

So Dana was here, Andrew thought. *What did they mean by 'the Bunker?'* Andrew left the porch and headed toward the barn. If he found nothing there, he would risk taking a look inside the large ranch house. Andrew peeked around the back edge of the barn and saw a door a few yards away. He crouched down and sprinted along the side of the building. The door was open. He didn't notice the security camera panning the entrance from its perch on a nearby tree.

Once inside, he let his eyes adjust and looked around. In the center of the room was a large platform with oil stains and vehicle tracks and what looked like a garage hoist. *Too big to be a mechanic's shop. It must be an elevator of some sort*, he mused. *Where did it lead?* Seeing no controls, Andrew searched the rest of the barn. At the far end were three large ventilation shafts, each six feet wide. *There was definitely something down there*. With the aid of a long steel rod, Andrew pried back one of the covers so he could squeeze in. A maintenance ladder in the shaft led to the lower levels…and hopefully to Dana. Three stories below, the duct leveled off and branched out in several directions. Andrew picked one at random and made his way along the narrow corridor. After crawling on his hands and knees for fifteen minutes, he arrived at a vent. Kicking the vent outward, he jumped down and looked around to see if anyone had heard the racket.

Outside the ventilation room, numerous hallways branched off a large corridor. Each hallway led to several numbered rooms. *This must be the sleeping quarters,* he thought. He scampered down the first hallway and finally found an unlocked door. The room had a pleasant décor, personalized with family pictures and artwork. *Judging by the number of rooms, this place had a lot of personnel,* he thought. *Perhaps it was a secret government site. That would explain the Senator's presence at the ranch.* But that wasn't Andrew main concern—he was there to find Dana.

Donning a white lab coat he found in the closet, Andrew hoped he would blend in as he searched the underground complex. When he left the room, he almost bumped into similarly-clad inhabitants coming around a corner. Fortunately, they paid no attention to him. He decided to follow them. By the time they reached the end of the corridor, he had his bearings. The concentric complex had five corridors that culminated at a central hub— a large circular room with panels, large plasma monitors and scores of people working at computer terminals. No one seemed to notice him as he wandered around freely, except for one security guard who glanced at him briefly before staring off into space again.

Andrew saw that everyone except him had security tags hanging around their necks. Sooner or later somebody would notice. Luckily, after twenty minutes of glancing furtively into cubicles and bumping into people, he found Dana. A guard stood watching several meters away. Andrew grabbed Dana's arm, forcing her out of her chair.

"Don't react, Dana. Just get up and follow me," he whispered.

The guard started to move. Dana stopped.

"Wait here," she whispered. Walking over to the guard, she pointed to Andrew and then to an area across the room and told him they would be reviewing a document. The guard nodded and went back to his station.

Halfway around the main circle, they veered off into one of the feeder halls, not bothering to look back to see if the guard had noticed.

"Andrew, how did you get here? How did you get away?" Dana hugged him after they made it into the hallway.

"I'll explain later. They're bound to notice if you don't return to your desk."

Backtracking to the ventilation room, they quickly made their way up the ladder to the surface. Unbeknownst to them, an alarm had been sounded when they reached the interior of the barn. Three stories down, the security room responded immediately. Doors were automatically sealed and personnel were summoned to intercept.

With only seconds to spare, Andrew and Dana crawled out of the ventilation shaft. Andrew cursed himself for his stupidity. He was tracking kidnappers and murderers...did he think they would just allow him to waltz in and grab Dana? These people were determined. It was time for his A-game...if he had one.

Grabbing a fencepost that was lying next to the barn door he flung it through the window, spraying glass fifteen feet onto the field beyond. Diving through the open space, he landed hard on his shoulder. Ignoring the pain, he turned to help Dana through the window. Once free of the sealed barn, they ran past the main house just as the security guards emerged from one of the smaller buildings behind the barn. Riding ATVs, the teams of guards headed in different directions in an attempt to cut off the escapees.

"They went left, to the back of the house," the team leader shouted. "Send half the men back. Cut them off near the pool."

"Subjects are in sight," was the immediate response.

"Alert the main house and watch the perimeter. Whatever happens, don't let them near the house."

"Yes, sir." To thwart all avenues of escape, the men converged, armed and ready.

Built in 1920 by a wealthy Eastern industrialist, the 10,000-square-foot main ranch house blended naturally into the rugged beauty of the Montana wilderness. Surrounding the house were numerous outbuildings—the kind you would expect to see on a stud farm in Kentucky. A white wooden fence surrounded the property. It was no ordinary white fence; this one had electrical charges and sensors to keep strangers out, not animals in.

Andrew and Dana rounded the house, barely avoiding the pool. One of their pursuers was not so lucky—the ATV and driver dove nine feet to the bottom. Andrew held Dana's hand as they sprinted away from the house toward the woods. Andrew attempted to leap over the fence, but an electrical jolt sent him flying. Running back, he helped Dana clear the fence and they bolted for the trees.

The second ATV was fast approaching, so they ducked behind a spindly birch tree. Andrew grabbed a dead branch lying on the ground. When the ATV came close to his hiding spot, he came out swinging, hitting his pursuer on the side of his head. He heard a sickening thud as flesh and wood connected. They followed the ATV as it careened down the side of a hill. Two miles later, Andrew stopped the commandeered ATV. For now, they were safe.

"Okay, Dana. What is going on?"

"I'm not entirely sure. Something to do with the model I've been working on." Dana told him about her discussion with Helmut and the conversation with Harry.

"They took Harry?"

"That's what he told me. But Harry has never done anything just because he was told to. He was at his desk working only a few hours prior to my abduction. How could he have arrived before me?"

"Whatever his involvement, something was done to implicate me after I uncovered a scandal at SuperMart."

"My model was run through SuperMart!" Dana stared at Andrew, incredulous.

"That's why I called. An accountant there told me about CSA. He was murdered later that night."

"Oh my God." Dana was shocked. "Who are these people?"

"I don't know, but I have to find out why they framed me."

"*We'll* find out, Andrew," Dana said emphatically. "We're in this together."

They embraced. The warmth of their two bodies blended in quiet comfort as they kissing slowly and then more urgently. A minute later, the sound of a helicopter disrupted their romantic reunion.

"We'd better get out of here and find a place to hide," Andrew said, starting up the ATV.

"If we can, let's go to my parents' place at Whistler. From there we can plan our next move."

Chapter 14

Thanks to Senator McDaniel, van Holder was able to build the underground research centre with Washington slush funds. The Senator was under the misconception that the information gathered at this facility would help the U.S. compete in the global marketplace. He didn't know the real reason for its existence—to prepare for what would occur in Amsterdam, now only a few months away. Van Holder intended to keep it that way. As far as the Senator was concerned, McLeod was a spy who had infiltrated the Bunker, and with the help of Dalton, had escaped with top-secret information. He would let McDaniel believe he would need to find them, but send Catherine to eliminate them before any more damage could be done.

In the span of a few hours, the Bunker went from calm preparedness to urgent pandemonium. How had someone penetrated the most sophisticated security system available to the U.S. military so easily? For some unknown reason, nothing had been done to block access through the ventilation system. Van Holder's plans were now in disarray. *That bastard Harry…why did he have to screw up his plans?*

McDaniel sat across from the Bunker's architect. When he had signed on with van Holder, he knew he was making a deal with the devil. Vanity and ego had caused this breech. They simply didn't think anyone would know or care what they were doing until it was too late. And now there were two spies loose who knew the Bunker existed. These interlopers would have to be stopped. They couldn't afford to lose six years of work. Leaders, businessmen, bureaucrats and academics were now in the palms of their hands. All was ready… and now this. He was fifty-seven years old. Without this arrangement, there would be no chance to gain the White House. Being a seasoned politician and well respected in Washington was not enough. Money—and the people who doled it out—made Presidents. McDaniel had found his man in van Holder. Van Holder had supplied all the equipment housed in the Bunker. Those in the know in Washington, those aware of the slush fund, thought the Bunker was a secret Government think tank for the economy. It had to remain secret, at least until the election.

The Senator was a California boy who had played football and loved cheerleaders and his old Ford pickup truck. He had a gift of the gab and could charm the tail off a rattlesnake. After two years of community college, he had started a small business in his hometown. He would do anything that didn't involve farming. His construction business grew, and by the time he was thirty, he had sold out for millions. He had it made. Soon after his 'retirement', at a Fourth of July celebration, someone suggested he run for state politics. He won his first election by a landslide; the incumbent just couldn't compete with McDaniel's charisma and charm. His oratorical talent had carried the day.

McDaniel stopped pacing and sat down to glare at Helmut across a massive tree slab that served as a coffee table. "Did the girl steal any secrets before she escaped?"

"Nothing that we know about," replied the security chief, glancing at van Holder.

"Dalton and the girl will be found," van Holder piped up. He wanted to be sure Helmut saw McDaniel as his superior.

"Helmut, put your best men on the job. Track them down," McDaniel ordered as he stood up to conclude the discussion. He had to get back to Washington. His trip had already been delayed by these unfortunate events.

"He still sees the research as part of an initiative to ensure U.S. competitiveness?" Helmut asked after the Senator left.

Van Holder smirked. "He does, and he's not far from the truth. Can we finish without the girl?"

"We think we understand the program enough to continue." Helmut made sure he knew the answer to the anticipated question.

"Implement the model on all the strategic industries we discussed. Let me know if there are any problems." Van Holder ordered.

"It has already begun," Helmut was relieved to report.

"We have three weeks to finish. I don't want anyone to sleep until this is done. And find those two." Van Holder left without waiting for a reply.

Nathan McDaniel boarded the government jet and immediately dialed the memorized number. The rundown to the election had started and he didn't want anything to get in the way. He would be the next President; it was part of the deal. But he still needed assurance.

"The timing is set. Don't worry, everything will work out. The White House is as good as yours, but not until we're done here." Van Holder assured him.

McDaniel was ready to assume the role of supreme commander. The world would be a different place. It was time to get to work.

"What about Amsterdam?" McDaniel was anxious.

"Nathan, I told you not to worry. The less you know about what's going on, the better."

"Will it be finished on time?"

"Yes," van Holder stated emphatically.

After the Senator hung up, van Holder picked up his satellite phone and dialed. He spent several minutes explaining the situation before asking Catherine about Tokyo. The response was a vivid reminder of her ruthless efficiency. After the conversation ended, he dialed the Bunker. Helmut's men had screwed things up badly enough. It was time to turn on the pressure. They had no idea what Dalton or McLeod knew, but it was enough. Involving Catherine would slow things down, but he had no choice. The leak needed to be sealed.

After calling her back from Asia, van Holder tracked down Harry. When he arrived at the ranch house, they didn't exchange pleasantries. "We need to flush out Dalton and McLeod. What cyber magic can you conjure up?"

"If they use their plastic, we can use the ASC network to track their location," Harry said.

"Do it," van Holder ordered. "Now!"

"Sure thing," Harry replied indifferently.

"And continue routing SuperMart funds to Dalton's account. Then download all the information you have on the Croft murder. The press will need the background. His numerous crimes are about to become public."

"What about Dana?" Harry asked.

"She's along for the ride," Van Holder replied.

"Do you think they'll be found?"

"They're as good as dead." Van Holder hung up the phone.

Harry stared into the phone for a few minutes. It was great conquering the cyber world, but nobody had ever died. He had no idea van Holder was so cold-blooded. He would have to find some way to warn Dana. In the meantime, he had better create some insurance.

Chapter 15

A torrential downpour soaked Andrew and Dana to the skin. At forty miles an hour, they weren't making good headway on the ATV. They would need a different mode of transportation. They had been traveling north for two hours across the rugged Montana wilderness, avoiding the main roads, knowing the backcountry would be safer.

"It's cold," Dana yelled over the drone of the ATV's engine.

"We'll stop soon. I'd like to find a spot to ditch this thing," Andrew screamed back.

Dana pointed to an outcropping of rocks leading to a small, concealed gully. "Over there."

After the ATV was covered with leaves and branches, they settled down inside a nearby rock enclave to get away from the rain.

"Do you think they'll find us?" Dana snuggled up against Andrew to stay warm.

"I suspect they'll go south, thinking we'll try and get home," Andrew replied.

"It was strange down there. They told me they'd kill you if I didn't cooperate."

"They tried to kill me right after you left." Andrew proceeded to describe the fight, leaving out the gruesome details.

"You killed him?" Dana couldn't believe what she was hearing. Maybe she didn't really know her former boyfriend. She shivered in silent fear.

"It was a fluke. Self defense," Andrew said, attempting to justify his brutal act. He had killed a man and yet felt no remorse. *What must Dana be thinking?*

"Something tells me these people are no strangers to killing," Dana said. "You had to do it." She kissed his cheek. They held each other for warmth, their bodies enjoying the closeness.

"I missed you, Dana," Andrew finally said, cupping her face in his hands.

"Why did we break up anyway?" Dana asked, chuckling.

"Work."

"Mine or yours?" Dana asked.

"Ours," Andrew said tenderly as he held her. It was nice to feel her touch again. For a few minutes, the two of them forgot about the danger they were in as they drifted off to sleep.

The sun was just coming up over the horizon when the noise shook them awake. The sound of whirling helicopter blades filled the canyon. Clambering to get out of the cave, crouching low to avoid being seen, they watched as the pilot disappeared over the horizon.

"Is that them?' Dana suddenly felt frightened.

"I don't think so." Andrew remembered the helicopter from the ranch. Its markings were different from the one that had just awakened them.

"We should go look." Dana asked.

They left the safety of the cave and made their way to where the helicopter had dipped over the horizon. An hour later, they saw the landing site across a small canyon.

"Stay here," he told Dana, thinking the two of them would attract more attention than a lone traveler crawling over the rocks. Reaching the other side of the small canyon, Andrew peered over the edge. The occupants of the helicopter were working with what looked like geology equipment. It appeared they didn't have anything to do with the ranch or the government. Andrew approached them confidently.

"Hello," he called out while he was still a safe distance away.

Startled by the voice, the two men looked up. "What in Sam blazes are you doing out here?" the surprised pilot yelled back.

Andrew had concocted a plausible story for the geologists. By this time, he had reached the men. "My girlfriend and I ran out of gas with our ATV last night. We're staying at a guest ranch about an hour from here. We went too far and couldn't get back before dark."

"Where's your girlfriend?" The second man asked, looking past Andrew to the canyon beyond.

"She's on the backside of the canyon. She hurt her foot, so I climbed the rest of the way by myself. We saw your helicopter, but it took us a few hours to reach you."

"Lucky for you, we're just finishing up and heading back to Kalispell. We'd be happy to take you back."

Andrew didn't have a 'lodging' to return to. "I'm not sure where it is anymore. If you take us into town, we'll call and get them to pick us up. Besides, my girlfriend should have her foot looked at"

"Good idea. We'll be about twenty minutes." The pilot returned to his work.

By the time they reached Dana on the other side of the canyon, she was frantic. Andrew jumped out of the side of the helicopter, remembering at the last minute to tell her to limp. Dana snuggled up to him during the flight to Kalispell, occasionally rubbing her foot in feigned agony.

Kalispell was a typical western town at the edge of America's farm belt where the shopping was passable and the people were friendly. After being dropped off at the local airport, Andrew and Dana settled for a nondescript motel in the centre of town. Despite the recent paint job and new curtains, the motel still looked its age. Putting the deposit on his credit card, Andrew left the room in search of groceries while Dana took a desperately needed shower. Afterwards, they would take an inventory of what they knew about why Dana was kidnapped.

At the cash register of the local grocery store, Andrew picked up a newspaper but failed to notice the article on the bottom of the first page.

CSA FOUNDATION CEO DEAD

Associated Press - San Francisco, Ca. – Alex Jacobson, the founder and CEO of the Centre for Strategic Analysis, was found dead in his home last night, apparently from a self-inflicted gunshot wound. In the past week the Foundation was beset with a series of problems commencing with the total loss of the twenty years of data and research. Experts say it was unusual to lose all data, particularly with the sophisticated backup systems available today. The virus that infected the CSA mainframe caused a chain reaction which destroyed the backup system. The only data left on the network were multiple streams of HALWASHERE – a reference to a computer in the 1970's Arthur C. Clarke's futuristic tale "2001 – A Space Odyssey."

Jacobson's Foundation was then hit with another setback when its main benefactor withdrew support, followed by the majority of its other sponsors. Unconfirmed sources speaking on the grounds of anonymity say that Jacobson was using the Foundation's research for his own gain. No charges had been laid prior to Mr. Jacobson's death.

The CSA, which was started by Mr. Jacobson over twenty years ago, provides research and data services to many Fortune 500 companies.

The police have not ruled out foul play.....

Dana noticed the article immediately when Andrew threw the newspaper on the bed. "Oh, my God!" she exclaimed. "Alex is dead!"

"What?" Andrew jumped up from his prone position beside her on the bed.

"Alex Jacobson, my boss. They say it was suicide, but think there might be foul play." Dana started to cry.

"Anyone close to this thing seems to have a short life expectancy." Andrew wondered how long it would be before they met the same fate.

"How could a Presidential candidate get mixed up in a murder? And why would ASC pull its support at such a critical time?" Dana asked, almost to herself.

Andrew sat bolt upright and stared at Dana as though she had two heads.

"What?" Dana asked.

"That was *him*!" Andrew might as well as had a light bulb beaming over his head.

"Who?"

"The ASC Chairman, at the farm, with the Senator. I recognized him but couldn't place the face." Andrew stated.

"Van Holder was at the ranch?" Dana asked incredulously.

"Why the big shock?"

"One of his companies is SuperMart."

"So what exactly are they doing down there?" Andrew asked himself.

They spent the next few hours speculating but came up blank. Suddenly famished, they headed to a small café down the street from the motel. They ordered a nice bottle of Oregon Pinot Gris, commenting on the depth of the wine selection at the small eatery. It was nice to be together again. They held hands across the table and stared into each other's eyes, giving anyone who saw them the impression that they were deeply in love. Only the waitress disturbed them.

After they had made love in their motel room, they held each other as though they had never been apart. For awhile, neither of them spoke, both lost in their own thoughts. Both hoping the nightmare would end. While Dana was in the shower, Andrew stared vacantly at the credit card receipt lying on the dresser. The entire picture of how the electronic payment system managed by ASC flashed though his mind.

That was it! He thought. ASC must be manipulating the payments going through their electronic data interchange system. Bob Craft said it had to do with a CSA study, but Andrew had a feeling these mistakes were deliberate and not part of any test. His theory would explain the mistakes during the Alberton's audit, but not the unexplained deposits going into his account.

Andrew outlined his theory to Dana when she got out of the shower.

"But the model was designed and run by CSA. ASC had nothing to do with our research." Dana countered.

"What about the guys who attacked me? Why would they do that?" Andrew countered.

"ASC is one of the largest companies in the world. Why would they steal pennies at a time, and from themselves?" Dana continued to question his logic.

"Why would they pull their support from CSA now? You and Harry were the ones working on the model."

"*Harry,*" Dana blurted out. She remembered laughing at him a few months earlier when he was waiting for the computer to process a complex algorithm she had asked him to run. "He had coaxed the computer along, referring to it as HAL."

"So he wasn't kidnapped," Andrew concluded.

"He knew they were going to take me. He mustn't have completely figured out the model…"

"So they kidnapped you." Andrew finished her thought.

Chapter 16

Sitting next to Harry was one of the most beautiful women he had ever met. She smelled of warm rain and cinnamon. Her soft touch electrified him.

He had traced Andrew's credit card to a grocery store, a motel and a restaurant in Kalispell, Montana, wherever that was. After van Holder instructed him to find the pair, he logged onto the ASC Financial Services computer and initiated a nationwide search for both Andrew and Dana's credit and debit transactions. He had secretly hoped they had gotten further by now, but they were still close by and his employers were eager to have them eliminated.

"Have you tracked them down yet?" Catherine queried the computer genius.

"No," he lied. "The system won't notify me until they use a credit card."

Catherine leaned in towards Harry, her mouth inches from his face, her perfume invading his nostrils. "When you know where they are, tell only me. They're mine. I don't want Helmut screwing up again."

Harry could sense her cruel desire. Now he knew why van Holder had insisted they meet. She scared him and now his lie made him vulnerable.

During the time he had spent working for van Holder, he had been able to design and implement dozens of spy programs, viruses and other gems that played havoc on an unsuspecting corporate world. Whenever CSA researchers launched their programs to gather data or study trends, there was a good chance that one of his code busters was somewhere in the background. But none of his programs was as insidious as his crowning achievement, the 'Debitfund' program, which contained the code that had caused Andrew to question the SuperMart accountant and had led to the demise of that pathetic CSA Foundation. He felt no remorse in focusing attention on Dalton; the jerk had dumped Dana. She had been heartbroken at the time, and now he decides to show up, endangering her life.

The beta version of the Debitfund should never have been launched, but to Harry it was all a game—a deadly game, as it turned out. The stakes had certainly increased. Harry knew he was safe for the time being, as the programming wasn't finished and only he knew how to implement the code. Some insurance would be needed, though, and Harry knew just what to do. When he shut down CSA, the final version of the program was transferred to the Bunker's computers and then to his own personal site. Van Holder didn't need to know the program still worked. Not yet, anyway. With silky precision, he entered SuperMart's network, erased the beta version of the program and uploaded the newest version. Initially, when the beta version was accidentally launched, the modifications he made caused a multitude of minute sums to be transferred to account number 1023-56678 – 9 at the California First Bank. Andrew Dalton's bank account.

Harry was completely unaware of the grief the initial glitches in the program had caused. Erasing the beta version from the data accumulation model allowed him to control the ebb and flow of funds to any account. The newest version also solved the loss of control problem. At van Holder's insistence, the funds had been redirected to Dalton's account.

Harry had designed Debitfund years earlier, but it wasn't until he met van Holder that he had the opportunity to implement it on a grand scale. The program allowed van Holder to steal from himself, thus providing a source of financing away from the prying eyes of regulators. It was pure genius. Running off EDI (electronic data interchange)—a method of paying bills through the computer—the Debitfund program would slightly alter the amount of money drawn from a vendor's account based on a complex formula to avoid detection. The initial beta version was ineffective, as it drew too much out of each transaction and didn't discriminate between vendors. The final version, on the other hand, extracted money from bulk payments that weren't attached to specific invoices. It would be impossible to trace.

Debitfund also contained a powerful element that could provide an even greater source of funding. Using ASC's financial services division, the second phase of the program extracted funds from a retail customer when that customer used a credit card to pay for purchases. Intended to fool the unobservant consumer, the program would increase the amount of money taken on certain transactions that met certain criteria. Harry figured that very few people took the time to compare their grocery receipts with the bank withdrawals at the end of the month. And those who did would hopefully miss the mathematically arranged changes.

As added insurance, Harry sent specific information to his private computer at server farm in Europe. He then sent an email to Dana's hotmail account, hoping she would take the time to look. (This information was vital to van Holder's plans, and only Harry knew of its existence and how to access the program remotely.) Next, he entered the ASC Visitrack system and deleted of Andrew and Dana's cards from the verification program rendering them useless. He hoped that by eliminating the cards, Dana would get the message that they were being tracked.

Finally, he called Catherine to let her know the fugitives had been found.

Catherine parted company with van Holder after a brief and satisfying visit. With news of Dalton and McLeod's whereabouts, it was time to get back to work. Much depended on their removal. Leaving the opulent surroundings of van Holder's private quarters, Catherine made her way through the maze of tunnels to the computer center.

"Is this all you have...three receipts?" Catherine asked.

"That's it. They seem to have settled down in Kalispell for a spell," Harry said, chuckling at his rhyme.

"Cute. Let me see the list," Catherine demanded.

Reviewing the information Harry provided, she noticed the information was a day old. After years of working undercover, she knew the man had lied to her. But for now this knowledge would remain hidden. Never eliminate an asset until it was no longer of any use. Harry might still prove helpful.

"Make sure I get any new information as soon as it arrives." She made no mention of the lateness of the current information, but the threat hit its mark.

A few hours later Catherine arrived at the motel, but her targets had gone. She got as much information as she could from the desk clerk—specifically that all the credit cards had been declined. It took only a few more minutes to convince the clerk to let her search their room. Their destination was written on a pad of paper by the phone. After highlighting the top page of the pad with a pencil, she left the motel and returned to the underground facility.

Andrew and Dana left the motel, hoping the clerk wouldn't call the police. Unable to explain the useless credit and debit cards, they gave assurances that money would be sent. Then they left, despite the raging protest. Heading west in their rental car, they drove along in silence for awhile, enjoying the scenery and the comforting drone of the speeding car.

Andrew broke the silence. "Who do you think cancelled the cards?"

"It might have been them, or possibly your bank," Dana replied.

"But why would my bank cancel *your* cards?" Andrew wasn't convinced his bank would do that without letting him know first.

"Good point. Let's assume ASC did it. If they had access to our cards, don't you think they'd use the information to track us?"

"Maybe someone is trying to send us a message," Andrew murmured.

"What sort of message?" Dana asked.

"I don't know. Maybe they found out where we were and decided to slow our progress."

"Do you think they could have located us that quickly?"

"Yes." Andrew stated emphatically.

Andrew knew the system that controlled electronic commerce and made modern living so convenient would also enable its architect to track their every move. With no credit cards, they would no longer be leaving an electronic map, but Andrew was afraid someone was already on their tail.

They drove for awhile in silence. They both realized they couldn't hide and must fight back, but first they needed money. After a quick call to Dana's father, they would need to head to the Western

Union in the next town. Dana told him she needed the money to buy a piece of art for his foundation and the artist took only cash.

As they waited for their money to be processed, Dana went to check her email. The last entry caused her to stop breathing for a moment. It was from Harry.

To: Dana7@hotmail.com
From: Harrythehammer@csalink.org
Subject: Model Study

The program was tracked, so all inputs stopped. Watch for soviet tail. Data sent g180Sx.com in France. Access via parent name. All info there. Hope you are okay. See you at the park in two weeks. HTH.

"What is g180sx?" Andrew asked.

"It's a server farm we use to store redundant data. Harry must have sent something there."

"Can you access it?" Andrew asked.

"Not without a proper connection. CSA has been shut down."

"Then we're screwed."

"I can probably use my Dad's network." Dana replied.

"There must be more to this. Harry wants to meet," Andrew said, referring to the comment about the park. "Do you know where?"

"Yes. It's his favorite place in San Francisco. He's mentioned the park to me several times, offered to take me out for lunch."

Andrew looked at her crosswise, but said nothing.

San Francisco looked beautiful from the sky as the commuter jet circled the city. The day was bright, and the bay glistened like a million diamonds—a perfect day to wander down to Fisherman's Wharf and enjoy the sights. But after their harrowing escape from the underground facility in Montana and with the prospect that they were now being hunted, Dana and Andrew were apprehensive about coming back at all.

The first stop was Andrew's office. Given the prospect of being hunted, they had decided not to separate, even though it would be faster. Andrew reviewed his week-old emails, looking for answers regarding the two audits he had left behind. The firm had been fired from the Alberton's file, which didn't surprise him. Thirty minutes later, he went to Frank's office to make his leave of absence official.

"Andrew, where the hell have you been?" Frank jumped up from his desk. "And Dana…what a surprise!" Frank gave her a warm hug.

"Hi, Frank." Dana sat down on the couch and turned around to enjoy the view of the bay.

"I need to have some time off, Frank."

"Don't you know what's happened in the past week?" Frank went to his desk and grabbed the morning paper. "There's an investigation surrounding your purported embezzlement at SuperMart."

"You were going to talk to them." Andrew felt his voice tighten.

"They wouldn't listen. Their parent company insisted on pursuing the charge."

"Frank, it's a setup. I need your help." Andrew told Frank as much as he knew about the money going into his account.

After taking a few moments to absorb the far fetched story, Frank responded in a fatherly way, "My hands are tied. Until this is straightened out, you're temporarily laid off from the firm."

Andrew stared at his mentor, stunned. "That's ridiculous! It's admitting to the world that I'm guilty." He couldn't believe the firm would do this to him.

"It was a unanimous vote, Andrew." Frank knew it wasn't fair, but he had no choice. He let the comment sink in. He had to protect the firm. The fallout could ruin them all if they didn't act quickly.

Andrew was furious. This was the one place he thought could help end this spiraling nightmare. His mentor and friend had turned on him. He tried to speak, but no words would come. After eight years, his contribution meant nothing.

Frank broke the awkward silence, "The firm can't afford a scandal. We have to distance ourselves from the controversy. Our major clients are already calling"

"That's loyalty," Andrew replied sarcastically, his fists clenched.

"If it's any consolation, I believe you." Frank said reassuringly.

"That and a buck and a quarter will get me a cup of coffee. Don't you get it, Frank? They're not just trying to ruin me. This thing goes much deeper," Andrew raised his voice, his anger getting the better of him.

"Don't be irrational, Andrew. They need a scapegoat so their European merger won't go off the rails. Once that completes, everything will smooth over," Frank said in an attempt to reassure his distraught friend.

Andrew slumped into a chair. He looked up at his mentor and began telling him everything that had happened since he had visited the SuperMart controller. When he was finished, it was Dana's turn to speak.

"The only thing he left out was what happened to me in Montana. Something about my model is fundamental to their plans. We have to find out what that is." She said.

"What are you going to do?" Frank was now fully involved.

"Go to Bermuda and locate the source of the deposits. I know they're originating from a bank called Island Capital. I'll need to track the payments to prove my innocence." Andrew went to the window and stared down at the street below. He could see police cars, their lights flashing as they made their way down Union towards the Brooks and Steiner building.

Frank knew the two young people in front of him were in serious trouble. Andrew was like a son to him.

"There's something else." Andrew laid out his plan to Frank, who was now eager to help in any way he could. They talked about the plan for a few minutes before he and Dana headed for their apartments to retrieve passports and clothes.

Mrs. Moyles, the nosey clerk at the cigarette kiosk in the lobby, saw Andrew exit the elevator. She remembered reading about the accountant in the paper…something about stealing money from the grocery chain where she shopped. And a CPA at that! She was very civic-minded and felt it necessary to do her duty whenever the occasion arose. She was in the perfect position to see the goings on, and made it her business to get involved.

As Dana and Andrew left the front entrance and walked to their rental car, they noticed the police entering the building. Before they got halfway to the curb, they could hear yelling behind them.

"There he is…the accountant! You're letting him get away!" Mrs. Moyles was standing outside her kiosk and pointing at Andrew. Andrew and Dana looked back, frozen in their tracks. Time stood still. In that instant, the world in which Andrew had lived—where police were there to protect, not pursue—changed forever.

"Run, Dana!" Andrew grabbed her hand and they raced to their car. Using the key fob, the doors unlocked remotely and the two of them jumped into the front seats. The car started an instant after Andrew found the keyhole. He jammed the car into gear and they leapt forward, barely missing one of the policemen.

"Andrew, maybe they can help," Dana gasped as they raced away.

The police also reacted quickly. The first bullet ricocheted off the rearview mirror. A second shattered the back windshield. The police took up their positions and aimed at the speeding car as it sped down the busy street.

"Whatever happened to shooting out the tires?" Andrew yelled over the whine of the subcompact's engine.

"Andrew, maybe you should shift gears," Dana yelled back, pointing to the stick shift. In his haste to escape, Andrew had thrown the automatic shift into the lowest gear. As soon as he shifted into drive, the motor started to purr and the car lurched forward with new momentum.

Behind him he could see the red and blue lights of the pursuit cars. Their small car was more nimble than the larger police sedans as they zigzagged through the traffic. He knew they would have to do something before the inevitable police helicopter showed up. Andrew turned off Battery onto Columbus Avenue and made his way to Russian Hill. He didn't relish a street chase, so he made a few quick turns onto side streets, driving under cover of the overgrown trees. The sirens blasting behind them grew quieter as he turned off into a residential neighborhood. Andrew slowed down the car and pulled over to the curb, intent on dropping Dana off so she could make her way out of the city by herself.

"I'll meet you in Boston. You need to find Harry's model and I'll go to Bermuda from there. I have to find proof of how the money was deposited into my account. Don't use the local airports. Take the bus."

"I don't think we should separate." Dana was adamant.

"Dana, we have to. It's me they're after, not you. Even if they capture me, we still have to find out what's going on in Montana. That will be impossible if we're both in prison," Andrew argued.

"Prison! Who said anything about prison?"

"They've created some trumped-up charges that they'll try to make stick. They obviously have friends in high places. Now go, before they find us." Andrew could hear the chopper on its way.

"I love you, Andrew." Dana realized how important he had become, had always been.

"I love you, too. Now go."

They kissed briefly, both reluctant to part. Dana opened the door and quickly disappeared, ducking under a large laurel hedge. *She'll be okay*, Andrew reassured himself. It was better this way, in case he was caught. Something told him that if they did catch up with him, he wouldn't make it into lock-up. The last thing these people wanted was publicity.

Suddenly, the street closed in on him. Oak trees flanked the sidewalks on both sides of the narrow street. Neatly spaced houses, old and well maintained, were set back at the ends of cobblestone driveways. He and Dana had often dreamed of buying a house in this same neighborhood when they could afford it. Now this place didn't seem all that important.

Andrew shook himself back to reality, revved the engine and drove down the narrow lane, hoping to avoid the police. Emerging onto Van Ness Avenue, he made his way south towards the freeway and out of the city. As he approached the ramp to the main highway, he saw two policemen ticketing another motorist. As he drove by them, Andrew looked away to prevent a visual, but his shattered back windshield had given him away. Through the rearview mirror he saw the two officers as they headed for their cruisers, leaving a stunned but grateful motorist in their wake.

Veering off the ramp at the last moment, Andrew crashed into a mail drop box before swerving back onto the road. The police were gaining on him. The rental car's smaller engine couldn't compete with the powerful engines of the San Francisco Police Department fleet. It was time to ditch the car. Taking a left, Andrew weaved through traffic into the Haight-Ashbury district of the city, made famous by the turned-on and tuned-out culture of the late 1960s. Nothing from its past remained in the neighborhood except the middle-aged, ex-hippies pursuing the American dream they had abandoned in their youth.

Andrew momentarily lost sight of the police cruiser. To avoid detection, he drove the rental car into a hidden driveway off a lane across from the entrance to the Golden Gate Park. He jumped out of the car, raced across the street and entered the park just as the cruiser was turning the corner. The cruiser stopped right in front of the driveway. Well hidden behind a towering oak, Andrew peeked around the tree to see if anyone was following him. The policemen didn't appear anxious to search the area and drove away after a few minutes.

Chapter 17

Andrew arrived in Bermuda out of JFK after reluctantly leaving Dana at the departure terminal. They both realized there was no time to spare, so she stayed behind to access her model from Harry's server farm. Andrew went to Bermuda to trace the source of the funds being deposited into his account

The heat hit Andrew like a blast furnace as he exited the customs building. The local officials wore the unofficial uniform of the island—short-sleeved shirts, shorts cut off just above the knees and socks that pulled up just below the knees. Andrew had never appreciated the style. To beat the stifling heat, he was dressed in a light polo golf shirt, khaki shorts, and Merrell hiking sandals

The island of Bermuda, situated 600 miles off the coast of North Carolina, is a favorite tourist spot for the residents of the eastern seaboard. Only twenty miles long and a mile-and-a-half wide, it boasts over a dozen golf courses. Bermuda, with a population of sixty thousand, was originally inhabited by British sailors and disenfranchised slaves. In its 350-year history, the tiny island had evolved from being a safe haven for sailors to being a haven for bank and insurance companies. Because of its lenient banking policies, businesses are eager to set up corporations on the island, which has resulted in thousands of international expatriates moving to Bermuda for short stints of work and pleasure.

At the airport, Andrew hired a taxi to take him to Hamilton, the main city and capital of Bermuda. As he approached the city, he could see that the island would soon be bustling with passengers from the two cruise ships docked in the harbor. To avoid the downtown congestion, he skirted the main thoroughfare and checked into a room at the Elbow Beach Resort hotel several kilometers outside the city. Nestled in the cliffs away from the main road, the resort lay only minutes away from the pink sandy beaches for which the island is famous. Andrew had stayed there on a vacation years earlier. He decided the best approach was to start in familiar territory.

After checking into his room, Andrew prepared himself for his meeting with the manager of the Island Capital. According to Bob

Craft, the grocery chain's now deceased accountant, all transactions processed by either credit or debit card flowed through this bank. Frank Tanner had agreed to send a letter of introduction in advance of his arrival. Despite being jilted by his mentor and the other partners at Brooks and Steiner, Andrew was thankful for the support. The letter requested help and instructions regarding an ongoing audit investigation. After a fitful sleep, Andrew awoke at six a.m. and took a short jog along the beach. Anticipating the British need for punctuality, he arrived at the bank precisely at nine.

Jeremy Plowstock was a jet-black, Bermudian national. He was six foot three, athletic and proud. Most people holding senior positions like his were ex-patriots from the various countries that controlled the local banking industry. He was a self made success story in the local community.

Jeremy Plowstock's accent was part Bermudian, part Bostonian. He had spent most of his childhood and young adulthood in Massachusetts, and had obtained an MBA from Harvard. He came around his desk to greet the accountant.

"My name is Mr. Plowstock. Our bank will be most pleased to assist you." Jeremy chimed.

Andrew was taken aback; for some reason he had expected an American. Finally, he stammered a brief "Good morning."

"Frank Tanner called and indicated what you required."

Andrew was relieved that Frank had come through. "It would be nice to get started. Where would I be able to set up my computer?" Andrew asked, showing him his laptop.

"We have set up a station in our trading bullpen. I have taken the liberty of allowing you access to some of our files."

Jeremy handed Andrew a sheet of paper with access codes to the bank's archived transaction files. Andrew set himself up, coffee in hand, and started searching. It was tedious, brain-numbing work. Somewhere in the archived bank records were the transactions that sent money to his bank account in San Francisco.

The next three days of analysis brought out the talents that had propelled Andrew to near partnership at Brooks and Steiner. He quickly identified relationships between transactions and remembered account numbers he had seen hours earlier. By the end of the third day, the concentration and focus had left him mentally exhausted. He had been successful in tracing several of the transactions that affected his bank account, but was still unable to discover the source of the funds.

Dana called every night. They kept each other informed of their progress and agreed that if Andrew didn't find anything in the next two days they would reunite and return to San Francisco to meet with Harry. On the third evening when Dana called, she couldn't contain her excitement. "Andrew, you're not going to believe this. I found it. I found my model!"

"Fantastic! At least one of us is having some success." Andrew forgot his dejection for a moment.

"Harry sent the source code of my model and stored it outside the CSA computer systems. I was able to download it on my father's network here in Boston."

Neither of them heard the click on the line as they continued to talk. After ten minutes they said goodnight and Andrew took a quick shower before drifting off to sleep.

When Andrew arrived at the bank on the fourth day, Jeremy suggested they go down to the Hamilton waterfront for an espresso. The city was decidedly British. Its pastel-colored stucco buildings and unique tiered roofs had a quaint island charm. The shops, which sold crystal, wool sweaters and island souvenirs, were crammed with passengers from the recently docked cruise ships.

"Mr. Dalton, let me be frank," Jeremy Plowstock began. "I have been requested by my head office to deny you any further access to our systems, effective immediately."

Andrew was stunned. How did they know he was there? He hoped Frank was okay.

"Mr. Plowstock…"

Jeremy cut him off. "I am not in the habit of listening to my head office, Mr. Dalton." He smiled. "Tell me. What is this really about? The audit introduction letter was obviously a ruse. It's clear that you are searching items affecting your personal accounts."

Andrew had not expected that his work was being monitored. He decided to trust the Bermudian banker, and explained everything he knew about the transactions affecting his personal account.

"It never ceases to amaze me how Americans will try to screw each other. But that is what keeps you in business, isn't it?"

"Make's me sound like a parasite." Andrew smiled.

"More like a pariah." Jeremy slapped Andrew on the back and stood up. They finished their coffee and headed back to the bank. Neither of them noticed the woman following them up the street from the café.

Jeremy Plowstock enjoyed a good challenge. He had risen to the senior position at the bank by combating resistance and prejudices throughout his career. Island Capital had never regretted its decision to elevate the local boy. Under his guidance the bank had grown to prominence in international circles. Part of the reason for this was that Jeremy didn't always do what he was told.

They walked up from the inner harbor along Court Street past the banking and legal offices that supported the tiny island country. Outside one of the more prestigious law buildings was a park bench with a bronze statue of a woman sitting to one side. Andrew wished this spiraling nightmare would end so he and Dana could wile away lazy afternoons sitting on the bench next to the bronze lady…

Once back at Island Capital, Andrew followed the bank manager to a private office near the back of the building. Leather chairs and mahogany desks were neatly spaced around the well-appointed room. A bank of humming computers lined one wall.

"This is the sanctuary of the private accounts, where details of the billions of dollars that have passed through the bank from unasked sources are forwarded to undisclosed locations," Jeremy explained.

It was here that the source of deposits going to Andrew's bank in California would be tracked. The bank respected privacy laws, but they made sure every cent could be accounted for. Their clients weren't the sort of people who trusted others, particularly those who handled their money.

"The servers in this room should hold the key to your mystery." Jeremy gestured to a leather chair.

"Without access to this room, would my search have proven fruitless?" Andrew asked as he sat down.

"Sorry about that. Your ruse to have your colleagues back in the States help you unfortunately didn't require access to these files. Not that they would have been available," Jeremy added with a grin.

"You must have quite the client base. I've always wondered where modern pirates of the financial high seas hid their stash. This is certainly more comfortable than a cave on some deserted island." Andrew knew he would have solved many more fraud cases if he had had access to these resources.

"True, but you still need a map to find the treasure—a password and a log-in sequence. With the right combination of keystrokes, voice commands and code words, anyone can access the loot…a typical, Caribbean-style Swiss bank account." Jeremy turned to the screen and instructed the computer to locate the required transactions.

The computers whirred away behind them as the two men discussed current banking laws in the U.S. and Andrew's frustration with international bank secrecy. The governments of the world stopped at nothing to find and locate ill-gotten drug profits. The countries with private banking and secrecy laws were forced to submit to the will of the powerful U.S. lobby. But the assistance stopped short of helping to uncover countless millions of clean, white-collar theft that regularly leaked out of the U.S. like a sieve. The IRS had tried with no success. There were too many powerbrokers in the country with money to hide from spouses or business partners. The IRS was the least of their concerns.

"Here it is," said Jeremy as the computer chimed to indicate it had completed the request. It spat out a list with each of Andrew's mysterious deposits, complete with a routing summary from the initial movement all the way to his account. Jeremy identified several of the routing accounts and wrote them down.

"This is better than I thought. With these details, at least I'll be able to prove there was no way for me to have embezzled the money." Andrew was ecstatic and a little surprised that it had been so easy. Leaving the sealed room, the two men returned to Jeremy's office. They agreed that Jeremy would send the package to Frank at Brooks and Steiner, along with a note of instructions.

"Thanks for everything, Jeremy. At least now they can start the process to clear my name and any suspicion directed at the partnership." Andrew stood up to leave. When he reached the door, he paused to turn around. "Please be careful. These people are ruthless."

Jeremy laughed. "Don't worry about me. My clientele are very rough. I have found ways to take care of myself."

After shaking the banker's hand, Andrew left. He was very grateful for the help he had received and hoped it wouldn't cause Jeremy any serious problems.

Bermuda was truly an island community. Those who came from abroad for work expected a hiatus from their careers. Business usually didn't get done quickly. The locals lived life at a much slower pace, and it took some time for these young professionals to become acclimatized. But several months and countless rum swizzles later, they would find it hard to believe they had ever worked as hard as they had back home.

The same was true of the services on the island. It took Andrew three hours to get the hotel concierge to contact the airline and have his flights changed. By the time they finished, it was too late to leave that night. The delay almost cost him his life.

Chapter 18

Nathan McDaniel rose to prominence in California politics during the heyday of the merger-crazed 1980s. Many people in Sacramento felt that only large California corporations could serve the state well. Nathan McDaniel was not one of them. In fact, he was instrumental in ensuring that large corporations did not gain monopolistic powers in his state. Not to mention the debt. He knew all to well the effects of over-leveraging by a government. The Californians have a voracious appetite for growth. If that growth comes at the expense of a screwed-up balance sheet, so be it. As a young state representative, he lobbied against any public works project that could not fund itself. He became a champion of the Average Joe taxpayer who recognized that large public work projects meant higher taxes.

His single-mindedness and uncompromising style would have landed him the governorship had it not been for Senator Billy Fortin. Billy Fortin had been the Senator of California for as long as anyone could remember. He died mid-term after 46 years in Washington. When the Democratic machinery started looking for a replacement, they fixed their eyes on Nathan McDaniel. They convinced him that whatever he could do for California he would do better for the country, and after a mid term election, landed in Washington.

By his second term, Senator McDaniel was appointed to the oversight committee for competitiveness. It was there that he met van Holder. ASC wanted to acquire a controlling interest in a competing financial services company, as this would afford it nation-wide bank clearing services. It would also eliminate one of the few competitors remaining in the industry. It was a hard fought battle against the Government that ASC won.

Nathan ruminated over the loss after the decision came down.

The ASC chairman approached him. "No hard feelings, Senator." Van Holder held out his hand politely, smug in his victory.

"Mr. van Holder. You may have achieved a victory here today that will not serve the American public well," Nathan replied bitterly.

"ASC only means to provide exceptional services to the American people, Senator." Van Holder's trademark smile was wry and condescending.

"But at what expense?" Nathan countered before walking away.

Van Holder had been impressed with the behavior and tenacity of the young Senator. Suspecting that ASC would be approaching this committee on many more occasions, he decided he had better get the young firebrand on his team.

Several months later, as Nathan was sitting in his office on the Hill overlooking the Potomac, a package arrived from ASC. It was a dossier listing corporations that had been denied mergers or combinations by his committee over the past decade. A staggering eighty percent of the target companies had failed within two years of the denial. The report went on to espouse the virtues of the denied mergers, which were normally turned away by his anti-competition oversight committee. A short note attached to the front page simply read "We should meet." It was signed 'Van Holder.'

Soft selling was not William van Holder's usual style. His normal tactic was to coerce or blackmail people who got in his way. But he saw in the Senator something larger, and knew that any skeletons he had created could come back to haunt him. Besides, he had bigger plans for the Senator from California. They met over dinner at the President's Club in New York. After a lengthy and at times heated three-hour discussion, Nathan was converted. Van Holder sold him on the patriotic argument that "Strong national companies were good global competitors. That could only be good for the country." After that night, the two of them had become inseparable.

Senator McDaniel resigned from the oversight committee and redirected his energies elsewhere. With his new source of unlimited financial resources, Nathan's star on Capital Hill rose to the point where he had become the front-runner for the White House. It was the ultimate prize—unlimited power. It was van Holder's design. Believing that he—as puppeteer, not puppet—pulled all the strings, Nathan McDaniel forgot who had given him his power. Now, as he sat at his desk and looked at the satisfying tributes to his success— the soft leather furniture, pictures of him with world leaders and

business tycoons, the expensive ornaments that adorned his office—
he realized that he had sold a piece of his soul in his unwavering
support for ASC's continued growth. But it was only one company.
After he had won the White House, he would distance himself from
van Holder's corporate shenanigans.

He stared out the window across the Potomac. The sun was
going down. The orange hew cast a soft light through the office
window. When the phone rang, it pierced the peaceful silence.

"McDaniel." Nathan's abrupt greeting had become his
signature.

"Nathan, we have a problem." Van Holder came right to the
point, explaining the situation.

"*You* have a problem," Nathan countered.

"This Dalton embezzlement. I think we should go national, get
the FBI involved. It'll help us round up the two of them quicker."
Van Holder was confident that Catherine would eliminate the
problem, but he didn't want to take any chances.

"It's not that easy telling the FBI what to do." Nathan
complained.

"This is getting out of hand. Do it." Van Holder was getting
angry.

"If I'm caught tampering, it could cost me the White House."

"I don't give a good Goddamn at this point. If you get there, I'll
have put you there. And I sure as hell want you there on my terms."
Van Holder was now yelling into the phone.

Nathan paused for a moment. His initial reaction was to lash
out at van Holder, at his audacity. But he knew he needed the ASC
chairman's resources and powerful connections to reach his ultimate
goal. He chose his words carefully.

"William, if we do something stupid now and word gets out
during the campaign, the White House will be lost. Let me handle
this my way. These two are as good as gone from your life."

Chapter 19

Andrew enjoyed his jog down to the beach. The humidity and heat warmed his joints and made his stride smoother. The sweat poured out of him, soaking his shirt. After a few miles, he began his ascent up the cliffs to the road.

Catherine was surprised that Dalton had left the bank empty-handed. Van Holder had insisted she recover whatever information was in Dalton's possession before he was eliminated. It was crucial that no details surrounding the transactions be released. With nothing to retrieve, it was time to get the job done.

Catherine went back to her room and put on a pair of black jogging shorts and a sports bra. The accountant was a creature of habit. Each night he jogged the same route. Catherine headed up the road to intercept. She would have to run quickly if she was going to catch him near the top of the cliffs as he came up from the beach. As she ran, the heat drained her lungs. The old days with the KGB were far behind her. She hadn't run much in the past few years. By the time she reached the path on the road leading to the cliffs, she was breathing hard. The Lycra shorts hugged her body. Using a familiar combat training technique, she quickly lowered her heart rate and body's demand for oxygen.

Andrew was cresting the cliff just as she was recovering. Before he reached the summit, she intended to push him backwards; a simple fall to his death. But a steep slope at the edge of cliff slowed her progress. As she rounding the last corner to the stairs heading down to the beach she came face to face with her target. He was about to say something when she whirled around and kicked him in the stomach.

"What the—?" Andrew collapsed and fell backwards into a palm tree, unable to breathe. Catherine was on top of him before he could react. She grabbed a hold of both his arms and tucked her feet inside both his thighs. He couldn't move.

"Who are you?" Andrew sputtered.

"Shut up," Catherine ordered. Her Russian accent told Andrew everything he needed to know. He remained silent.

"What did you do at the bank?" Her breath warmed his cheek as she spoke.

"Audit work for my employer." Andrew did his best to lie.

"Bullshit. You have been fired by Brooks and Steiner. This has to do with the money going into your account." Catherine was breathing slower now. She enjoyed the power of control. He was young and athletic—not like the old cronies van Holder normally sent her to.

"How do you know so much about me?" Andrew asked, trying to squirm free.

Catherine laughed. "Just relax…you'll only hurt yourself. I was sent here to finish the job that was botched in Montana."

"You're going to kill me." Andrew stated in an unexpectedly calm voice as panic set in.

"Yes." Catherine smiled.

Fear clouded Andrew's thoughts. He had to do something, say something. Her grip tightened.

"Maybe we can make a deal. You can do better than that egomaniac you're working for." Andrew tried to calm down, even though he saw no way of escaping. Her grip on him was amazing. He had wrestled in high school and never had anyone pin him so strongly.

"What do you have to offer?" Catherine loosened her grip slightly.

"Five million." Andrew blurted out.

"You don't have that sort of money." Catherine didn't believe him, but she listened anyway.

"I know where to get it." Andrew remembered his conversation with the Bermuda banker. *Just a voice command, password and code were needed.*

"No deal. Besides, I do what I do for more than just the money."

"What if I told you that van Holder planned on eliminating you after Amsterdam." Andrew was grasping at straws.

"Nice try. But just to humor you, how would you happen to know that?"

"When I was in Montana, I overheard him talking to the Senator. McDaniel said you'd be a liability." Andrew stretched the story as best as he could.

"That bastard." Catherine muttered under her breath. "I still have a job to do." She tightened her grip around Andrew's neck. He was powerless to stop her.

The six of them were waiting on the beach as promised. Nothing was to be done until they got the word from their boss. The leader, Timothy Gibson was a tall, strong, black construction worker. He augmented his meager wage by taking on odd jobs. His boss always had work, and the boys were paid well for their efforts. Tonight was different, though; they had been told to bring weapons. That meant the job would be dangerous and someone would likely get hurt. It was unusual to meet on the beach. The boss must have his reasons. But tonight, the leader didn't know the reason. He had left his boss that afternoon, shaking his head at the strange request. The money was better than normal so he didn't question the information.

They were to go to the Elbow Beach Resort and wait on the beach. If an American matching a certain description came out, they were to follow him and ensure he made it back safely to his hotel. It was dusk before the American emerged from the hotel and started running down the beach. The group followed. Nobody ran after him—that would be crazy in this temperature, something only the idiot foreigners did. By the time they had reached the base of the cliff, Andrew had disappeared over the top and was pinned to the ground by Catherine.

"Let's go up," Timothy instructed his group.

"Are you crazy, man? It's too bloody hot to climb that hill," protested the man standing next to him, who happened to be his best friend. Judging by the looks on the faces of the rest of the group, he spoke for everyone.

"We have to. This is important. Besides, a little exercise never hurt anyone." He knew no one in the group needed an extra workout, as most of them spent several hours daily at the gym.

"What do we have to do… baby-sit an American out for a jog?" the youth continued.

"Don't ask questions. Now get going." Timothy pointed to the path leading up to the main road.

At the top of the hill, the men heard voices. Timothy motioned for the group to stop and held his index finger to his mouth for quiet. He signaled his best friend to follow. Peering though the underbrush, they saw their man being held down by a gorgeous white woman.

"What do you think?" the youthful friend whispered.

"I think I'd like to be him." The older Timothy smiled at his underling, his white teeth shining.

As they watched, it became obvious the scene was not as it appeared. The man was being held against his will. For whatever reason, they had been told to keep this man safe until he boarded his flight the next day. It was a plum assignment and it paid better than many of the jobs of late. The two of them sank back into the bushes and quickly formulated a plan. It was decided that a frontal open assault would be best. The crash of the ocean against the rocks muted their advance as the six men threaded their way through the underbrush and surrounded the pair. On Timothy's signal, they emerged from the surrounding foliage.

Catherine looked up to see a group of black youths surrounding them. "Oh shit," she cursed under her breath.

The distraction was all Andrew needed. He pushed himself up, forcing Catherine to fall backwards, her head landing right between the feet of the group leader. Stunned, she stared wide-eyed at the smiling black face. Andrew rolled over and stood up, shaking his arms to regain the circulation. He looked at the motley crew who had taken up positions in a circle around him and the Russian, brandishing knives and bats and ready for action.

"Evening," said the man standing over Andrew's assailant. He spoke as politely as he could, just in case they were mistaken about the intrusion.

"What do you want?" Catherine hissed from her prone position on the ground. As she tried to rise, the black man placed his foot on her shoulder.

Ignoring her question, the man directed his attention to Andrew. "Leave. Now."

Andrew didn't hesitate. He didn't know who these men were, but his brush with death had been enough to send him scampering down the path. When he reached the road, he hesitated, wondering if he should go back and help the Russian woman. Then he came to his senses. She was going to kill him! What made him think she would reconsider if he attempted to save her? He turned and ran back to the hotel, deciding he would pack and head to the airport and wait there for his morning flight.

Once the American had left, the youths closed in on the woman. The instructions had been very clear. *Make sure the gentleman boards his plane.* They would have to restrain the lady until the next day.

"It looks like we arrived just in time. What were you going to do...strangle him?" Timothy asked. His men stared down at the beautiful woman, who didn't appear remotely dangerous.

"Fuck you!" Catherine snapped. "It's none of your business." She wanted to kill this moron. Her luck was crap when it came to that bloody accountant.

"I'd like not to have to hurt you," Timothy replied, trying to be conciliatory. He relaxed his grip, shifting his feet. That was his first mistake. His second mistake was not having his knife handy. With lightning speed, Catherine lifted her legs over her head and hit the black man squarely in the balls. He doubled over in pain and shock from the unexpected blow.

Wheeling around, Catherine lunged for the next closest man, hitting him in the gut. Number two down. The remaining four edged back until one of the bigger men moved in on the woman. After all, they had weapons and the woman was clearly unarmed. Catherine fought hard and would have escaped if the leader hadn't recovered in time. Her sport top was ripped and she had several cuts to her arms and legs, including one particularly nasty gash on her left thigh. As she backed away towards the cliff, Catherine was cut off by the risen leader.

"That's some kick you have." He was friendly, despite the pain. "But, I'm afraid I still can't let you leave."

"You have no idea who you are dealing with," Catherine hissed.

"Perhaps not, but you still can't leave." The black man positioned himself between Catherine and the path while several members of his gang picked themselves up and joined him.

Not one to give up easily, Catherine attempted to escape through the underbrush, crawling her way toward the beach path. As she emerged, she went straight for the leader, fingers poised to gouge his face and hurl him backwards off the cliff. As she approached, the glint of a six-inch bowie knife caught her eye. The point went through at shoulder height, hit bone and exited out the back. As the leader extracted his knife, she fell forward towards the cliff and slipped over the edge. The water and rocks lay thirty meters below. Any scream was drowned out by the crashing waves.

"Should we go down and look?" the leader's best friend asked as he peered over the edge, cradling his broken arm.

"Even if the knife didn't kill her, nobody could survive that fall."

Timothy turned away. He had killed only once before, in self-defense. He was certain the woman who had fallen off the cliff would have many sins to recant as she approached the pearly gates. They turned and headed down the road to stand vigil at the hotel.

Wearing shorts, a golf shirt and a ball cap to hide his face, Andrew sat near the departure gate, anxious to board the flight to JFK. The previous night's experience had him wondering how he'd been tracked to Bermuda. He thought they'd been careful, using cash to pay for everything and booking several different flights to separate locations. It had to be luck, or someone at the passport control had tipped off his pursuers. Lost in concentration, he was startled by a familiar voice behind him. He wheeled around and came face to face with Jeremy Plowstock.

"What are you doing here?" Andrew asked.

"Good to see you made it to the airport safely." Jeremy sat down in the seat next to him and extended a hand, his broad smile indicating satisfaction in seeing Andrew in good condition.

"I'm no worse for wear. It was a rather uneventful night." Andrew didn't want to elaborate on how much danger he had been in.

"So I didn't get my money's worth." Jeremy let the comment linger. It took a few moments for it to sink in.

"*You* sent those men to protect me!" Andrew exclaimed.

"Good guys. They do me the occasional favor."

"Quite the favor. They couldn't have arrived at a better time. Ten minutes later and I'd have been dead."

"I came to tell you not to worry. Things got a trifle nasty. Apparently, the woman who attacked you fell off the cliff." Jeremy explained.

"Is she…dead?" Andrew asked.

"It was over 30 meters to the water and rocks. When the boys went back this morning, they couldn't find her body. It must have washed out to sea." Jeremy stood up to leave.

"Are your friends okay?"

Jeremy laughed. "Apart from the cuts and bruises, their egos are shattered from having been whooped so badly by a lady…and not a young one at that."

"She was tough. Can I repay you somehow?" Andrew said.

Jeremy stopped short. He did need help from someone on the outside, but wasn't quite ready to commit. He had come to relay the news about the woman to Andrew, but also hoped to solicit his help. He was sure this accountant was the right guy, but he hesitated. Instead he said, "When you get to New York, send me some of that famous east side pastrami. Fresh food is hard to come by here."

"It'll be on the next plane after I land." Andrew stood up and shook the banker's hand.

Jeremy waved as he left the terminal. He couldn't help wondering if he should have asked Andrew for help. It was only a matter of time before something had to be done.

Chapter 20

In a quiet corner table at the Village Kitchen Restaurant in Greenwich, 'Hatchet man' Charlie Booker listened attentively to his dinner guest. Charlie Booker always listened carefully. The conversation was momentarily interrupted as a waitress set two water glasses down then quickly retreated from the awkward silence. Unlike what the name implied, the Village Kitchen was an upscale restaurant that served entrées at $75 a plate. Its dimly lit, forest-like décor was the ideal setting for discreet meetings. The owner lived up to his reputation, attracting many of the who's who that didn't want to be seen.

'Hatchet man' was not an accurate description of Charlie Booker. More precisely, he could be described as a surgeon with a scalpel. Both were designed to severe things, but Charlie did it with such flair and finesse that he had no trouble keeping busy.

"Three million. Here's the account it's to be wired to. Half now and the rest when the job is done." Charlie slid a piece of paper across the table to his dinner companion. "Wire instructions."

"When?"

"As you said, it is to be done by the end of August. No later. No other specifics." Although Charlie was a stickler for his own details, he rarely shared his timetable.

"Fine. Just make sure all information dies with them." The guest slid his plate to the side, having only nibbled at his dinner. Then he stood up and left.

As Charlie Booker watched his guest leave, he took a sip of the three-hundred-dollar Merlot that complemented his steak. Afterwards, he sat back to enjoy the rest of his meal, already contemplating the new assignment. After this job, his last, a comfortable home in the Cayman Islands would suit him just fine.

Chapter 21

The airbus 320 touched down on the tarmac at JFK airport. After several anxious minutes at customs, Andrew walked briskly up the concourse, spotted Dana and pushed his way as politely as he could through the crowded hall. They embraced, each eager to share their experiences of the past few days and plan their next move.

"It's so good to see you." Andrew stared into Dana's eyes, holding her face in his hands, his thumbs slowly rubbing her cheeks.

"Yes," Dana cooed. "You, too.

"No, seriously. You won't believe how close I came to not being here."

"What do you mean?" Dana stepped back. "What happened?"

Andrew grabbed his bag in one hand, Dana's hand in the other and headed toward the exit. "Let's get out of here first."

On the freeway heading north to Boston, Andrew told her what had happened the previous night. He left nothing out.

"Do you think she died?" Dana asked.

"It doesn't matter. They'll just send somebody else." Andrew didn't mean to be cynical, but it was unlikely their pursuers would leave the game just because one of their players dropped the ball.

As the city turned into countryside, Dana stared ahead, silently praying the nightmare would end.

"I'm sorry I dragged you into all of this," Andrew said.

"Dragged me into all of this? If it weren't for you, I'd probably be chained to a desk three stories underground in Montana until they finished with me. And then, God only knows what they would have done." Dana reached over to stroke Andrew's arm.

"Yeah, well, they don't know who they're messing with," Andrew replied with mock heroics.

For the remainder of the drive they talked about the good old days, how work seemed so irrelevant and how their lives would be when this was all over. Several hours later, they pulled into the gated driveway of the McLeod residence and came to a stop at the end of a long, circular driveway at the front of the house. It was dark in the eighteen-room beachfront home, situated on the Atlantic Ocean south of Boston. Dana's parents were spending the summer in Greece.

Andrew plunked his suitcase in the hall and followed Dana to the den. The den was his favorite room. The trophy mounts and sailing pictures that adorned the walls were a testament to her father's business and personal exploits. The brass fixtures, deep brown leather furniture and bearskin rugs created a comfortably masculine atmosphere.

Brushing away a wisp of hair from her eyes, Dana began laying out the reams of paper. When she leaned over the desk, the sun illuminated her breasts through the sheer blouse. Andrew parked himself in a nearby chair, mesmerized by her provocative stance. His mind was not on the task at hand as Dana explained what she had found out since they spoke the night before.

"Are you listening?" Dana finally looked up to see why she was not getting a reply to her comments.

"Attentive as always." Andrew smiled into her eyes.

"In other words, not very well," she replied, laughing.

He stood up, lifted her off the leather chair and pushed her up onto the desk.

"Later. We have work to do," Dana protested weakly. "Don't mess the papers." But she really didn't care as they both fell softly to the floor, rolling together onto the grizzly bear rug next to the desk.

During the next few days, the two of them were lost in a blissful world of passion and intrigue, as they spent hours in front of the computer screen sorting through the results from Dana's study. For hours the corporate servers of the McLeod computer network would grind away, applying Dana's model as it had been intended. The afternoons were spent down at the beach. Occasionally they would take one of the small sailboats into the harbor. In the evenings, they relaxed in the Carriage House where they had decided to stay. The guest accommodation—closer to the beach than the main residence—was a large home in its own right, giving the two of them plenty of room.

Andrew called Frank in San Francisco every day to find out whether or not the information he had forwarded from Bermuda would be helpful. On the third day, Andrew received word that the police investigation had been dropped and that no further action was pending. Frank sent a report to SuperMart, politely apologizing for the misunderstanding but making it clear the indictment was unacceptable. For Andrew, it was a tremendous relief, and the two of them went out to celebrate that evening.

Mario's, a quaint Italian restaurant in the downtown business district, was a McLeod family favorite when it came to celebrating birthdays, anniversaries and other landmark events. That night it was bustling like a mid-morning farmer's market. The smell of garlic and olive oil permeated the room as they sat down at their private table. The starched white tablecloth and single rose lying in the crystal vase complemented the elegant atmosphere. Andrew moved the vase so he could reach across and hold Dana's hands. It was as if they had never been apart; they were indeed soul mates. Between dishes of tomato and onion insalada, fettuccini with Portobello mushrooms, brochette and tiramisu, they talked about the past and how ridiculous they had been about their work. It all seemed pointless now.

"You always hear people saying you should live for the day. Now I know what they mean," Andrew commented as they sipped their cappuccinos.

"I was still scared being alone," Dana admitted.

"They've set the rules of this game, but we're going to win. We just have to take some precautions." Andrew was confident they could avoid another incident. "Whatever they're doing, they certainly won't risk exposure."

"That's what I'm afraid of. We don't know anything, and they think we do. That's why they tried to kill you in Bermuda." Dana squeezed his hand.

"We'll be more careful, Dana."

"From now on, we do everything together. If you're going to get yourself killed, I want to at least have the opportunity to save you," Dana said, grinning.

The plan was to go to San Francisco in four days, which would give them two days to set up before Harry was due to arrive. Now that the SuperMart problem had been sorted out, traveling wouldn't be a problem, but they still feared their movements could be traced through the airlines. They discussed various options to avoid detection.

With a few days to kill, they decided to go sailing. The trip took them up Massachusetts Bay towards Marblehead, a trip Dana had taken often in the 34-foot family ketch. The emerald green sailboat sliced through the waters of the Bay, leaving a smooth cresting wake. Andrew and Dana shared a day of laughter and lively conversation. After dinner, they finished cleaning up the galley, found a harbor in a small upstate fishing village and made anchor. The two lovebirds hiked up to a bluff overlooking the small harbor and after some searching found a suitable outcropping of rock to sit and rest.

"Sorry for taking you away from the research." Andrew had a habit of apologizing to those he cared about.

"This has been great. I've almost forgotten about the predicament we're in," Dana replied.

For awhile they gazed silently at the boats in the harbor, holding hands and enjoying each other's company. Neither one believed in fate, but neither would argue that the last few weeks had been serendipitous.

Light dew coated their vessel as they headed north early the next morning, taking them closer to the maze their lives had become. The cool breeze and gentle swells of the Atlantic lapped at the bow as the boat headed out to sea.

Charlie Booker watched them leave the harbor. Sitting on the deck of the 50-foot two-engine cabin cruiser, he eyed the sailboat through high-powered binoculars. Perfect. Now that they were both on board, he could finish the job by nightfall. The hatchet man gunned his powerful boat, set the automatic pilot for the horizon, and smugly sat back to wait. This would be the easiest three million he would earn in his long and illustrious career.

Three days before, he had set up operations in an empty house a few doors down from the McLeod's. The first night, he had disengaged the alarm system and set up surveillance in the study and guesthouse. Charlie Booker was very patient. He could have gone in with guns blazing the first day and finished the job, but there was no finesse in that approach. He looked forward to watching the news after one of his jobs and hearing the analysts conclude that the tragedy was due to an airplane engine failure, freak storm or poisoning from bad food. He was an expert at making problems go away without suspicion, which was why his unique services were so highly sought after.

Charlie glimpsed the tall mast on the horizon. First, he would commandeer the sailboat. Then he would tow the vessel from shore and capsize it in the rough Atlantic waters her, ensuring its occupants wnt down with the ship.

For three hours, Andrew and Dana sailed northeast out to sea, challenging their skills. Once they caught the wind at the wrong angle, broaching the boat. It scared them so they brought in the sails to slow down the pace. At mid-day, they turned the boat back towards shore, wanting plenty of time to reach land before dusk. As the sailboat turned westward, a glint off the starboard caught Dana's eye. A cabin cruiser was bearing down on them at full speed. The large boat was cutting through three-foot swells so quickly that water was splashing over the rails onto the deck. They were transfixed as the boat beat its way through the ocean swells toward them. Two hundred meters away, the boat showed no sign of slowing down.

"The guy is crazy! Bring the boat around, Andrew. He's coming right at us!" Dana hoped they could maneuver the nimble sailboat quickly enough.

"Hoist the jib sail. We'll have to go hard around," Andrew yelled over the loud roar of the cruiser's engines.

"I don't think it's going to give way. Can we come around fast enough?"

"I'm trying." Andrew gritted his teeth as he fought to hold the wheel steady.

The growing shadow of the cruiser as it headed straight for the sleek sailboat paralyzed their efforts. Each time they maneuvered out of the path of the oncoming powerboat and changed direction, the other boat followed suit. After forty minutes of dodging and running, the cabin cruiser was close enough to throw a line over. Running parallel to the much smaller sailboat, the lone individual on the deck of the much larger boat held up a megaphone.

"Heave to, or I'll ram your boat," Charlie Booker calmly instructed. "Lower your sail and come alongside."

Andrew was about to bolt when the man replaced his megaphone with a rifle. He looked at Dana. She watched in horror as the red marker of the laser-guided scope danced about on his torso as the sailboat rocked in the water. Andrew shot her a smile as if to say, 'Don't worry. I know what I'm doing.' Locking the wheel, he set about lowering the main sail, indicating to Dana that she should do the same to the jib. As they crossed each other in the boat, he leaned into Dana. "Once we come alongside, go below deck and hide. We'll make him come and get us."

"Andrew, are you sure. What if he rams us?"

"The rifle tells me this isn't a social meeting." Andrew tried to sound lighthearted. After everything that had happened, this attack in the middle of the ocean didn't faze him.

After lowering the sail, Dana went below deck and crawled into a cubbyhole next to the galley. Covering herself with a blanket, she held back sobs, hoping Andrew would be alright. Dana could hear muffled voices as the sailboat scraped alongside the larger boat.

"Where's the girl? Get her back up here!" the man shouted from the deck of his boat.

"What are you talking about? I'm out here by myself," Andrew yelled.

"Do you think I'm stupid? Go get her and come on board."

"There's no one else," Andrew insisted, trying desperately to think of what to do next.

The sound of the rifle echoed over the water as the bullet sailed harmlessly out to sea. Charlie had missed on purpose. In order for his plan to work, there couldn't be any blood. This was to appear to be a sailing accident. Charlie was precise about everything he did.

"Okay, I get your point." Andrew scrambled below deck as the gunman yelled for him to hurry up. *Come and get me you bastard*, he thought.

"Dana... Dana. Where are you?" Andrew called out. He walked quickly from one end of the boat to the other. No response. "If you can hear me, stay where you are until I give the all clear signal." He hoped she'd stay wherever she was. It was time to find a weapon, and the best place to look was the galley. He knew whatever he found couldn't possibly compete with a high-powered rifle. As he was grabbing a knife, Andrew suddenly remembered a previous conversation he had had with Dana's father. He raced to the storage locker in the stern of the boat.

The sea calmed down enough to prevent serious damage to the two boats, now strapped together with cable and rope. Charlie finished securing the lines, which allowed him to bring the sailboat further out to sea to finish the job. *Where the hell were they*, he wondered. *Did they really think there was a way out?* Satisfied the boats would stay together he grabbed the rifle and jumped onto the deck of the boat.

"Mr. Dalton!" Charlie raised his voice so it could be heard over the waves slapping against the hull. "Don't make this any harder on yourself. Come topside now and I'll end it quick and painless. Otherwise…"

"Otherwise what? Dead is dead. If you want me, come and get me," Andrew shouted, moving away from his position to prevent the gunman from following his voice.

"Have it your way," Charlie answered as he proceeded to the bow, intending on a surprise attack through the hatch at the front of the boat. He thought about going back and ramming the sailboat to end this cat and mouse game, but the thrill of the hunt was too enticing. He turned to focus on the challenge ahead. Ducking under the boom, he opened the hatch and went below into the galley. The sloshing of the waves made it hard to hear. He grabbed a ladle from an overhead hook and banged it against the hull. The sound reverberated throughout the boat. He banged it again and listened carefully as the echo died down. Ahead in a storage locker, he heard a whimper. He edged toward the cupboard.

Dana screamed when the light hit her face. Unable to see, she started kicking. She was able to land a few shots before Charlie grabbed her leg.

Andrew was waiting. "Don't move," he ordered.

Charlie spun around to see Andrew behind him, braced against the wall, a spear gun pointed in his direction. The close quarters made it difficult to move. Charlie let go of Dana's leg to grab for his gun.

"Don't move," Andrew repeated sternly.

"Listen kid." Charlie tried to calm himself down as he thought of a strategy. "Have you ever killed a man?" He realized he shouldn't have come below deck without knowing the location of his targets. He hadn't figured on this…on anything.

"As a matter of fact—"

Having created the necessary distraction, Charlie reached for the knife strapped to his ankle and lunged forward in the cramped space. Stepping back to avoid the attack Andrew pulled the trigger. The spear shot out of the gun, hitting Charlie mid-thigh. Blood gushed out of the wound onto the floor of the boat. The pain was excruciating, but that didn't deter the professional killer. He flung his knife. It settled harmlessly into the wall next to Andrew.

Andrew carefully reloaded the spear gun.

The readied weapon didn't stop the killer. No longer attempting to reason with his intended victim, Booker rolled onto the ground to get out of the way, causing the spear to break off at the back of his leg. Charlie reached down, and with a painful groan, pulled the shaft out. Blood now spurted from the opening. Charlie tossed down the blood-stained spear and stared at the shooter. He raised the rifle.

"Don't move." Andrew commanded.

Breathing heavily, Andrew aimed the spear gun at Charlie. The injured man bolted and was out of sight before Andrew could take a second shot. Andrew crouched down and moved around the corner into the hallway. As he rounded the corner he took aim and fired just as the blast from the killer's rifle echoed through the enclosed space, drowning out the sound of the spear gun. Dana tried to catch Andrew as he fell backwards into the room. He grunted as he hit the floor.

Not anticipating Andrew would come around the corner into the hallway in a crouched position Charlie's bullet sailed above Andrew's head and lodged in the oak paneling at the far end of the room. The second spear found its mark in Charlie's chest, pinning him against the door to the galley. Charlie's last thought as blood filled his mouth was that he should have just rammed the sailboat.

After he recovered from the fall, Andrew settled Dana into the salon with a stiff drink. He then wrapped Charlie's body into an old sail, weighted it down and tossed it over the side. Jumping onto the cabin cruiser, he started the engines and set the autopilot on a course to the north Atlantic. Loosening the ropes that secured the boats together was tricky, but he finally freed the sailboat and leaped down onto its deck. Turning their boat around, he filled both sails and headed for home, more determined than ever to regain their lives.

Chapter 22

Harry had grown up on the filthy rich side of Malibu. Preoccupied with lives that didn't involve raising their prodigy, his parents farmed him out to whichever school sucked up the most to their over-inflated egos. Everyone wanted to boast that they had Mr. and Mrs. George Compton's son at their academy, and the Compton's milked it for all it was worth. Harry attended eight different private schools by the time he graduated from high school. Neglected and pampered, Harry rebelled, and instead of going to Stanford as expected, he headed east to develop video games in New Hampshire. After two years, he dropped the charade and enrolled at MIT. His brand of genius had finally found a home. For fun, he worked evenings and weekends for a gaming company. His trust fund made certain that the creature comforts were available, and to Harry that meant frequent trips to his favorite store, Computer World.

Harry thrived on viruses, worms, Trojan horses and spy-ware. Late at night after cramming for midterms, nothing gave him more pleasure than watching networks crumble and companies panic in the aftermath of his destructive meddling. His third year invasion of the MIT central computer got him expelled. Despite the carnage, however, the Dean couldn't help but congratulate Harry as he handed him his walking papers.

Harry saw the men following him as he approached the park. They were pathetic at covert surveillance. He thought back on the past 48 hours with growing unease. Having been chased to San Francisco after what he thought was an effective evasion, had him doubting his intentions. After leaving the Bunker on the pretense that he needed to access a government database from an independent source, he had driven to Billings and hopped onto a commuter plane to Reno. From there, he had rented a car and driven west. Somehow they had managed to track his entire trip. He would have to be more careful from now on. Maybe Dana wouldn't show up, even though he hoped to see her again. He had to warn her of the danger she and Andrew were in.

The grey-haired couple sat down at a window seat with a clear view of the park across the street. The greasy spoon had been carefully selected. Before sitting down, the man had gone to the bathroom, noting the best way to exit from the back. After a few minutes of idle conversation, their coffee arrived. The man's hand shook as he brought the coffee cup to his lips, leaving behind several droplets of coffee in his long mustache. The two companions looked anxiously across the table at each other.

"I don't want to do this anymore." The woman sighed in resignation, smoothing her skirt as she spoke.

"The sooner we get this over with, the better," the man replied as he scanned the park. He hated the waiting, the anticipation of the unknown.

"Do you think this was wise? Coming here, I mean."

The old man nodded, not bothering to reply. They had discussed it many times. They both knew it had to be done. It was agreed that when the time came, the man would leave the restaurant first; he would be the only one put in harm's way. If things didn't go as planned, the woman was to leave by the back door and go to the designated rendezvous.

Halfway through their coffee, the man saw what they were waiting for. He stiffened. It was time. He leaned over and whispered in the woman's ear, "I love you." The man left the restaurant and stumbled slowly into the park, getting as close to his target as he could. Passing the man with the wild hair and horned-rimmed glasses, the old man tripped and fell, slipping a note in the pocket of the computer genius.

"Be careful." Harry was not one to take the blame.

"No problem. My fault." The old man continued on his way. He stumbled out of the park, picking up the pace when he was out of view.

From her vantage point at the window of the restaurant, the woman watched to see if they could trust Harry and if anyone else was watching. Hopefully, they had recruited an ally. It didn't take long to find out. After the old man left the park, the target was approached on three sides. The woman recognized one of the attackers and saw the gun at his side. She knew that Harry hadn't expected the company by the look of fear reflected though his glasses. If she didn't react immediately, he would be lost.

Despite their carefully laid plans, Dana left the diner by the front door, pulled off her wig and ran to the other side of the street. After ten days of research, they had begun to formulate a theory. Whatever Harry could tell them would fill in the blanks—if he survived.

"Harry!" she yelled. "Watch out!" After she screamed, Dana turned and fled through the restaurant with two of the men in hot pursuit. The others continued to approach Harry.

Stupid, she thought as she raced out of the restaurant. She hoped it wasn't too late to catch up to Andrew. Dana donned her wig, hoping the grey hair would make it harder for the men to spot her. At the end of the alley, she glanced over her shoulder, avoiding detection by only a few paces. Picking up speed, she spotted Andrew in the next block. The men were catching up to her. She yelled out, hoping he could hear her plea for help. Realizing she wouldn't be able to reach Andrew in time, she ducked into a clothing store.

Andrew heard Dana yell and turned in time to see her run into the store with her assailants in tow. He sprinted back up the street he had just left, all signs of aging gone except the makeup. As he crossed the street, a taxi turned the corner and clipped him in the hip, throwing him to the ground. The driver of the cab jumped out to help, but Andrew was up and limping toward the store before the cabbie could make it around his car.

Bolting through the door of the clothing store, Andrew searched through the jungle of racks and saw Dana's pursuers corner her in the back. Grabbing a pole used to hang clothes on the higher racks, he lunged at the closest attacker. He missed his mark and fell into a rack of suits. The man whirled around and shot at him. The bullet whizzed by Andrew's head as he carefully moved down the row, watching the approach of feet under his temporary hiding place. When his attacker grabbed the clothes rack to move it out of the way, Andrew applied all his strength to thrust the pole through the rack, connecting at pelvic height. Bull's-eye! He kicked the gun out of the downed man's hand.

Out of the corner of his eye, Andrew could see the second attacker moving in his direction. A moment later a burning sensation in his arm came just before the pain registered in his brain. The bullet entered above the bicep, traveled through a rack of coats and planted itself into the wall. Andrew felt faint when the pain registered. He howled his best rugby yell, rushing directly at the shooter, hitting him head on just as the second bullet sailed harmlessly overhead. Andrew head connected, breaking the attacker's nose and sending him crashing into the wall of the storage room.

The next few minutes were a blur. Andrew whirled around to see what became of the first attacker just as the man reached him. It was then that the gun went off. Andrew looked to see where he had been hit when the man collapsed in front of him. Turning around, Andrew saw Dana staring straight ahead, pointing the gun at the downed man. She froze. Only the tears trailing down her cheeks indicated any sign of life.

"It's okay. You can lower the gun now," Andrew reassured Dana, as he gently removed the weapon from her hands.

"Oh my God! What have I done?" Dana began to shake uncontrollably.

"You saved our lives. Now come on. We have to leave." Andrew guided her toward the front door.

"We can't leave. The police will want to know what happened." Dana wanted to throw up.

"If we stay, we'll certainly be dead. The people who want us killed will get to us if they know where we are."

Dana reluctantly agreed. She knew it was the best move for them but was still hesitant to leave the scene of her crime. Before they left, Andrew wiped off the gun and placed it in the right hand of the unconscious man in the storeroom to make it look like he had shot his partner. Their anxious looks as they ran past the frightened and confused clerk implored that he forget they were there. They ran out without waiting for his response.

Andrew's pain was unbearable as they raced through the streets to the address they had given Harry. The blood had soaked through his shirt and was running down his arm and side. He didn't want to stop. It was crucial that they beat Harry to the location and ensure he was alone, but Andrew's failing strength required that they address his injury. Two blocks later, they crossed the street to a Walgreen's and bought bandages, antiseptic and the strongest over-the-counter painkillers they could find. At a fast food outlet next to the drug store, they ducked into the bathroom. Crammed into the small space, Dana carefully unbuttoned Andrew's shirt to expose the wound. The bullet had pierced the flesh under his arm below the shoulder.

"Hold still and try not to scream," Dana implored, holding his arm as she opened the bottle of antiseptic.

"Who, me? Mr. Tough Guy?" Andrew replied, unable to suppress a grin.

"Yeah, right. The tough guy who practically fainted when he cut his foot on the side of our balcony door. Remember?"

"You must be thinking of some other guy." Andrew smiled, remembering the night he tripped and almost severed his baby toe.

The blood had congealed on both sides of his arm. Neither of them particularly liked the sight of the oozing wound, but now was not the time to be queasy. Dana poured the antiseptic liberally over the two holes.

Andrew could not stifled a cry. "Ouch! That hurt." It was one of those times that his machismo male demeanor took a back seat to raw emotion.

An hour later, they arrived at the abandoned warehouse across the street from the address they had given Harry. The street offered several routes should they need to escape. Their particular location was not very well lit from the front, but floodlights shining from the waterfront would blind anyone coming toward the building. If Harry had been followed or was part of a dragnet, the warehouse had direct access to the water where earlier they had tied up a small rented powerboat. Andrew's painkillers kicked in about the time the sun went down. The seriousness of their stakeout was entirely lost by Andrew in his drug-induced euphoria. He moved close to Dana in the darkness of their hideout.

"You know I love you, Dana. I'm so sorry to have involved you in this mess," he began, but was quickly cut off.

"Not now. We need to pay attention. If we miss Harry, there may not be another chance."

Even though he had taken only limited precautions, Harry had thought he would be safe. But van Holder obviously wanted to control his movements. They couldn't possibly have known he was coming to San Francisco or why, yet somehow they knew. Something told him his days were numbered if he didn't disappear, but the attack in the park made Harry more determined than ever to find out what Dana and Andrew were up to. Now that he was officially being hunted, the thought of being a pain in van Holder's side was appealing. He didn't care much for the ego driven entrepreneur who reminded him of his parents.

By the time Harry reached the waterfront, darkness had fallen. The dockside floodlights were casting eerie shadows on the pavement. Even though the lane between the warehouses was wide enough for two semi-trucks to pass, Harry hugged the edge of the building across from where they were to meet. As he approached the end of the building and was preparing to cross over in the safety of darkness, he felt himself being hauled backwards into a doorway, a hand clasped over his mouth. He and his captor fell awkwardly onto the dusty cement floor and slammed into a dusty support beam in the abandoned warehouse. Harry was about to strike his assailant when Dana's face came into view. A laugh was forming as she stared at the two men grabbing each other.

"That wasn't exactly how I meant for you to get his attention." She directed her comment to Andrew, who had released Harry and was picking himself up off the floor.

"You did say no noise," Andrew grunted in reply, helping a startled and bruised Harry to his feet. "Sorry, Harry. Just following orders." Andrew brushed a piece of garbage off Harry's shoulder.

Harry brushed the dust off his jeans and then shook his ball of hair to free any debris that may have been embedded. He was just glad to see Dana. "What the hell is going on? I knew van Holder was crazy, but is he really trying to kill you?"

"We were hoping you could tell us what was going on?" Dana replied. "We've figured out a little, but there are other things we haven't been able to piece together. When you asked to meet, we thought you were coming to tell us what was going on."

"In particular, why was I framed," Andrew interjected accusingly.

"It seemed like a good idea at the time. Van Holder thought it was a great idea, not." Harry chuckled about the trouble he had caused the unfortunate accountant and the irony that he would have to find a solution for the havoc he had created.

Andrew scowled at the confessor. "Shit! Did it ever occur to you that you could be ruining someone's life?" Even the painkillers couldn't erase his contempt.

"Not particularly," Harry replied.

"Great. Why are you here anyway?" Andrew shot back.

"I was worried about Dana."

"You got her into this mess!" Andrew shouted.

"And I'm here to help get her—and you—out of it." Harry replied, his voice calm and amused.

"It's already in the works," Andrew replied, his tone still edgy. "Hopefully, the authorities will at least stop looking for us. Do you know anything about the others?" Andrew told him about their recent encounters in Bermuda and Boston.

"Shhh," Dana interrupted.

The sound of a car engine coming down from the waterfront ended the conversation. Dana peered around the corner of their hideout as a van roared past the building. Its presence reminded them that they shouldn't stay in one place very long.

"Harry, do you think anyone followed you here?" Dana asked.

"It would have been difficult. I spent hours wandering through deserted streets. I'm sure I would have noticed something."

"How do we know you aren't setting us up?" Andrew asked suspiciously.

"Good question. Let me ask you something…do any of your credit cards work?" Harry asked.

"No. In fact, they stopped working shortly after we left Montana. After the cards were rejected, my Dad wired us some money." Dana said.

"They had me trace you through the ASC Visitrack system," Harry explained. "That psycho Russian lady kept pretty close tabs on me until I told her where you went. After she left, I shut down your cards so at least the system couldn't continue the trail."

"Thanks." Andrew was starting to realize that perhaps Harry wasn't the enemy.

Dana was anxious to leave. "Let's get out of here. We rented a boat in case we needed a quick getaway. It's past the last warehouse."

"Did you give them any ID?" Harry asked.

"Give who ID?" Andrew replied.

"The marina where you rented the boat."

Andrew remembered giving the clerk his driver's license and California CPA membership card. It was either that or no boat. Harry was right. It would be foolish to return to the marina now in case they were traced to the rental.

Dana came up with a quick solution. "Plan B. We'll take the boat across and leave it tied up near the marina. Then we fly out of here."

"To where?" Harry asked as they made their way to the dock.

"To Amsterdam, eventually."

Chapter 23

Nathan McDaniel was furious. He hadn't heard from his specialist in three weeke, and now this—Dalton and McLeod were back in San Francisco and his million-and-a-half was gone. As soon as the U.S. security machinery was under his control, he'd track down that bastard Booker and kill him personally.

He was sitting with van Holder in the strategy room three stories below the Montana night sky. The room, designed with post-nuclear requirements in mind, had been built specifically for ASC.

"Handle it yourself." Van Holder was chastising the inept senator, but McDaniel wasn't listening. *What could have gone wrong? Booker was the best.*

"I repeat…what do you plan to do now?" Van Holder thrust a copy of the email he was holding at McDaniel—a picture of the now dead hit man with a spear through the chest. "Dalton sent a message."

McDaniel stared at the digitally reproduced photo. This was not what he expected. It was definitely not what Booker had expected. "Does Dalton have any military training… Navy Seals, Rangers?" he asked.

"None whatsoever. In fact, our research has him profiled like a lamb. No aggressive tendencies," van Holder replied.

"Tell your team to get new profilers." McDaniel hated stating the obvious.

"How did they disappear?" Van Holder couldn't believe they had let Harry and the other two slip though their dragnet. "It's like they fell off the face of the earth. No banking or retail transactions, no border-crossings. They simply disappeared. You used the FBI like I suggested?" Van Holder was smug.

"They came up empty." McDaniel wasn't about to tell the head of ASC that he hadn't called the FBI.

"They'll show up somewhere. That picture…" van Holder said, pointing to the email, "means they've thrown down the gauntlet. We'll just have to wait until they make a mistake. If all goes well, you'll be in the White House in November and I'll have what I want, more or less."

Van Holder had no intention of divulging his plan to McDaniel. *McDaniel will serve his purpose and be gone in four years*, he thought. The remnants of his legacy would live on forever without him even knowing it. But the stage wasn't set yet. Trying to track down Dalton and McLeod for the last three weeks had prevented Catherine from finishing the last few assignments. It was time to get back to work. With only three weeks left, the priorities had to change.

Chapter 24

Catherine sat across the room looking at the plasma screen. Her gaze moved to the man sitting in front of the screen—van Holder. They had been through a lot together, but the words of that kid Dalton still rang in her head. Did van Holder really intend to eliminate her after Amsterdam? He would certainly be the first to make sure there were no loose ends. Was she considered a loose end? She decided to keep her suspicions to herself for the time being, but remain cautious.

Staring blankly at the large screen displaying the organizational structure, she recognized most of the names from her recent escapades. "It was my fault Dalton got away."

"He's either very lucky or very talented," van Holder retorted.

Catherine snickered. "I'd like to think it was all talent, that he was a formidable adversary. But the truth is I just screwed up. I should have killed him in Bermuda as soon as I caught up with him. Instead, my little game-playing saved him."

Catherine rested comfortably in van Holder's office. After falling off the cliff, it was a miracle she missed the rocks down on the beach and landed just above a natural underwater cave. Over eons, the tide had eroded the rocks and ocean floor inside the cave. The waves had pushed her inside the open-air cavern where she had stemmed the flow of blood with the elastic from her sports bra and then rested for the night. It wasn't the worst condition she had ever found herself in after a fight. Once she had hiked twenty miles in a Siberian snowstorm with a bullet lodged in the small of her back.

The next day, she considered tracking down the locals who had fouled her up, but chose instead to head back to the States. She assumed that speaking to the banker would yield nothing. She vowed to come back and deal with them later. Nobody threw Catherine Demitrikov off a cliff and lived.

"I won't make that mistake again," Catherine grinned as she stood up to leave.

"I don't believe you will." Van Holder smiled back as he watched Catherine walk to the elevator, her body smooth, her stride determined, despite the beating she had taken just a few weeks earlier.

London was enjoying one of the best summers in years. The weather was cooperating and tourists were flocking to the bastion of colonialism. To far-flung Britons, London was the centre of the universe. To Catherine, it was a homecoming. After years of training with the KGB, it was her first taste of true decadence and freedom from the drab soviet lifestyle.

Catherine stretched out on the king-sized bed and reviewed the dossier on Audrey Newcastle—the matriarch of the global mining company, Newcastle Mines Incorporated— which also included a summary of the family holdings. Few people knew about Newcastle's control of the world's iron ore, cobalt, gold and copper supply or the other family secrets outlined in the brief.

In the late 1890s, Audrey's ancestor, Colonel Terence Newcastle, set up a series of blind trusts to control his burgeoning colonial mining enterprise. With each passing decade, the company continued to expand, each arm of the conglomerate growing without knowledge of what other subsidiaries were doing. Companies Newcastle controlled often competed with each other, supported opposing sides during military coups and endured hostile takeovers from each other. Only the head of the company—always a family member—knew about the complex web that held the conglomerate together. The Colonel's great-granddaughter, Audrey, assumed that position ten years earlier at the age of thirty-four.

After two days of following the mousy, hypertensive Brit, Catherine approached Ms. Newcastle as she dined alone one afternoon at a quiet restaurant off Bank Street. The restaurant was the epitome of understated elegance—white linen, full service and sterling silver dessert forks. Taking a seat opposite the woman, Catherine acted the distraught, frightened harbinger of bad news.

"Ms. Newcastle, I must speak with you," Catherine implored in halting English.

"Who are you and what do you want?" Audrey was already looking around for the maître d.

"Please. It is important. Do not send me away. I have traveled a long way to meet with you." Catherine spoke with a rural accent she had perfected while stationed in Mexico.

"This is very unorthodox. Call my secretary if you must meet. Please leave now." Audrey handed Catherine her business card while continuing to search for help.

Catherine took the card, her hand shaking. "Please, just a few minutes. If you want me to leave after that, I will go."

Disappointed that no one from the restaurant had come to her rescue, Audrey abandoned her search and granted the distraught woman an ear. Catherine reached for the water claret and poured herself a drink, gulping the liquid as though she had just spent a fortnight in the desert.

"Thank you. I have just come from San Paulo. You have a mine there, no?" Catherine began.

"How do you know that?" Audrey queried the woman.

Ignoring her question, Catherine continued. "Last year a man was killed at the mine. He had been accused of stealing and was murdered before the police arrived. He was not a thief; he was my cousin." Catherine paused. The previous year, one of the workers—a union sympathizer who had threatened to organize the mine—had been killed at the mine. There had never been an investigation. She wanted to see if Newcastle would acknowledge her awareness of the death.

"Newcastle Mines is a very large company. I am not aware of everything that goes on," Audrey replied cautiously.

"I understand, but some say the owners were involved. That is why I am here."

"Surely the police investigated." Audrey stated.

"No, they were bought off," Catherine retorted. "And now he is dead and no one will know why."

"I'm sorry to hear about your cousin, but how can I help?" Audrey regretted the comment as soon as it left her mouth.

"It is okay. He was a bastard anyway," Catherine responded using a stronger tone. She reached into her purse and produced a piece of paper, which she slid across the table.

"What is this?" Audrey picked up the single sheet of paper, her eyes widening in shock as she read the short communication. The email was a perfectly forged document— an internal email from the mine boss to his head of security. Audrey was not mentioned, but it was clear that action had been taken at her behest. Studying the woman's body language, Catherine guessed correctly that the overly controlling Ms. Newcastle had indeed been aware of the suspicious events regarding the death.

Those idiots, Audrey thought. She would now have to deal with this woman who obviously wanted money. "You've come all this way to present me with a threat. How much do you want?" Audrey put down the sheet of paper and glared at the blackmailer.

"It is not that simple. The family wants justice." Catherine sat up straight, ready to pounce.

"Justice from whom? Clearly my employees are at fault. I'm afraid I cannot help you." Audrey got up to leave.

"But you were involved," Catherine argued.

"This piece of paper isn't enough to prove anything."

"No, but this signed affidavit from the mine manager will be enough," Catherine affirmed, holding up another forged legal document. "He is prepared to testify."

"To save himself. That spineless piss-ant…" Audrey spat.

"I can make the piss-ant go away." Catherine avowed.

Audrey took the bait. "So that is why you are here," she replied with a knowing smile. She breathed a sigh of relief as she sat back down, knowing that redemption was just around the corner.

"Yes."

"How much?" Audrey got down to business.

Catherine laid out the details and Audrey listened and responded. The entire conversation was caught on tape. The assignment was complete.

Chapter 25

Harry logged into the McLeod computer network and proceeded to eliminate Andrew and Dana's movements. Fueled by Pepsi and Twinkies, he worked non-stop at a downtown Boston hotel to expunge their identities from the passport system and install new identities. After this was completed, he went to Boston for a few days to visit an old school chum from MIT who worked with a private security firm funded by unknown government sources.

Harry returned from Boston with new passports, complete with recent travel stamps, and triumphantly entered the suite and announced they were ready to leave. Andrew and Dana were huddled around the coffee table plotting out a plan. They knew ASC was accumulating a vast amount of information on international conglomerates. They knew Harry had developed a program for ASC to extract money through the Visitrack system. They knew van Holder wanted them dead. The only thing they didn't know was how it all fit together. What was it they supposedly knew that made their lives expendable? Andrew's theory that ASC was in financial difficulty and needed Harry's program to shore up a failing financial empire was quickly shot down by Dana. Her research showed too much cash flowing out to buy companies, with no indication of debt.

"What about the information generated by my model? I was kidnapped to complete something on that model," Dana challenged her two conspirators.

"Yeah, but thanks to me that couldn't happen," Andrew declared proudly.

"Not so fast, super-hero. The model was completed by a second team of researchers. Van Holder reverted to his backup plan after you escaped," Harry said, slapping the accountant on the back. He pointed out that the model had been up and running before he left. He had sent the final working version to Dana.

"We've used that model. It didn't seem any different from the version we were experimenting with at CSA," Dana said.

"The difference was in the execution. While your model searched only public or semi-public sites, the final version was modified to include spyware," Harry informed them.

"So why did they need me? I would never have installed that in my program." She said indignantly.

"It wasn't that. They need you to interpret the information," Harry said.

"How do you know this?" Andrew asked, becoming suspicious.

"There are a couple of computer heads like me working in the Bunker. One of them talked about Dana coming in to read all the crap they were generating. It meant nothing to them."

"I wouldn't have given them any help," Dana said.

"What else do you know, Harry?" Andrew pressed, continuing his line of questioning.

"Back off, bean-counter."

"You seem to know an awful lot for someone they let walk away," Andrew shot back.

"Did you see how many men they had tracking me? Or were you too busy playing spy-man to notice."

The two men were now standing face-to-face, separated only by a table strewn with coffee cups and empty plates.

"That doesn't mean anything. For all we know, you all flew to Frisco together—a nice, neat package," Andrew replied angrily.

"I don't need this shit!" Harry shouted.

"Boys, stop it! Dana placed a hand on each of the quarrelling men's shoulders. "Harry, if you want to leave, I'll understand, but if you want to find out what's going on, we'd like your help."

Harry backed down. He grabbed his half-finished cola and mumbled apologies.

"Andrew, we have to trust each other if we're going to solve this thing. Harry's done enough to prove he's here to help."

"I guess you're right." Andrew conceded, extending a conciliatory hand. "No hard feelings, Harry."

"All for one," Harry said, saluting with his can.

The loose alliance the three of them had formed was based on a mutual dislike for van Holder, the ASC chairman. Admittedly, Harry was in it more for the challenge than the revenge. With that knowledge, both Dana and Andrew decided to be cautiously wary of Harry's actions.

Dana took a break and went out for some fresh air and a latté. It didn't occur to her to be cautious. Their supposed departure from San Francisco had taken place weeks ago and Harry's magic had made them invisible. It was a warm summer day. The breeze off the water was fragrant and refreshing, and the pink-orange clouds looked like puffs of cotton candy. Settling down in a small coffee house across from the Boston Common, she was comforted by the café's inviting ambience. She momentarily forgot about their predicament and the last harrowing months of danger. She was anxious for it to be over—not just forgotten, but done, finished, kaput.

It had taken some time, but the structure of ASC with its intricate web of corporate holdings was now complete. The model had performed flawlessly. By applying probability tests to data gleaned from the world's databases, it had identified relationships in share structures and trustees of blind trusts and connected the entities. And ASC had many—van Holder had created a behemoth over twenty years. As long as the ASC madman thought Andrew and Dana knew something, he wouldn't stop his search-and-destroy tactics. So what if he was stealing from his own company? It was a private company. Did he intend to use the Debitfund program to steal from the world? To her, this was the most ridiculous idea ever conceived. Too many people would be accounting for every penny. The scam would be discovered within days. Someday, Harry would have to explain the algorithm to her. And what did any of this have to do with her model? That was the real issue. What did van Holder intend to do with that information?

Pondering the situation, she was oblivious to the patrons coming into the coffee shop. Totally absorbed in her thoughts, savoring the smells of the pastries and coffee, she didn't notice the movement behind her. By the time the arms were around her shoulders and the hands over her eyes, she had started to scream. The dozen or so customers all turned in unison to see whose scream had pierced the peaceful atmosphere. One patron standing a few paces away made a move towards Dana, but then drew back.

"Hey, honey, it's just me." Andrew let her go as he leaped over the back of the couch.

Dana punched him hard on the bicep and then kicked his right calf. "Jesus, Andrew, you scared the hell out of me!"

"Yeah, and everyone else in here, too, thanks to your scream." Andrew put his hand up and mouthed "Sorry" to the curious patrons. He got up and ordered an extra hot no foam grandé latté, the west coast coffee lexicon falling off his tongue like a familiar song. Sitting back down, he described his day, sipping the hot coffee during pauses in the conversation.

"Have you deciphered the ASC web, come up with a game plan and planned the rest of our life yet?" Andrew joked.

"Almost to the first, no to the second and definitely to the third," Dana said as she squeezed Andrew's arm, spilling some coffee onto his lap.

"Ouch! That plan of yours may not happen if you spill too much coffee on me." Andrew replied.

"Payback for the scare," she said, getting up to leave.

It was eleven p.m., and the two of them were sitting up waiting like parents of a teenage boy. Over the past week, the three of them had lived together in close quarters in the two-bedroom suite at the hotel, working, thinking, eating and planning. Harry finally arrived back at the suite, exhausted and excited. Everything was ready; they would leave first thing in the morning. From Washington they would fly to Montreal then Paris, and take a train to Amsterdam. Untraceable, he said.

Chapter 26

Van Holder first established a kinship with the city of Amsterdam years earlier when he came to trace his heritage and ended up buying a three-hundred-year-old merchant house on Herengracht. His ancestors hadn't been a part of the wealthy merchant class. By day they worked the streets with cart and horse; by night they cleaned horse manure off the cobblestones before retreating to the outskirts of the city. It was this constant struggle to survive that eventually drove the desperate van Holders to move to America. It was fitting that van Holder should have this special meeting here in Holland. Of all people, the Dutch understood global commerce, drawing strength from the vast riches their traders had brought home from around the world.

A picture caught his eye—the three founders of ASC on a hunting trip in Oregon. He wasn't sure why he kept it or why he had brought it to Holland when he was furnishing the residence on the top floors of the building. It reminded him of his power and what he was prepared to do to succeed. The lives that crumbled around him in his quest meant nothing to him. Most of them were weak, and he enjoyed sending Catherine out to take advantage of their failings. The briefings from his head of internal security never failed to arouse him. She had a way of controlling her prey that left him wanting more. Somehow she was able to get close to her victims without getting personal. He waited for her to finish the debriefing then led the way to the bedroom.

Afterwards, they sipped cognac, enjoying a rare moment of intimacy. Catherine enjoyed the attention. Van Holder was one of the few men who really possessed her, and she liked it. She had met and destroyed many powerful men over the years, but none of them had his unwavering commitment to domination. Soon, he would be unstoppable.

Even on such a remarkable night, work was not far away.

"That Newcastle thing was brilliant," van Holder said.

"Yes, short notice and all. But she was a pushover. Most of these people think their positions exempt them from the pitfalls of the real world. Most of them have crimes or indiscretions to flaunt. You'll have to find something more challenging for me."

"Dalton."

"Do you know where he is?"

"No, but he and the other two will be found and eliminated. Next time, you will not fail."

Chapter 27

Andrew trailed behind the others in the Amsterdam airport concourse after a departure from the U.S. that would have made the CIA proud. They couldn't possibly have been followed.

Taking up residence in a house on Keizersgracht, the trio set up a computer network and strategy room. At dinnertime the first night, they wandered to the Leidseplien and ordered Heinekens and paprika chicken with frites.

"I just know something will happen here," Dana said. "That's why we had to come. Everything I worked on for CSA involved van Holder and the Amsterdam round of the Global Trade Commission (GTC) talks. All my research points to ASC's continued dominance in key industries."

"Together with McDaniel. Could he be working for the government?" Harry asked, even though they could not believe their government would plot to kill them.

"McDaniel has too much to lose. We need to concentrate on van Holder," Andrew quickly pointed out. "We know this round of talks is about global competition. A lot of cloak and dagger commerce is going on behind the backs of governments and their regulators. I presume the GTC doesn't intend to promote those aims." Andrew explained.

"But what can van Holder do to stop them?" Dana asked.

"Stop who?" Harry asked.

"World leaders, economists, the President of the GTC and numerous other interested parties," Dana replied.

"Do you know which major business leaders are attending?" Andrew asked.

"Audrey Newcastle of Newcastle Mining Corp, Bill Phillips of UsCorp and Marion Fletcher of Fletcher Communications, to name a few. Each of them will speak about the need to think globally. In particular, Marion Fletcher will address the need to act and behave like a global village. Recently, she has been outspoken about child labor laws and product dumping rules that have hurt the poorer countries." Dana had read many of her speeches with rapt attention.

"According to the ASC internal memo I downloaded from his confidential files, van Holder is hosting a reception for many of the corporate attendees. Are these people invited? Harry asked.

"Them and a handful more. As well the President of the GTC was invited." Dana had studied in detail the information downloaded from the agenda.

"We need to get close to that party," Andrew and Harry chorused.

The usual trick was to go in as caterers. Andrew went so far as to rent the uniforms and arrange for a truck, but the plan fell apart after the others exploded in a fit of uncontrolled laughter.

"I changed our names, not our faces. Did you rent fake moustaches?" Harry exclaimed between bouts of snickering.

Cupping her hands far in front of her chest, Dana said, "I think a breast enlargement would hide my identity."

"Go ahead and yuck it up, guys. Do you have any brighter ideas?"

"Actually, yes. We don't go inside!" Harry exclaimed.

"What do you mean?"

"We've been around and around the building. The surveillance is tighter than a gnat's asshole. But if we can't get in, we can at least get through. A high-powered, directional microphone from across the canal should be sufficient to pick up the conversation. Directly across from the ASC building was an advertising agency. Every time we've walked past it at night it's been dark inside. If we can get onto that roof, we can scan the meeting from there and transmit onto our servers back here."

"What about the guests? How do we identify who's attending this meeting?" Dana asked

"We could take pictures and enhance them later," Andrew suggested.

The next day Andrew and Harry headed out to buy the necessary equipment while Dana rented a houseboat on the canal close to the ASC offices. She was nervous wandering the canal by herself to view the boat, but it was better than spending time in electronic heaven.

Later that night, wearing the disguises Andrew had purchased, the two would be spies crept along the narrow walkway across the street from ASC's headquarters to the houseboat. It was a short jump down onto the derelict craft. The loud creaking of the antiquated vessel drowned out their whispers as they placed small remote control cameras under the eaves of the cabin. Using staples and Velcro, it took fifteen minutes to secure the devices. Later, sitting in the kitchen of the houseboat sipping a cold Amstel lager, they wondered if it would be better to relocate during the evening of the meeting.

"It would be closer," Harry said.

"Yes, but I don't like our escape route if we're discovered."

"Just over the edge into the water."

Andrew peered out the window. "Not on your life. Look at the crap in there."

The canals fed into the sea and were drained by the tides twice a day, but the daily tourist pollution made them very uninviting. Not to mention the countless houseboats—not unlike the dilapidated rental they were sitting in—that dumped sewage into the waterways without authorization.

Straightening his moustache and coveralls, Andrew grabbed the empty duffel bag and headed for the door. He turned to Harry. "I'm glad we got to know each other better. I always thought you had it out for me when Dana and I dated."

"You were the competition."

Taken aback, Andrew stared at him for a moment. "I'm sorry. I never realized you liked her."

"She's a beautiful creature in both mind and body. You're a very lucky man, Andrew. I hated you for the pain you put her through," Harry said.

"So did I." Andrew exclaimed, staring for a moment into his beer.

"Even though I worship the ground Dana walks on, our karma would never be right. She likes to play by the rules, and I like to break them," Harry said, laughing.

Andrew held out his hand. This time Harry grasped it.

"Whatever happens…" Andrew began.

"Whatever happens, I'll personally kick your ass if you don't do whatever it takes to make Dana the happiest woman alive."

"After we foil van Holder's evil plot," Andrew reminded him.

"Consider it foiled," Harry replied smugly, as he flicked the switch on the router hub for the remote camcorders.

Chapter 28

The sun glanced off of the canal as it set below the Amsterdam skyline, silhouetting the first limousine as it pulled up to the entrance of the old merchant house on Herengrachtstraat.

Van Holder sat at his desk watching the proceedings on closed circuit TV. The guests continued to arrive throughout the afternoon and early evening, most of them having flown into the Schiphol, country's ultramodern airport on the outskirts of the city. He ensured a waiting car and driver personally greeted each of them upon their arrival. Numerous digital cameras and microphones captured and stored all the activity. The information was then instantly transferred to the ASC servers for review and analysis.

The large ballroom where they would meet was decorated with antiques from the bygone merchant era, each piece having been carefully restored to its original state by craftsmen who did so as more of a labor of love than for financial gain. Except for the area surrounding the massive boardroom table in the centre of the room, the lighting was subdued. A small halogen light illuminated each of the fourteen place settings where a Mont Blanc pen sat beside a pad of stationary of similar quality.

The nine men and four women had been invited to the meeting in a carefully worded request sent several months earlier. They had come to observe the latest round of GTC talks. ASC Chairman's offer to dine was met with various degrees of acceptance, but in the end, they all agreed to attend. Van Holder suggested it was mandatory. All of the guests operated large multinational companies and were highly successful in their respective home countries. Having anticipated a more intimate meeting, most of them were surprised by the large attendance. In fact, the unexpected formal business setting seemed to dominate most of the conversation. These titans operating in the upper echelons of business were not accustomed to surprises, so they speculated amusingly about the night. Most of their companies did multi-million-dollar deals together, but no one was willing to disclose their private interests. It was a game of chess, where the pawns were moved without the aid of a chess master. The game played itself.

At one end of the room, an Australian woman—Marion Fletcher, head of Fletcher Communications—was deep in conversation with a small, barrel-shaped Greek. Mikos Popokulas was an influential oil producer working outside of OPEC. Marion's company had been the first to construct a worldwide satellite system to provide multinational conglomerates with private communication networks. Mikos had been her first client and visionary for the global strategy. The partnership had made Marion a very wealthy woman and Marion's company a household name. Thanks to his communication system, Mikos was always one step ahead of the OPEC bandits, as he liked to call them. His network had been modified to provide eavesdropping capabilities, thus keeping him well informed of oil deals around the world.

"So, are you still marrying a new girl every couple of years, Mikos?" Marion teased her old friend. He had had at least three brides over the years.

"My dear Marion, they are all very happy with millions to spend. It gives me such great pleasure to watch them all enjoy my money. But none of them can hold a candle to you." Mikos looked up at the five-foot-eleven business diva. He loved the tall, graceful woman, although her drive to succeed had prevented them from becoming romantically involved. She had never had an interest in him other than for business.

The other eleven attendees were in various stages of discussion when the door to the anteroom opened and van Holder entered. "Gentlemen and ladies, welcome." His voice boomed across the room. "Please take your seats and we will begin." Van Holder moved into the room and took his place at the head of the table. Lieutenants marched in behind him to stand in the background like the Swiss Guards, inactive but attentive.

"What is the meaning of this meeting? Why are we all here?" Monsieur Pierre Michaud, the CEO of Lyon Avionics, didn't approach his designated seat. He had attended only out of curiosity, and was not about to be told when and where to sit.

The room fell silent as the who's who of global commerce waited for van Holder's response. Those who knew the Frenchman had expected nothing less. He had risen to prominence in the armaments industry by destroying his competition. Nobody pushed Pierre Michaud around.

"Monsieur Michaud, humor me please. I am but a crude American businessman who has a proposition." Van Holder settled into his seat, reached out and selected a Belgian truffle from a nearby plate.

"This is a somewhat unorthodox approach to doing business, even for an American." Choosing discretion, Michaud moved to his chair.

"Yes, indeed. It is somewhat clandestine. I can assure you, however, that by the end of the evening, you will all be intrigued, if not anxious to participate."

Mikos switched name tags so he and Marion could sit together. (He felt an evening sitting next to a Russian Mafioso would not be enjoyable.) They shared a private laugh before directing their attention to their host.

The room fell silent. Van Holder looked down the table, savoring the moment. He observed the smug arrogance of the highly successful and motivated magnates of business, safe in their unbridled power of achievement—it was time for the Amsterdam Protocol to begin.

The men previously standing in the shadows placed two dossiers in front of each guest. The dossiers, one red and one black, were sealed with a wax stamp—a special crest that van Holder had purchased from the estate of a sixteenth century Dutch merchant family. A serpent guiding a ship through a hurricane to a safe harbor would be the symbol of the new economy.

He cleared his throat to gain their attention. "Gentlemen and ladies. For years the world's governments have strived to keep our companies from reaching their true potential. Trade barriers, anti-competition laws, unfair tariffs, closed borders and socialistic subsidies have damaged world trade to the point where we have to lie and cheat in order to succeed. We are forced to set up blind trusts, artificial management deals and dummy corporations to meet the demanding protectionist sentiments of each of our host counties."

The men and women around the table nodded in agreement. They had all felt the sting of government clampdowns on their global vision. Van Holder now had their undivided attention.

After a brief theatrical pause, he continued. "And I for one am sick of paying lobby groups and crooked politicians in order to make a decent profit."

"What do you propose?" The Russian Mafioso couldn't keep quiet. He effectively owned his government, but every day the liberals were gaining a foothold in the Politburo. Soon he, too, would have to succumb to their demands.

Van Holder was now ready to deliver his vision. He had their attention. Soon he would have their obedience.

"A partnership, if you will. It is my proposal that each of you hand over controlling interest in your companies to ASC. You will each remain heads of your enterprises, but my company will direct how and when trade occurs. Together we will direct and determine world prices for every conceivable product. Government influences will become irrelevant. Industries not currently under our control will be harassed until they join the group."

The room sat in stunned silence at the absurd proposal. After a few moments, the silence was broken by Pierre Michaud's laughter. He thought it was a joke. "Our collective companies are but a drop in the ocean of world commerce," he stated boldly, waving his hands. "Even if we were to agree to your ridiculous proposal, which I would not, how could the combined trade of our paltry businesses make a difference in your grand scheme?"

Van Holder glared at the troublesome Frenchman, but held his temper. "Two dossiers lay in front of each of you. Each of the red dossiers contains a complete list of all companies, ventures, partnerships, trusts and foundations that are ultimately controlled by each of you. The dossier contains the organizational charts of your respective businesses. You may review the dossiers for accuracy if you like." The magnates seated at the massive oak table may have boards and shareholder groups who thought they were running their businesses, but van Holder knew better. He had spent years funding the research at CSA to prepare for this moment. Before tonight, only a handful of people even knew this information existed, three of whom were still at large.

The room fell silent as the dossiers were opened and scanned. Audrey Newcastle, the CEO of Knightsbridge Mines, broke the silence, speaking slowly as only British faux nobility can. "But how could you possibly have found out so much about my company? Only I control the files outlining our vast holdings. Nobody else knows the extent of this company. It is impossible."

"Rest assured, Ms Newcastle, it is very possible. There are corporate filings and records for each of your projects. My researchers have been very thorough."

"Indeed. But that still doesn't compel me to join your wild plan. I have no intention of relinquishing control, particularly to an American." Half of the startled entrepreneurs around the table nodded in agreement, and a few of them got up to leave.

"Perhaps just a few more moments of your time." Van Holder gestured to the black dossiers sitting in front of each participant. This was his insurance. The men and women sitting around his table that evening had earned their positions of power by taking control, not by being controlled. Soon that would change.

Catherine had been very thorough. Each dossier contained pictures, events, recordings and affidavits collected during her private encounters with each of the business leaders. Most of them had skeletons that she had unearthed and exploited. For those few pure souls like Marion Fletcher, who had hidden their indiscretions well, she had created scenarios to help the process along. As each of the guests combed through their private dossiers, reactions of shock, anger, dismay and humor filled the room. Each of the men and women seated around the table had previously enjoyed a reputation unblemished by scandal or deceit. What lay before them would demolish any reputation created by gracious living or careful design.

Van Holder raised his voice above the din. "Forgive my crudeness, but without such tactics this partnership I am proposing would not have continued past tonight. I have no interest in sharing your little secrets with the world. So let's begin." He stared directly at Marion Fletcher as he spoke, which made her blood run cold.

Embarrassed at being caught off guard by the woman sent to fabricate her story, she finally turned away.

The room was eerily silent. Subdued by the private revelations and shocking invasion into their lives, the attendees fell so silent that only the rhythmic tone of the antique ship's clock could be heard. The Frenchman, Clyde Michaud, broke the silence by flinging his thick dossier at van Holder, missing by only inches.

"This is preposterous," Michaud said, pointing to the dossier. "I for one will not let some criminally insane Yankee tell me what to do. You are crazy. You will burn in hell for your sins."

Michaud rose from the table and walked briskly past his host to the door. Van Holder nodded to his right and one of the porters silently followed the Frenchman through the door. Moments later, the resonating blast of a gunshot filled the air.

"Suffice it to say that Monsieur Michaud will not be joining our partnership," van Holder announced calmly.

Admiring the man for his nerve, the Russian Mafioso jumped to attention. *A strong ally and even stronger enemy,* he decided. The murmurs subsided as they all turned their attention to van Holder. It was time to subscribe to the new global trade strategy that would be created under the Amsterdam Protocol.

Chapter 29

The vision of the Amsterdam Protocol unfolded before them in stereophonic sound, each syllable captured by the computer to be analyzed later. Several times Andrew shook his head in disbelief, amazed at what great lengths van Holder had gone to in order to accomplish his goal. These titans of business were ruthless in their own corporate dealings, so why had they capitulated so easily? Something in the information van Holder presented had forced their hands, but the eavesdroppers could only speculate on what that might be.

Dana was the first to speak. "I don't get it. When you look at the printouts and analyze the information generated by my model, van Holder is involved in every major industry. In addition to his financial services network, he's involved in steel, real estate investments, shipping, electronics…the list goes on."

"There has to be more to this. It must have something to do with the GTC talks," Andrew said.

"What's exactly does this GTC do?" Harry asked.

"The Global Trade Commission is a policy-setting board that regulates global commerce. It deals with international trade disputes, fair business practices and third world development, among other issues. Representatives from various countries are presented with trade issues to determine if countries are treating each other fairly."

"Maybe van Holder wants to make the GTC redundant. With enough world business leaders behind him, he'd be able to do anything anywhere and governments would be powerless to stop him." Dana reasoned.

"And it would work. Whatever brought those business leaders to this meeting and whatever hold van Holder appears to have on them would be irrelevant if he could enhance their corporate profits," Andrew said. He had seen firsthand what this man was prepared to do to accomplish his objectives. He would stop at nothing. So neither would they.

When the gunshot rang out, followed by the hollow silence over the speakers, the three of them stared at each other. "Obviously not everybody was there of their own volition," Harry commented as he downloaded the digital files collected by the surveillance equipment. He wrote down the web address of his offshore server and handed the information to Andrew and Dana.

"Do you think we should keep the surveillance equipment set up?" Andrew asked. He had presumed they would disconnect everything after the meeting.

"We may as well keep it aimed at the house. Who knows what other tidbits of information will arise."

"We'll need help. We should approach one of the participants," Dana said.

"Which one do you suggest? They're all on in this global conspiracy," Andrew countered.

"I can't believe Marion Fletcher would be involved. I read her biography, followed her career. I can't imagine her true character could be so well masked." Dana wasn't convinced a corporate pirate was running Fletcher Communications.

"Even though we know everything that was said at that meeting, we still don't really know what's going to happen. I say we go with Marion Fletcher." Harry signed off his computer, stood up and walked over to the coat rack. "I'm going for a walk." He indicated two hours by holding up his figures like a peace sign.

Dana and Andrew eyed each other suspiciously. Harry caught the gaze and laughed. "That's right. I'm going to head out right after the big meeting and run over to Mr. William van Holder and tell him everything we know. I may not have many convictions in life, but I do know who my friends are."

"I'm sorry, Harry. It's just that... where are you going?" Andrew asked.

"You have urges. I have urges. I'll be gone for two hours," Harry said, walking out the door.

When the door closed Andrew and Dana looked at each other. "Two hours. I should be able to track down Marion Fletcher by then," Andrew said with a wry smile. Dana was already heading for the bedroom, leaving a trail of clothes behind her.

Harry headed for the famous Amsterdam Red Light District. *While in Rome—or in this case, Amsterdam,* he thought to himself. Harry had never paid for sex before, but somehow being in the city that embraced the profession convinced him it was okay. It was mesmerizing. Crowds of people filled the streets, from junkies to fat, middle-aged American couples toting their gawking children. It was easy to distinguish the curious from the serious, the tentative from the bold. One father walked with his teenage boy as though shopping for a tutor.

Harry enjoyed the sights and knew he would have a difficult time choosing. The Nordic beauties and African temptresses were enticing with their friendly smiles. Settling on a dark-haired, well-proportioned European, he entered the tiny, dimly lit room as the proprietor drew her curtain. Afterwards, overcome by a mixture of satisfaction and guilt, Harry realized the woman had reminded him of Dana. Lost in thought, he failed to notice the flurry of activity as he passed a café on his way back to the apartment.

Catherine sat at a sidewalk café on Rembrandtsplien, sipping her espresso and listening intently to her companion, Mikhail Gorky. She knew her former colleague would be anxious to get together; he had even postponed a family dinner to meet with her. It had been several years since she had had time to sit down with a former comrade of the KGB and hear about the complete overhaul of the Soviet spy machinery. Mikhail was now a security consultant in Amsterdam, supposedly safeguarding European companies from post-communist Russia. What he really did was operate a private army comprised of ex-elite soviet KGB and military men. Their prices were high, but their methods were effective.

Then, to her surprise, Harry walked past her, his head lost in the clouds. By the time her brain had registered his presence on Rembrandtsplien, he had disappeared around the corner. She jumped up, told Mikhail she would call him and then ran after the computer guru. Turning the corner onto a small side street, she saw Harry's silhouette against the backdrop of a streetlight. He was only a block ahead. She sprinted to catch up.

Harry wandered through the alley, unable to get his mind off Dana. The longer they were together, the more he realized his love for her would increase. He would have to leave. A loud clatter of high heels shook him out of his daydream. He turned around and saw Catherine racing down the alley. "Shit," he muttered. He turned on his heels and ran.

Cursing her loud approach, Catherine pulled off her high heels and pursued him in her stocking feet down the narrow lane. By the time she reached Dam Square in the centre of the city, Harry had a sizeable lead. Hindered by her lack of footwear on the rough cobblestones, Catherine stopped her pursuit when saw him turn off into a small alley next to the Munttoren. She wasn't concerned. By morning, she would have people scouring the streets to find him.

Harry's heart lay in his chest like a dead paperweight. *"She's alive."* He resisted the thought. Looking behind him, he slowed his pace after entering the alleyway, realizing he had lost her. "Shit," he repeated again as he bent over a traffic control stanchion to catch his breath. *Of all the dumb luck.* Up until now, they had adopted Andrew's suggestion and worn crazy disguises. This was the first time he hadn't done so. As he rested, he mentally calculated the ridiculous odds of him being spotted by the one person the three of them feared the most. Someone they thought was dead. *Should he tell Andrew and Dana they should leave immediately?* By the time he rounded the corner of their apartment block, he had decided not to say anything about the encounter. If they left now, they wouldn't be able to find out what was really going on. "Besides," he rationalized, "what were the odds he would be seen again?" He would be extra careful in the future.

"But they are here, William! I have someone with a private army at his disposal. I can find them in a day or two." Catherine was adamant. She wanted her nemesis dead. Not only had they caused her severe pain, they had tarnished her otherwise impeccable reputation.

"Not yet. I don't want any distractions until this is finished. We do this my way. There will be enough time to eliminate them after the GTC talks. You can do it at your leisure, make a sport of it."

"I hope so, for your sake, William. Now, if you will excuse me, I am going to go clean up." Disheveled and dirty, Catherine turned and walked away, having already decided to ignore her boss' order.

Chapter 30

Despite the eagerness of the Dutch to accommodate, Andrew and Dana had a difficult time tracking Marion Fletcher. After lying to the Australian receptionist of Fletcher Communications; mentioning the dossier, the Amsterdam Protocol and its repercussions, they eventually succeeded. The callback came fifteen minutes later. Marion was very tentative. Knowing they were taking a huge risk, they went with Dana's theory that Marion Fletcher couldn't be compromised. Andrew introduced himself and explained who he was and why he was contacting her. Marion softened and started to divulge her reaction to van Holder's meeting the evening before. Uncertain that the phone lines were safe, Andrew stopped her. They agreed to meet in the lobby of her hotel.

It was starting to rain as Andrew and Dana crossed the bridge separating the three main canals from the rest of the city. The outer shell of their not-so-rainproof jackets had soaked through by the time they rounded the corner and spotted the hotel. Marion had placed bodyguards at both ends of the establishment. Immediately upon her return to the hotel the previous night, she had hired the bodyguards. The security company had come to her aid on several other occasions when she had needed to safeguard company equipment and personnel in countries where lawlessness was rampant.

"It's a real pleasure to finally meet you, Ms Fletcher," Dana gushed. "You're a real inspiration to me. Such a success story."

"My success had more to do with timing than ingenuity. And my being female had nothing to do with it," Marion stated flatly.

Dana was disappointed. She was about to refute the communication giant's comments when Marion interjected. "Well, maybe being a female in the male-dominated echelon of multinational conglomerates is difficult at times. Most get there by knifing somebody in the back…call it 'climbing the corporate ladder.' Many of my female peers had to sleep their way up the ladder. Fortunately, I did neither." She glanced at Andrew.

"No knives in my climb, Ms. Fletcher, but I've thrown a few since crossing paths with van Holder."

"He's on the sunny side of crazy town, that's for sure. I don't think any of us are safe at the moment." Marion said.

"How well do you know him?" Andrew asked.

"Met him briefly a few years ago. Our company installed a private satellite network for his ASC to provide secure downlinks of debit terminal transactions. He insisted on gaining access to our proprietary software, which I refused. At the time he laughed it off, but something tells me he carries a grudge," Marion said.

"He eventually got your software?" Dana enquired.

"I suspect he did. About three months after the deal, our mainframe was hacked into and the hard drive was swiped. We thought the company had been a victim of a crank hacker. The day after the firewall was cracked all the computer screens flashed one phrase over and over again. The only thing gone was the software we had refused to provide. It took our technicians three weeks to eradicate the virus."

"Was the phrase 'Hal-was-here'?" Dana asked.

"Yes, as a matter of fact. How did you know that?" Marion sat upright, curious.

"Harry Compton. It's his calling card. He used to work for van Holder. Now he's part of our little team," Dana said.

"I'd like to meet him. According to my computer people, he's the best they've ever seen."

"He's the best and he's now on our side," Andrew said, beaming.

Dana shifted gears and got right to the heart of their dilemma. "We know a lot about van Holder's company, including what transpired at last night's meeting, but we haven't been able to piece together what he intends to do?"

"Last night's meeting?" Marion asked, puzzled.

"Directional mike from across the canal," Andrew explained.

"We know what was said, but not why the group was selected. We also got the gist that each of you received information that was unexpected," Dana added.

"And that not everyone went home." Andrew formed his hand into the shape of a pistol, pretending to shoot.

"You heard that? Van Holder is psychotic. He had his security people dig up some scandal involving each of us. It was his way of saying 'Welcome to the club, whether you like it or not.' But I have no intention of participating in his little game."

"What did he do to you to try and influence your future decisions?" Andrew asked.

Dana kicked him under the table. She could see that Marion Fletcher was embarrassed. "I'm sorry, Ms Fletcher. Andrew shouldn't have asked you that."

"That's okay. It'll probably be made public anyway, once he sees I'm not on board. I'll have to be prepared for the reaction. About a year ago, I was approached at my country club by a woman claiming to represent an Arab sheik. She said she had come to negotiate a contract for telecommunication services for his Kingdom. She was very alluring. We spent two weeks together. We did *everything* together. We were inseparable."

"So what? You spent time with another woman. What does that make you…irresponsible?" Dana asked naively.

"No, it makes me a lesbian," Marion said, almost relieved as the words escaped.

"Oh, I'm sorry. I mean… there's nothing wrong with that. I mean… do you have a shoe horn?" she asked Andrew, trying to take her foot out of her month.

Marion laughed. "It's okay. In fact, it felt good to say it out loud. I've been very discreet about my choices in life. The people on my board of directors are very 'old school.' They have a tough enough time accepting that the company is being run by a woman, let alone a lesbian." Marion already felt comfortable with these two young people, even though she had just met them.

"I thought it was your company," Dana said.

"It is. I mean it *was*. During our rapid global expansion, the company required a lot of capital—more than we were earning. We raised venture capital money but weren't able to meet the repayment terms because of the continued growth, so we went public. I became extremely wealthy, but lost control of my company."

As the late day turned into evening, the three of them continued to discuss van Holder's agenda. Looking up, Andrew noticed it had become dark and suggested he and Dana return to the apartment. It was clear to all of them that something had to be done. The Amsterdam Protocol would be difficult to expose. Regardless of the blackmail, too many of the participants in the room the previous night would be anxious to increase their personal wealth.

"So what happens now?" Marion asked.

"We need to gather enough information to build a case—details of deals, documents, collusion…whatever will implicate van Holder. It has to stick. And we have to find people and politicians who aren't in his pocket." For the next ten minutes Andrew laid out his plan.

"We have the contract to supply the ASC Group with its intranet and other global telecommunications needs," Marion said when Andrew finished describing his proposed course of action.

"Can we tap into it, bug his system?" Andrew asked, excited about the possibility of accessing their enemy's private communications.

"If we get caught, we could all go to jail," Marion cautioned him, even though she had no intention of backing away from the proposal.

"If we don't get caught, we could prevent the end of free trade," Dana added.

Marion stood up and extended her hand. They shook hands and agreed to meet the day after the GTC talks.

"I can't believe we're the first people Marion told," Dana said as they left the meeting.

"She's lived with her secret for a long time. Van Holder's blackmail finally gave her the courage to come out of the closet."

"Now she won't have to worry about repercussions when she doesn't participate in the conspiracy." Dana was glad they had chosen her. Finding some way to stop this madman would take a lot of work. Having someone like Marion Fletcher on their side was a huge advantage.

"Except maybe her life," Andrew murmured ruefully.

The walked along for awhile trying to blend into the Amsterdam surroundings. Passing under the archway of the Reichsmuseum, they didn't notice the shadow of a man blending into their footsteps on the cobblestones. The man continued his observation at a safe distance. When the two of them turned onto Keizersgracht, the man quickened his pace, silently closing in on them. As they unlocked the door to their apartment, he passed by on the other side of the canal, committing the house number to memory. As the door closed behind them, the man moved on, dialing his cell phone as he rounded the corner.

Chapter 31

Senator Nathan McDaniel was not well traveled. He had grown up in California and reluctantly moved to Washington when he was elected. Once he became President of the United States, he planned to hold court at the White House or Camp David. The world leaders would have to come to him.

This was his first visit to Amsterdam, and so far he didn't like it. With the election less than three months away, the last place in the world he wanted to be was out of the country. Too many things could go wrong. His election staff and his running mate had begged him to send an under-secretary instead. But van Holder had been adamant. "What happens here is crucial to my corporate strategy. Three days only, and then you'll be back kissing babies and hosting teas for little old ladies." Deciding that it was not the time to argue, McDaniel had relented. November would come soon enough. In his mind, he had already won the election. Sitting so far ahead in the polls, the Senator from California appeared to be a shoe-in for the presidency. But there was good reason for this. Van Holder had spent the last four years grooming his 'boy.' Anyone who even got close to being a contender was quickly wiped out, discredited or otherwise made impotent.

His running mate was Jessica Poole. While it might have seemed risky to have a female on the slate, Jessica was one of the reasons they would win. At the tender age of forty-two, the talented woman from Wisconsin was a seasoned politician. The papers described her as 'attractive, smart beyond belief, and genuine.' Her only flaw was that she saw the good in everyone. It had already gotten her into trouble a few times. Several years earlier, the Fanny Mae mortgage scandal had landed a senior executive in jail. She knew the man and had attested to his integrity before a Senate sub-committee investigating the affair. Afterwards, McDaniel had taken her aside and told her the facts of life. She had endured the scolding, but continued to believe in the goodness of people—just not quite so vocally.

Van Holder had described a grand vision for McDaniel and his presidency. The two of them had met frequently over the past year, van Holder acting more like a mentor than a manipulator. According to van Holder, global commerce was about to explode and the U.S. would benefit the most.

He preached, "U.S. interests were at stake. It was imperative that the GTC recognize the plight of the multinational."

The Global Trade Commission (GTC) was spawned from the post-WWII framework formally known as GATT, or General Agreement of Trade and Tariffs. Near the end of the twentieth century, governments started to recognize the need for a more sophisticated organization that would promote world trade on an even playing field. Eliminating child labor, preventing anti-dumping duties, the protection of the environment and generally fair play amongst nations were some of its objectives. Except for a minor consultative role, corporations were excluded from the decision making process.

McDaniel agreed to present van Holder's grand vision as his own policy. Although the research conducted in Montana failed to satisfy his curiosity about the ASC growth strategy and how it would increase U.S. jobs and, hence, the economy, van Holder made a compelling argument; the statistics he provided to make his case were real and frightening. Foreign corporations were gobbling up U.S. companies with lightning speed, and nothing was being done to stop the exodus of capital.

Deep in thought, the Senator was startled when van Holder entered the room where he had been waiting.

"Thank you for coming, Nathan. I know it's a difficult time to be away from the campaign trail." Van Holder was aware that the GTC ruled by consensus and the presence of the soon-to-be next U.S. President would carry a lot of weight. In fact, he was counting on it.

"It's been an uphill battle. The Senate was not exactly tickled pink by the numbers you gave me. Some of them were ready to abandon the GTC altogether," McDaniel said.

"Morons. Don't they know their protectionist attitudes will only serve to alienate us in the eyes of the world? There's a big economy outside of America. One day the sleeping giant will wake up and fight back. The floodgates of international commerce need to be opened. The GTC is all about fair trade. If you deliver what we discussed, your presidency is guaranteed." Van Holder smiled. He had poured millions into McDaniel. Now was not the time to lose him. The Senate was jumping onto his bandwagon of prosperity and his boy was falling off.

"What if they don't agree? Your proposal is a two-edged sword," McDaniel argued.

"They have to agree. You have to *make* them agree," Van Holder emphasized.

"I'll try," McDaniel stammered.

"You'd better do more than try," Van Holder warned. He didn't give a damn about the floodgates of global commerce. It was the floodgates of profits he intended to open.

Chapter 32

Catherine stared at the address she had written down. Mikhail had come through, just as she knew he would. They were meeting at a small café near Dam Square, a favorite spot of visiting Russian diplomats and ex-patriots. The fare was decidedly Slavic, borsht and cabbage rolls being the favored dishes. Seated by the window, Catherine waited impatiently. It was as if a race had started and she was stuck in the blocks. Why couldn't he have just given her the information over the phone? After what seemed like hours, Mikhail arrived, taking the time to appraise Catherine with a visual body scan as he sat down.

"Hello, Catherine. A pleasure once again." Mikhail was charming as his lips brushed her hand.

"Sorry about the other night," Catherine said apologetically.

"No problem. Is everything okay?" Mikhail leaned forward, his eyes fixed on her sweater's plunging neckline.

"Do you have the information?" Catherine asked.

"For a price." Mikhail wanted to set the terms. He wasn't ready to hand over the details. It would have to wait until the morning. The men guarding the Fletcher woman were trained well. "As I said…terms."

"How much money? I have the authorization."

She let her skirt rise up her thigh, giving Mikhail a glimpse of the garter clasp holding her sheer stocking tightly to her leg. The contrast of the lily-white garment on the pale skin invoked a release of air from his lungs that blew audibly through the floral arrangement in the center of the table.

Mikhail reached over and caressed her arm. "We can come to some other arrangement."

Catherine had never found members of the Russian KGB appealing. They acted like rutting dogs. Why couldn't he just extend her this courtesy as he would any other colleague?

"So, we go." Mikhail could hardly contain his excitement. As he jumped up, he spilled hot espresso, staining the white linen tablecloth.

She would get what was needed, but would make sure the evening left no doubt as to their activities. She would leave him something he could wear like a badge. Something for the wife to see.

Chapter 33

As the city maintenance crew recovered the items from their watery canal grave, they hung them over the railings or laid them down on the sidewalk beside the canal for collection. While the tourists gawked, the locals looked on with mild interest at the kitchen sinks, bikes, toys, furniture and other sundry items that lined the streets.

Each year, together with the flea market paraphernalia, the Amsterdam maintenance crews dredged up bodies in various stages of decomposition. Two days after van Holder's reception, Andrew watched as city workers lifted their dredge from the water cradling a body. Following procedure, the foreman shut down his rig, called it in and then lowered the scoop to get a closer look. No identification could be found. The man had been shot once in the back of the head, his watch and rings gone. *Most likely a robbery,* the worker thought. The well-dressed man had died recently.

Andrew knew exactly who it was and went to inform the others.

Marion Fletcher had been able to provide them with the names and descriptions of the Amsterdam Protocol guests. They identified each in the ensuing days, matching faces to names from web-based biographies. By the time the GTC round of talks had ended, they had names and bios for all but two—the Russian mafia man and the Swiss banker. Marion didn't know much about them, so they labeled them as hostile until future information could prove otherwise.

Marion's description of Michaud the Frenchman was accurate. There was no doubt that his body was the one being removed from the canal.

"What should we do?" Andrew asked.

"Nothing yet," Dana replied. "We don't have enough evidence to lead the murder back to van Holder."

"Van Holder has a habit of covering his tracks," Harry chimed in, pausing from his work on the computer.

"Any luck in cracking the ASC computer for details on the Amsterdam Protocol?" Dana asked.

"I don't think they're stored within ASC's system."

"What about in Montana?" Dana was certain everything originated from that facility.

"Not from what I saw. He must have a separate network. If we keep monitoring his communication, I'll find it eventually." Harry pointed to the computer behind him whirring away 24/7 to track all communication through ASC. The uplink was thanks to Marion. The day after the GTC talks had ended, she had called to give them the necessary satellite codes.

It was the last week of September. They had been in Amsterdam for a month. Van Holder had departed the week before, and with him the immediate threat of exposure. Harry had forgotten about the Russian killer. He was convinced she had stopped looking for him after he had eluded her. No sense bringing it up. All that was left was to pack up the equipment and ship out. It was time to go to Bermuda and trace the money used to acquire the companies on van Holder's immediate target list.

Andrew phoned Jeremy Plowstock. "We'd like to come this week," he said after explaining the plan.

"This may not be a good time." Jeremy was evasive.

"Why not?" Andrew asked.

"Bank auditors are here. They are looking at the data logs. Somehow they must have found out about the information I gave you." Jeremy's voice was muted, as if he were cupping the receiver with his hand.

"What auditors? Where are they from?"

"The mainland. They called last month just after you left and arrived yesterday. Didn't say how long they would be staying."

"I'm sure they'll be gone before we arrive." Andrew was beginning to think they would never get to the bottom of the conspiracy to frame him for embezzlement.

"There are other matters…banking matters that affect me. Transactions that I signed off on." Jeremy said.

"Are you in trouble, Jeremy?" Andrew queried his new friend.

Jeremy changed the subject. "Is it important that you do this now?"

"If we don't, we'll never be safe," Andrew said.

"Then you'll come," Jeremy agreed.

"Not just that. We need your help." Andrew explained what they needed in terms of space and supplies. After assurances from Jeremy that all would be ready, he hung up the phone. Bermuda would provide the base they needed to carry out the financial assault. There was a lot of work to do. Research that required massive computer power.

When the van arrived to load the final crates of equipment, Andrew accompanied every box down the flight of stairs. Harry had left early that morning with little indication of where he was going and when he would return. Andrew still didn't completely trust the computer genius. He was holding something back. Andrew could feel it whenever they ventured far from the apartment.

On the first landing of their building was a sharp corner that precluded the use of the trolley. Andrew and the courier hoisted the equipment onto the trolley at the top of the second story landing around the awkward corner. One crate slipped and fell down half a flight of stairs before Andrew was able to stop it. The box contained the stereo and listening equipment. It would have to wait until Bermuda to be fixed.

Dana had already left to meet with Marion Fletcher and arrange the setup of the communication links in Bermuda. The Fletcher Communications satellite codes were crucial in their preparations. She and Andrew would leave later that day and meet up with Harry in Bermuda at the end of the week.

As Andrew tidied up after the courier had gone, he didn't hear the front door open, despite the squeak that had been a constant irritant since they arrived. The sound of high heels clacking across the hardwood floor captured his attention.

"Call your friends back!" Catherine demanded, her legs straddling him as he sat on the floor wrapping up the last of the cables. She had her Glock out, but didn't intend to use it...not yet. Mikhail's information had proven to be invaluable. She had been watching the house, waiting for the right time to strike. But she had waited too long.

"You're alive." Andrew stammered.

"And kicking. Call them back." Catherine pointed to the cell phone.

"They're gone," Andrew replied calmly. "They left yesterday."

Catherine laughed. Shifting her weight onto her left foot, she glanced around the room and then at the back window. She wandered over to it and moved the curtain back, getting a perfect view of the ASC offices. "Perfect location, hiding in plain sight. It's a good thing I saw your friend Harry heading back from a roll in the hay in the red light district. Otherwise I would have never known you were here. I would have caught up with you sooner if he hadn't lost me in a chase."

Andrew felt he had been hit by a sledgehammer. That's why Harry must have seemed distracted.

She turned around and looked at Andrew. "They left twenty minutes ago. I watched them leave. Now call them back."

"And if I don't?"

"Your death means nothing to me, but how I do it will mean everything to you. Don't be so gallant. By the time I'm through with you, you'll tell me the world is flat if that's what you think I want to hear." She threw him the cell phone.

Knowing Catherine's capabilities, Andrew made the call. He didn't want to drag Dana back into this, but realized they stood a better chance of escaping if they were together. It would have to be timed right. Maybe he could catch Catherine off guard when the taxi pulled up with Dana. Settling into one of the utilitarian leather couches, he placed his heels onto the glass top of the coffee table and waited. Sitting across from the sleek woman, Andrew asked himself why he was there. What did he care what van Holder did? It certainly wasn't worth getting killed over.

"What are my other options?" he asked.

"What do you mean?" Catherine leaned forward, directing her attention across the glass table.

"I don't care what van Holder does, and why should you? Why not cut and run?" Andrew proposed.

"After everything you have done, you would turn like the tide? What about everything you said in Bermuda? You don't strike me as the type to throw in the towel," Catherine said.

"I call it survival. This is all about the money. Are you still interested in my offer of five million?"

"He has a vision," Catherine replied.

"What vision? He'll discard you like an old suit once your approach is out of style, once you're not needed anymore."

She paused to contemplate his words. "Still spouting the same line," she sneered.

They waited in silence. Catherine paced the room, pausing often to look out the front window at the street below.

Her Glock was on the coffee table, six feet from Andrew. He gazed at it several times. It would be so easy to grab. It would only take a moment to reach over and palm the instrument of death. He had never fired a pistol before. She'd be across the room and he'd be dead before he even figured out how to release the safety.

The car door cracked the silence like a whip, bringing both of them to the front window, the gun forgotten. Seeing Dana emerge from the taxi, Catherine moved to the table and picked up the gun, disappointed that the accountant had not taken the bait. She motioned to Andrew to open the door downstairs. Catherine stayed in the shadow of the stairwell, keeping the Glock leveled on his back. She had killed many people in the past and it had never bothered her. As far as she was concerned, they were all guilty of sins the world did not need repeated. She enjoyed her work.

Andrew could sense the black hole of the gun barrel boring into his spine. He glanced up the stairs. Catherine had stopped on the first landing and was waving the gun for him to continue. This was the moment. The door opened inward, leaving only a small space to shift around before exiting. His fear was that if he tried to run, Dana would be standing on the steps outside in the line of fire. Andrew hadn't planned for this contingency. They hadn't thought about escaping from inside the apartment. They had been in Amsterdam so long they figured it was safe. *Shit, Harry should have told them he saw her rise from the dead.*

Andrew slowed down his pace as his mind raced though the blur of choices. An instant later he knew what to do. Clarity had returned and he was singularly focused on what to do next. Time slowed to a crawl. At the bottom of the stairs, an umbrella stand stood next to the door. In one swift movement, Andrew reached for the doorknob with his left hand and the stand with his right. He took a step backwards, flattening himself against the wall as the door swung open. Pivoting sideways, he hurled the umbrella stand up the stairs at Catherine. Using the distraction to his advantage, he pulled open the door, let go of the knob and pushed his way outside as the door swung back, effectively blocking the view from the first landing.

The first bullet zinged past his head and embedded itself in the doorframe. The umbrella stand provided the necessary cover. The second bullet caught Dana high in the shoulder as the door swung open, sending her sprawling onto the pavement. The hit saved her life. The next two bullets sailed past them and came to rest somewhere on the other side of the canal.

"What's going on?" Dana cried out from her position on the ground. The groceries in her backpack had spilled out and were scattered all around her bruised body.

Andrew grabbed her arms with the strength of a desperate man racing against a deadly foe. "Later!" he shouted, lifting her up onto her feet. They raced down the cobblestone street, finding shelter between the cars parked along the canal. Slowing down, the two of them turned back to watch a horror unfold.

Harry had rounded the corner from the opposite direction just as the door had swung open. Deep in thought, he had looked up just as Dana fell to the ground and Andrew stumbled out. Before he could yell out, the Russian killer emerged from the apartment. Standing with her legs wide apart, arms outstretched and both hands on her pistol, she took aim at the fleeing figures. Just as she pressed the trigger, Harry rammed her like a linebacker. The two bodies fell forward onto the hard pavement and rolled toward the edge of the canal. The bullet splintered a wooden signpost beside Andrew's head. The gun flew out of Catherine's hand and landed on the raised curb of the canal, the barrel teetering over the edge.

For a split second their eyes locked. A moment later they both scrambled for the gun, jockeying for position on the pavement. Catherine's experience paid off. She instinctively grabbed the handle, while Harry held onto the barrel. The two of them struggled to free the gun. Harry twisted the barrel away from his body and tried to swing it back when Catherine's finger found the trigger. The last two shots in the magazine exited, ripping flesh and crushing bone.

Andrew and Dana watched as the intertwined bodies slipped off the curb and into the canal. Dana went into shock as she watched the bodies disappear under the water. Her screams rippled down the canal street like the water consuming the bodies.

After setting Dana down behind a late-model green Peugeot and wrapping her tightly in his sweater, Andrew ran to the edge of the canal. The two combatants had separated upon entering the water. Harry was floating down the canal with the current. A trail of blood spread out behind his body, staining the murky water.

At first, Andrew couldn't see the Russian. He searched the waterway and peeked under the few houseboats floating in the canal, he caught a glimpse of her heels underneath the rudder of an old permanent canal home. Blood was seeping into the water around the inert body. As he watched, the body worked itself free and followed Harry's body downstream toward the sea. The woman who had tried to kill him in Bermuda and again at the apartment was laying face down, blood gushing from a deep gash on the top of her head. He went back to Dana.

"I think they're dead," he said matter-of-factly.

"Harry?" Dana looked pale and gaunt.

Andrew nodded. "The Russian showed up when you left. It was a set-up."

"I guess we're even now." Dana tried to laugh.

Andrew massaged the wound he received in San Francisco. "We're even."

"Are you sure she's dead?" Dana was skeptical.

"I think so. There was no movement. And she was face down for at least five minutes. I watched." Andrew tried to sound convincing, not succeeding. They could not shake the feeling that the Russian was indestructible.

"I want all this to stop!" Dana whined, clinging to Andrew.

"We have to keep going. Unless we can prove something is going on, no one will believe I'm not guilty of the crimes pinned on me."

"But what about Harry? The poor guy's dead and he didn't do anything except try to help us," Dana said ruefully.

"Harry!" Andrew retorted angrily. "Harry's the reason my name is mud in the U.S. He used me as a scapegoat. I'm in this mess because of him. Harry's the reason that demented killer knew we were in Amsterdam." The adrenaline pumped though his veins like jet fuel.

Dana pulled away and started to cry. "That's not fair. At least he tried to help. He didn't have to do that. What do you mean, his fault."

Andrew looked at Dana and immediately regretted his outburst. He was sorry he had put Dana in jeopardy. It was his fault that they were in this mess. He had called Dana for help. It was his fault they were on the run. Whatever Harry did could have been solved with a few phone calls. Andrew cursed at having to be right all the time, needing all the answers. If he had just done what the partners at the firm had told him to do—shut down the audit and bill it—none of this would have happened.

Dana read his thoughts. "It's okay. We'll finish this together."

"Let's get this van Holder bastard," Andrew said with renewed conviction. He explained how Harry's outing uncovered their presence in Amsterdam. He reassured Dana that he knew it was just a fluke; that Harry didn't mean to be seen. He hugged Dana tightly into his chest.

They stood under the awning of a small bakery, holding each other for a long time before heading for the train station to take them to the airport.

Chapter 34

The burgeoning organizational chart was obscured as the walnut panel descended. Van Holder smiled as he watched the screen disappear. In a few more days, everything would be in place. McDaniel was poised to ascend to the White House and he would have a true puppet dictator in place. Any deviation from his instructions would abruptly end the Senator's political career. He had plenty of insurance.

ASC was housed in a sprawling complex of buildings south of New York. Van Holder chose not to locate in downtown Manhattan like the rest of the corporate lemmings. This facility, together with the underground bunker in Montana, served as the heart and lungs of his corporate body. His office on the twenty-fifth floor of the main building took up an entire floor. His divisions below controlled various business groups. In some cases, they didn't even know they were all part of the same company.

Plucking a Mont Blanc pen from its brass and jade cradle, van Holder signed off on the latest merger with Euronet Financial Services SA. Actually, it was more of a palace coup than a merger, thanks to the Amsterdam Protocol. A broad stroke of ink across the paper sealed the deal. His Amsterdam Group had withheld contracts and payments until the Euronet board relented. In an unexpected turn of events, Audrey Newcastle proved to be his strongest asset, lobbying the EU politicians until they had no choice but to accept the merger.

Now a true financial services monopoly existed. Euronet, ASC and Rising Sun Transact Inc.—a Hong Kong-based company that had been acquired earlier that month— processed over ninety percent of the world's electronic banking transactions. Smaller competitors would soon be made extinct. Ultimately, it was control he was after, not size. Control of the arteries of commerce was crucial to the success of the new partnership. It would determine where, when and how the world would trade.

Audrey Newcastle had become the unofficial Vice-Chair of the Amsterdam Group. She had championed the global trade model to an even greater extent that van Holder. She had quickly seen the advantages of active participation, and was instrumental in convincing many of the Protocol signatories to forget van Holder's underhanded tactics and move forward with his broad plan. Only two had refused to commit. They would soon find it impossible to conduct business. If they still didn't yield, they would meet the same fate as the Frenchman.

Van Holder's direct line to Montana pierced the silence of his empire building. Only three people knew the number, and no one used it to deliver good news.

"Van Holder," he answered.

"We have a problem with Debitfund," the tentative voice replied on the other end. Bruce Peterson was the head of computer operations in Montana. A twenty year veteran of ASC, he was one of van Holder's most trusted lieutenants. Like most of the upper echelon employees, they had no idea of the true nature of their actions.

"Can it be fixed?" Van Holder dove into the heart of the problem.

"The problem is that it's gone," Peterson said.

"What do you mean…gone?" van Holder said, suddenly alert.

"About an hour ago, the program stopped working. The balance hit $16.2 billion and change then it stopped," Peterson replied.

"It took you an hour to call me?" van Holder shouted into the phone.

"We tried to restore the program. That was when things went really wrong." Peterson voice was barely a whisper.

"What happened?" van Holder demanded.

"We don't know," Peterson replied meekly.

Van Holder was getting angry. "Find a way to fix it."

"Sorry, sir, but we can't find it. We scanned all backups. It doesn't exist on any of the servers. It's gone."

Van Holder hung up the phone. It was as though the program had died with its creator. What a shame to lose such a valuable tool. To keep up the momentum, he would have to find other ways to gather funds. He couldn't show any weakness now. As he turned his attention to the next deal, van Holder was again interrupted.

McDaniel barged past the flustered receptionist and stormed in, knocking an antique globe off its stand.

"What the hell is the meaning of this?" Nathan yelled, barely able to contain his rage. He thrust a newspaper article in front of van Holder, the relevant section circled with red pen and highlighted:

"...ASC staged another coup this week, gobbling up more companies in its wake. This time the merger-crazed conglomerate completed a deal with Euronet, a German-based financial services company providing transaction flow-through for banks and retailers. The company will compliment the financial services provided by ASC via its proprietary program Visitrack. .... Sources close to the company say that as many as 15,000 US based jobs will be transferred to other service centers currently operating in Eastern Europe by Euronet. The move will save millions of dollars for an industry already awash with cash..."

Van Holder picked up the paper, glanced at the article and casually set it aside. He stood up and smiled at the apoplectic politician. "Well, you didn't really think I'd pass up the opportunity, did you?"

"This stinks, van Holder. My name is all over that merger. We supported the globalization of financial services because you said it would be good for America. How are fifteen thousand lost jobs good for America? How is this good for my election?" Nathan's voice was quivering.

"Settle down, Nathan. The election is as good as won," van Holder said reassuringly.

"The political pundits are going to kill me in the run up to Election Day. We're not that far ahead in the polls." Nathan simmered.

"The deal isn't done yet. Put some political spin on it. Tell them this type of deal is exactly what you'll stop once elected." Van Holder was toying with the distraught man. There were many more surprises to come. The Euronet deal couldn't have waited. Just like a germinating seed, it was ready. He couldn't waste it.

Nathan settled into an overstuffed leather chair, his arms dangling over the wide, rounded ends. His twitching fingers dangling down. He closed his eyes and sighed. Something deep inside told him this was a harbinger of things to come. A small, salty taste of an ocean of change crashing down on the world…on America…on what was soon to be *his* America.

"Why me?" he finally asked, looking up at the confident, smug face of his mentor and liberator.

Van Holder wasn't ready to go there. He still needed the man to do battle, to want to win for himself. Instead of an answer, he provided fuel. "This election is for you. Don't think about how or why. Embrace it. Embrace your victory and savor it. There's far more to win than what pittance was lost here today."

"Things won't be the same." Nathan looked up, still wanting clarity.

"They'll be better. Remember the good things you've already accomplished," van Holder said.

The flattery had its desired effect. Nathan started to expound on his many virtues. He forgot the article and its paltry shifting of workers. There was much to do and he was the one who would lead the change. Van Holder listened politely until time pressed him to end the meeting. As Nathan was leaving, van Holder stroked Nathan's ego one last time. "I picked you because you could win."

As if to dramatically herald in the new era and usher out the old regime, the ring from van Holder's desk phone broke the cycle of accolades. Excusing the interruption, he waited until Nathan had left the room before answering the private line connecting his office to the Montana. Knowing that the call meant action, he settled comfortably into his leather chair. Hopefully, they had restored the program. Sipping his gin and soda, he picked up the phone.

"We have them." The voice on the other end dispensed with introductions.

Van Holder leaned forward as if to pounce, the tips of his fingers tingling, "Where?"

"Bermuda. A small house on the outskirts of Hamilton," the man replied.

"When do you leave?" van Holder's voice was palatable now.

"The plane takes off in an hour."

"This has to be done right. No screw-ups this time. Are you going personally?"

"A crack team has been assembled. I'll be leading the assembly team when we land. It shouldn't be a problem. We have the element of surprise this time." Helmut flinched at the reference to San Francisco.

"Are they both there?"

"According to our sources, the two match the description of Dalton and McLeod."

"How did you find them?" van Holder asked.

"Your source proved accurate. We were able to monitor the satellite signals to triangulate their exact location with a GPS scanner." Helmut could feel van Holder's cold, piercing eyes staring at him through the fiber optic phone line. He had failed again and tracked the couple down only with van Holder's help. His team hadn't even thought of looking in Bermuda. *Dalton had almost been killed there once, so why would he go back? Who was helping him?*

"Nothing is to be left behind. They've been constantly hacking their way into our servers. I want *everything*," van Holder said icily.

"It'll be done," Helmut replied.

"And we need the McLeod girl alive. Bring her to Montana."

"What about Dalton?"

"We need the McLeod girl," van Holder repeated before hanging up.

Chapter 35

With the help of Marion Fletcher's satellite codes and Jeremy Plowstock's computer systems, Andrew and Dana quickly accumulated an impressive amount of data documenting the ASC's expanding corporate structure. What might have been inconsequential to the casual observer represented shining examples of complacency and manipulation to Dana's training. The paper began to pile up in their tiny office on the outskirts of Hamilton. Intrigued by the corporate buildup, the two of them almost forgot what they were trying to accomplish.

Dana was excited to see her program work as it tracked multiple transactions culminating in block purchases of stock or the acquisition of entire companies. Using blind trusts and friendly intermediaries, ASC had illegally bypassed Securities regulators around the world, allowing it to gain control of a myriad of companies without obeying government anti-combines laws.

There was more to this than just academic curiosity. Andrew wondered whether he could also use the information to prove his innocence of theft and murder. So far, they had concentrated their efforts on building a case of corporate theft and securities fraud. They hadn't yet linked van Holder and his company's activities to Andrew. But Andrew was convinced a link existed and that it involved the 'Debitfund' Harry had created. The program was an integral part of van Holder's plans. Andrew's discovery of the money siphoning had catapulted him and Dana into this swirling nightmare.

"Coffees." Jeremy placed the steaming mochas on the vacant desk near the door as he entered.

"Jeremy, you're a lifesaver. How do you always know the exact time when we need a caffeine fix?" Dana smiled, jumping up to grab the sleeved latte.

"Because that time is always," he replied, laughing. Sitting down in an empty chair in the corner, Jeremy directed his attention to Andrew. "Any breakthroughs?"

"Nothing significant today. Just the purchase of a block of shares of a small telecommunications equipment maker in Finland. Dana thinks it's the start of a new series to control the sector."

When he and Dana had first arrived in Bermuda, Jeremy had shown so much interest in their 'work' that Andrew initially became suspicious. Jeremy's insight and quick mind, his questions about transactions he shouldn't know anything about, and his numerous visits had made Andrew question his loyalty. He needed to be more trusting. His suspicion of Harry was misdirected. But he needed to be careful, even if Jeremy did save his life from the same people he was up against. They had the same enemy, although Andrew hadn't yet figured out why the Bermudian was threatened.

"How much?" Jeremy made his way across the small office.

"Sixty two million," Andrew replied.

"Exactly that amount?"

"No."

"What was the exact amount?" Jeremy sat next to Andrew and stared at the computer screen.

Andrew turned to look. Their eyes settled in on the number on the screen—$62,513,250. The amount was paid to Credit Suisse via a London clearinghouse.

"What is it?" Andrew looked at Jeremy. He was staring off into the distance, eyes bouncing rapidly as he processed the information.

"That money—the exact amount—left our bank this morning through an Internet transfer to Credit Suisse. Trust money held for ASC on behalf of one of their clients," Jeremy replied.

"You mean inter-day transfers created by the collection of the debit and credit card activities," Andrew clarified.

"Over the past year, I've received instructions to transfer money directly out of these accounts. I thought it was strange and was nervous about the direct request. Usually the money goes to the payee named on the account, but not in these instances," Jeremy explained.

"This was the dilemma you tried to tell me about at the airport," Andrew said.

"I lost my nerve at the last minute," Jeremy confessed.

"These funds come from the accounts managed by the servers in the back room." Andrew remembered the private room at the bank with the servers that had initiated the barrage of deposits into his personal account.

Jeremy nodded.

"Are you thinking what I'm thinking?" Andrew asked.

"We should cross reference the other transfers," Jeremy replied.

"What are we waiting for? Let's go." Andrew was already on his way out the door, agreeing to meet Dana later at the house. Jeremy would drive him to the cabin when they were finished.

At the bank, the two sleuths headed straight for the back room, ignoring the receptionist's pleas to sign the security register. She was adamant, and after chasing them down the hallway, Jeremy finally scrawled a quick signature and entered the private banking room. The records were confidential and any access had to be documented and approved by two bank officers. Jeremy hauled in a junior manager to sign them into the server.

Within minutes they were pouring over computer files, looking for fund movements. Andrew brought a list of all the ASC acquisitions they had uncovered since arriving in Bermuda.

"I've got one." Jeremy located a low-level transfer from his First Island branch to a lending house in Iowa. It matched to the penny a purchase by an ASC subsidiary of a regional grocery chain. The money flowed out of a clearing account Jeremy thought his bank was managing on behalf of a major US credit card company.

The matches continued, and by late morning they had six positive traces. It was proof that someone was manipulating the funds through Jeremy's bank. Not all the deals could be matched, so it appeared other banks were also involved.

"Harry said that the 'Debitfund' was designed to siphon small amounts from millions of transactions. He built it for van Holder but always thought it would be for internal cash manipulation like the entries at SuperMart," Andrew explained.

"Did he ever see it activated?" Jeremy asked.

"Absolutley."

"Maybe van Holder had other designers."

"Like a secret source of money to fund the Amsterdam Protocol," Andrew said.

"The Amsterdam Protocol?" Jeremy asked. "What's that?"

Andrew explained what the three of them had discovered in Amsterdam and about their subsequent meetings with Marion Fletcher. He deliberately omitted information about the Frenchman's death. The story was farfetched enough.

"What is the man trying to do?" Jeremy asked, chuckling. "Make governments obsolete?" The whir of computers created a background white noise, enveloping Jeremy's comment as he spoke.

"What did you say?" Andrew fell back in his chair and stared at the black man. Something twigged in the back of his mind. Something Harry had said about Senator McDaniel.

"Make government obsolete. A borderless, unregulated global free-for-all like the movie 'Roller Ball'…you know, with James Caan…"

"Never seen it," Andrew confessed.

"It's a futuristic movie from the seventies," Jeremy explained. "Violence and crime are eliminated from society and replaced with the brutal blood sport of 'Roller Ball', a blend of football, hockey and motor-cross. In the movie, the game is sponsored by the multinational corporations that control the world following the collapse of traditional politics. James Caan plays the hero."

"That's it!" Andrew sprang out of his chair. The casters spun wildly as the empty seat slid across the room and crashed into the servers. He closed his eyes and held his breath.

"That explains the secret fund. It explains his affiliation with the lame duck McDaniel. And it explains what he was trying to do at the GTC. He wants to set global economic policy and needs a loosely knit group of corporate titans to launch his assault on the world. He wants total domination." He needed to test his theory on Dana.

"Come on. Let's go." He yelled over his shoulder as he left the secure room. Jeremy followed in tow.

Chapter 36

The army surplus troop plane buzzed over the horizon, skimming the waves as it approached the coast. The dozen battle-trained men sat in a semi-circle on the floor of the plane facing the leader as he outlined the attack on the whiteboard. Sitting at the back, Helmut watched as his former Marine lieutenant summarized the movements the team would need to make in the next six hours. Each man listened intently. They were well paid for their services—more than they would make in a year traipsing through some puny African country teaching thirteen-year-olds how to fire a Kalashnikov.

Max Drummond shouted over the roar of the engines as they came in low near the private airstrip in the Southampton Parish of Bermuda. He reached Helmut in three long strides. "Ready."

"Remember," Helmut repeated for the fifteenth time. "The girl must be taken alive."

"Piece of cake." Max smiled. He loved insurgency work. It didn't suck that they were infiltrating an island paradise during peacetime. He could easily get used to this type of work. He checked his rifle. "What about the other subject?"

"It wouldn't hurt my feelings if you disposed of him," Helmut replied.

The plane touched down with a jolt, sending several crates sliding forward. Helmut grabbed the mesh hanging down the sides of the cargo bay used to secure equipment during flight, and was thrown heavily into the wall. Max braced himself against the superstructure, his eyes focused and set.

As soon as the plane taxied to the tiny hut of an office, the men emerged from the open jaws at the back of the plane. In less than five minutes, the surplus carrier was heading back down the runway. This was a daylight raid. Four hours to objective. Max studied the laminated map Velcroed inside his bush jacket, then jumped into the jeep and headed in the direction of the house circled on the map. A second team drove into Hamilton. Looking at the vehicles as they left the abandoned airfield, one might expect to see golf clubs in the back. It was a military operation only to those involved.

Helmut stood in the improvised tent underneath the toppled remains of the airstrip hanger. GPS and satellite communications gear lined the tent. Two operators watched the LED screens as the tracking signals emitted a faint light on the inlaid map of Bermuda. Technology allowed complete and direct contact at all times. Once the small blips changed direction and reverted back to point zero, the plane circling a hundred miles offshore in a holding pattern would be called back.

"Tango base, do you read? This is Blue Dog." Max checked the feed. Although no longer performed, the procedure had been necessary when high frequency radios were used. Now communications were digital and beamed off a satellite three hundred miles in space, so he could talk to his com-ops a mile-and-a-half down the road. The message was encrypted as it entered the small mike next to his cheek. The voice signature activated the receiver in the communications tent where Helmut waited. The computers were set to receive communication from individual team members. Even power was no longer an issue, as each piece of equipment was powered with miniature NcD batteries recharged continuously through solar cells.

"Blue Dog, you are live. Happy hunting." Tango base replied.

It took less than thirty minutes to get to their destination. It was 1245 hours. Based on the information provided, this was where the subjects would be. Max and his men took up positions around the pale pink house set back from the road. Built on a small incline above two houses situated north and east of it, the property had a commanding view of the water from the front porch. The unkempt shrubs and high grasses were well suited for the operation. Like many houses in Bermuda, this one had a small suite on the ground floor. The subjects were housed on the main floor. Max stared at his target as he waited for a report on the surrounding houses.

"North property is vacant," the scout reported.

"This is Spotter. East property has eight occupants."

"Visual on subject property?" Max queried.

"Negative. Occupants are on the opposite side of the house. Appear to be playing cards. Probably bridge."

"Why do you say that, Spotter?" Max asked.

"Two tables of four. The women appear to be winning, Blue Dog." Max smiled at the comeback. His men were very observant. If all went well, they should be gone in twenty minutes.

Even though they could talk to each other, the soldiers preferred the use of hand signals. It was safer and left less room for error.

"Do we have a read on the occupants?" Max asked the Tango operator.

"According to our fact sheet, the subjects usually come home for lunch. They should be inside now."

Max made a wide, sweeping gesture with his arms and the two men on the perimeter swung to the back and far side of the house.

"Ready, Gunner. Give me a visual." Max wanted to be sure.

"Roger, Blue Dog." The mercenary rolled through the undergrowth to the edge of the house and peered though a window. The house had an open design. Gunner recognized the woman from the laminated picture given to each member of the team. After circling the house and looking through each window, he reported. "Visual on girl. No sign of other subject."

This was better than he had expected. "Get the girl and go." He contacted the second team. "Red Dog, this is Blue Dog. Report."

"This is Red Dog. We have entry and are removing contents. No sign of either subject."

"We have the girl. The male subject not located."

"The secondary objective is not crucial," Max responded. It was time to act. "Set to go. Positions."

"Gunner ready."

"Spotter ready."

Max fired a stun grenade. "Go on impact."

The operation had begun.

The two vehicles almost collided on the last turn of the steep driveway. Andrew jolted forward as Jeremy slammed on the brakes and skidded to a stop inches from the camouflaged four-wheel-drive jeep. What was it doing in his driveway? Suddenly, a bullet shattered the windshield and lodged in the seat between them.

Jamming the vintage Ford Escort into reverse and keeping his head low as he backed onto the main road, Jeremy narrowly avoided clipping the bumper of a pink public transit bus as it bounced slowly into town, spewing diesel in its wake. Two more bullets harmlessly entered the confines of the small car before a corner in the road took them out of range.

"Looks like they found out where you are," Jeremy shouted as he shifted into first gear and headed down the road after the bus. Moments later, the jeep appeared in the rearview mirror.

"More importantly, how did they find us?" Andrew yelled back over the din of the noisy engine.

"How many are there?"

"I saw four. We'd better not let them catch us. I don't think they'll want to talk."

"What about Dana?" Jeremy asked. "Do you think they were coming or going?"

The realization hit Andrew like a blast of cold arctic wind. Dana! Did they have her? Was she dead? He broke out in a cold sweat as he quickly reached for his cell phone. Dialing was not easy as Jeremy swerved into the ongoing traffic to pass the lumbering pink bus. The stench of diesel filled their nostrils as they came alongside. Jeremy ignored the 20mph speed limit posted on the main arteries of Bermuda. The fine for speeding was higher than the fine for drunk driving. Jeremy looked like he was guilty of both as he careened past the startled passengers on the bus. Although the small Ford was going 65mph and speeding up, the jeep was gaining on them.

Andrew hit the speed dial button on his phone, pressed send and then waited as the phone rang. No answer. He tried again with the same results. "Go back," he screamed over the engine.

Jeremy threw him a sideways glance, his bright teeth grinding together. "Okay, it's your funeral," Jeremy said. "Hang on."

Jeremy spotted the road he was looking for and abruptly turned the car onto a narrow path leading up into the hills. The road was one-way but doubled back onto the main road a mile later. Andrew whipped his head around in time to see the Jeep miss the turn and continue on in the same direction.

"I don't have a very good feeling about this," Andrew remarked as the Jeep disappeared into the distance.

Jeremy stopped the car. "Let's follow them. Call Timothy Gibson. Tell him to go to the house and check it out." He gave Andrew the number. Timothy had come around a few times since they arrived in Bermuda. Andrew couldn't thank him enough for saving his life from the Russian.

The small car skidded back onto the main road and followed the Jeep from a safe distance. They lost sight of the vehicle a few times, but Jeremy was unconcerned. "The only place they could be going is the abandoned airfield in Southampton Parish. The Jeep they were driving was not from the Island."

"How far?" Andrew asked.

"About ten minutes at this pace." He had slowed the Escort to fifty-fve.

As they neared the turnoff, the drone of twin props filled the air. "They seem to be in a hurry. They must have gotten whatever they came for," Andrew said.

"Or *whoever*," Jeremy added.

Racing down the dirt road onto the airfield, they were met with a barrage of gunfire. One of the bullets met its mark, blowing out the right front tire. The car spun clockwise, exposing Jeremy to the sentry's continued firing. Fortunately, the car landed in a small ditch and the remaining bullets sailed overhead. The two of them quickly climbed out of the crumpled sedan and dashed to a grove of hibiscus bushes. Peering through the dense foliage, they saw one of the Jeeps drive up into the belly of a plane. Following on foot were several men carrying equipment. When a second Jeep drove up the ramp, Andrew spotted a figure in the back seat. It was Dana.

Chapter 37

"Stop pacing," Jeremy said, trying to calm Andrew down.

Since their arrival at the small, pastel green shack surrounded by lush fields of poinsettias on the outskirts of Southampton Parish, Andrew had been walking from one end of the small room to the other, pounding his fists on the wall and cursing and swearing. Outside in the early morning, the workers were gathering for the harvest.

Andrew stopped pacing and peered through the window, berating himself for allowed them to take Dana. "What the hell am I going to do now?" he asked as if talking to a room full of waiting minions.

"At least now we can fight back. They didn't get you," Jeremy consoled him.

After realizing they wouldn't be able to rescue Dana, they had left the airstrip and traveled to Jeremy's secluded home where they would stay until they had formulated a plan. *Whatever Dana knows must be very important for them to launch such a massive operation. What does she know?* Andrew asked himself.

"They won't kill her," Jeremy said, interrupting Andrew's thoughts.

"How do you know they won't kill her? They seem to have an appetite for killing people who get in their way."

"They won't kill her because they need her. Otherwise why take her off the Island."

"What does she know that is so important? They had no trouble leaving me behind, so obviously I'm not a threat anymore." Andrew's head was spinning. "What does she know?"

The rehearsed plans they had been working on since arriving in Bermuda two months earlier would have to change.

"What about the document Marion was forced to sign—the Amsterdam Protocol. Could she have told Dana something about it?" Jeremy queried.

"Dana would have told me."

"Where do you think they're keeping Dana?" Jeremy asked.

The two of them were silent as they pondered the question. Only the sounds of a hinge rattling on the shutter and the workers cutting the plants outside filled the empty space. *Where was Dana?* Jeremy was probably right. They would have killed her at the house if they didn't need her. Harry was dead. Dana was kidnapped. How would he find her? Andrew knew he needed a powerful ally. The information they had been gathering, the trail of conspiracy between multi-national giants overseen by ASC, was almost complete. Luckily, their attack had occurred away from the small office housing the files they had accumulated. It was time to retrieve the files and leave. Andrew would finish packing up and transfer the documents to the mainland. They were ready to go public, but it would have to wait. Disclosing what they had found out now might eliminate the need to keep Dana alive. He couldn't risk it.

It took them a long time to get back into town. Skirting the main road, the two of them trudged through fields and small neighborhoods. The choice was to remain hidden, in case others were left behind to deal with Andrew. As there was only one major artery on either side of the mile-wide island, it was likely that both routes into town were being watched. Neither of them had any illusions about the commando unit that had descended upon them. Climbing through the large garden and over the rocks near the entrance of the town, they quickly weaved their way through the streets. Jeremy proved tremendously agile for his large size, moving like the gymnast he had been at university. Andrew labored under the stifling humidity. By the time they reached the back alley behind their office, his breath was coming in short bursts like a man starved of oxygen.

Jeremy laughed. "You need to spend more time on the island!"

"You need to come to Colorado and ski so I can be the one laughing," Andrew wheezed.

The office door was jammed as they tried to enter. Pushing it open with his shoulder, Jeremy led Andrew into a room that was in shambles—monitors smashed, computers ripped apart, wires sprawling over the ground like spaghetti. And all the boxes were gone.

"Looks like they were here," Jeremy said ruefully as they sifted through the mess.

A note was tacked in the middle of the corkboard on the far wall. Andrew walked over and removed it. "Well, at least we won't have to wait long to hear from them."

Hearing a sound outside, Andrew paused. Both men looked at each other. "Run!" they exclaimed in unison.

Dodging splinters from the door, they dove through the fire escape window. A bullet zinged over their heads and lodged in the crumbling stucco of a tenement house across the lane. They ran down the stairs and down the ally. Looking over his shoulder, Jeremy saw that the shooter was a Bermudian constable.

"It's the police, and they came to shoot. Somebody must have told them a very believable fabrication," he managed to say as they rounded a corner to safety. They didn't stop running until they had reached the other side of Hamilton.

Jeremy pulled his cell phone out of his pocket and dialed a number. "The police will be swarming the downtown core in a few minutes. We have to get you back to the States, and I have to reclaim my island!" Jeremy exclaimed.

A few hours later, the two of them sat on the edge of a small dock jutting out into an isolated bay at the edge of the tiny island. A floatplane bobbed listlessly in the water as the pilot climbed onto the pontoon in preparation for flight.

"Are you sure that thing will fly?" Andrew stared at the ancient plane held together with a handful of rusty rivets.

"It hasn't failed old Frank in thirty years," Jeremy replied confidently.

"Will it make it to the mainland?" Andrew asked.

"Old Frank ran contraband rum and black market electronics to the mainland and back until he was caught and had to spend six years in jail. Now he does local sightseeing trips. The plane is designed to fly the distance. Each of the pontoons carries two hundred gallons of extra fuel."

"Why is he doing this for you?" Andrew asked.

"It is a long story. Frank's wife and kids needed help while he was in jail. I gave them a loan and then wrote it off when old Frank got out of prison. What did the note say?" he asked, changing the subject.

Andrew fished it out of his pocket. In their haste, he had forgotten about it. He reread the note and handed it over to Jeremy.

"What do you make of this?" Jeremy asked, returning the note to Andrew.

"Scare tactics. A desperate plea to get me to back down."

"But if he wanted you dead, why leave a note?" Jeremy asked.

"Maybe killing me was only secondary. They didn't exactly make an effort to track us down at the airstrip."

"Then why send the police?"

"Tie up the evidence if they couldn't carry it all," Andrew suggested.

"Are you always this logical?" Jeremy grinned and slapped the young accountant on the back.

"It's a curse." Andrew smiled.

The note was unsigned, but Andrew had no doubt as to its author. Dana wouldn't be safe if he did nothing. It was time to fight back. Fortunately, Andrew's penchant for duplication paid off. Copies of most of the key documents were stored securely in the vault at the bank. Jeremy would send them stateside when he was ready. In the meantime, nothing further would be done until Dana was safe.

Jeremy waved at the pilot and stood up on the dock. "Ready to go, Frank?"

"Yep." Old Frank came over and introduced himself to Andrew. "Pleased to meet you, son."

"Thanks, Frank. I appreciate you doing this for me." Andrew extended a hand and returned the introduction."

"It'll be fun to buzz the mainland again." Frank smiled through gaps in his teeth.

Three hours later, they neared the shore, coming in ten feet off the crest of the waves. Frank explained that in his rum-running days it wasn't necessary to fly so low to the water, but the new homeland security measures made it impossible to sneak into the country. As soon as the plane touched down, Andrew was to jump and then swim to shore. Once there, he would be on his own. When the authorities arrived, Old Frank would claim he had been lost at sea. There was nothing in the plane but scattered tourist maps and charts. Hopefully, the story would be credible enough to fool the authorities.

As the pontoons skidded against the gentle waves inside the narrow bay, Frank eased the weathered airplane as near to shore as possible. Andrew opened the passenger door, shook Old Frank's hand and jumped into the water. Within minutes after he had crawled onto the beach and hidden in the underbrush, the pontoon plane was surrounded. The light from a helicopter overhead illuminated the plane as the Coast Guard made sure it could not take off. Frank was standing on his pontoon, hands up and smiling. He was having the time of his life. Hearing sirens in the distance, Andrew knew it was time to move.

It was a chilly winter night on the coast of North Carolina as Andrew made his way to the main road, staying in the shadows. At a small resort motel, the night clerk looked at him suspiciously when he unzipped his body belt and handed her two wet fifty-dollar bills. Inside the belt was $20,000, his fake passport and driver's license. He had decided to risk coming back to the States using his new identity. He would just have to stay below the radar.

After turning the knob on the small space heater as far as it would go, Andrew undressed and laid his clothes on the chair and small desk to dry. In the hot shower, he formulated a plan, letting the stream fill the room until the walls were dripping. He had put Dana's life at risk. Maybe he should give up, go to Montana and turn himself over to van Holder. Take his chances. But that would be foolhardy and he knew it. Dana would want him to keep going. Too much was at stake. He had the information. It was time to take action.

Chapter 38

McDaniel was conspicuously absent from the room on the eve of his presidential inauguration. His platform of fiscal strength through global strength driven by strong U.S. interests and underpinning the need for continued social change had led McDaniel and his team to a landslide victory.

The room at the Four Seasons had been reserved for a private party. The inner circle of McDaniel's presidential team and his close confidants and friends had gathered for an early celebration. The who's who of Washington's political and social scene mingled in a jubilant mood. Waiters and hostesses circulated throughout the crowd, offering canapés and champagne. Streamers hung from the ceiling in chandeliers surrounded by bags of balloons ready for the next day's celebration.

Since the November election, McDaniel and his team had wasted no time in preparing for this day. After the backlash from the GTC summit had almost turned the election against him, McDaniel had used statistics provided by van Holder to squelch the naysayers, who quickly grew out of favor as people turned their attention to an era of renewed prosperity.

Standing regal and attentive amongst a small group of her supporters, Jessica Poole surveyed the room. She felt privileged to be a part of such an auspicious group, but was confident that many believed McDaniel had only made the White House because she was his running mate. They were already talking about her succession in eight years. When the conversation turned to social services, she detached herself from the group and approached her assistant.

"Have you seen Nathan?" Jessica asked as she again panned the room.

"I think he went up to his suite," her assistant replied. "Would you like me to go find him?"

"It's okay. I'm sure he's just overwhelmed." Jessica continued her rounds.

In his dimly-lit suite twenty-three stories above the ballroom, McDaniel was slumped in the chair at the desk, staring at the dark night closing in on the city he loathed. He looked at the unfolded letter on the desk. A young man had approached him at the party and thrust the letter in his hand, urging him to read it. When he had shoved it in his coat pocket and resumed talking to his guests, the young man had approached him once more, reiterating the urgency of the request.

McDaniel picked up the letter again and reread the two pages. Was it true? When his political star was on the rise, had he been so blinded by van Holder that he allowed himself to think the man was his salvation? Deep down he knew he had signed a contract with the devil, but had convinced himself it was only backroom lobbying and politicking. Van Holder had wanted him to believe Booker was sent to track down corporate spies and opportunists. He almost had their blood on his hands. Although the facts spoke volumes, he refused to believe what the letter said was true. How could he have been so stupid? The letter referred to Calico Pharmaceutical's recent approval from the FDA for their myelin regenerating technology. What did this kid know about Calico? He remembered van Holder talking about it the last time they had met and how important it was for the European company to receive the appropriate FDA approval. A friendly call to the head researcher had secured the drug's entry into the U.S. This kid now says the company is actually owned by ASC, his chief benefactor. After the inauguration, he would look into their application.

The other information in the letter was too farfetched to believe. Had he funded and built the bunker in Montana so van Holder could use it for his private research arm? How could he be so unaware of what was happening? As soon as possible, he would head out to Montana and find out if the allegations were true, if they were indeed holding captive the young girl that van Holder had told him was a spy, it was time for immediate action. He placed a call to the Pentagon.

In the meantime, he wanted to speak to the letter writer face-to-face. He picked up the phone and called the FBI deputy director. The two of them had graduated from university together, so he should be more than willing to help the next President. Not wanting to leave a trail to compromise his executive position, he fed the two-page letter through a shredder before returning to the party.

Andrew's heart was pounding so hard he feared it would burst through his chest. He wasn't sure how McDaniel felt about his involvement with ASC and its founder, van Holder. At least he had succeeded in giving him the letter. He had felt very self-conscious wandering through the private party handing out drinks, waiting for the chance to get near McDaniel. He knew it was the right thing to do, since McDaniel knew about the facility in Montana. Hopefully, the letter conveyed what he had intended to say, which was 'I know more than you think.' The next step would be to place a seed of doubt in the minds of his enemies in the event they derived comfort from his or Dana's death. The second letter in his pocket, to be delivered tomorrow during the inauguration, burned against his thigh.

Riot police lined the street outside the Four Seasons Hotel, creating a seemingly impassible cordon around the hotel. A mob of protestors—more vocal than dangerous—marred the jubilant celebrations going on inside, their breath rising in the biting cold like smoke from smoldering ashes. A generation earlier, these noisy, swarming demonstrators would have been called hippies or beatniks. The leaders of the demonstration, who made appearances at most world trade events, considered it their God-given right to protest. On the night of McDaniel's celebration, they had come out to show their disapproval for his 'global trade, no borders' policy.

Andrew weaved his way through the crowd looking for an entrance into the hotel. It had been easy the night before, but now security was tighter than blue jeans on a cow. He stood at the edge of the crowd and stared at the line of masked, baton-wielding stickmen. Just as he was about to abandon his plan, the crowd suddenly shifted towards the far side of the hotel, as if guided by an unseen force. The police stickmen tensed and leaned into the shrinking space separating them from the crowd. News camera crews panned the scene from hovering copters. Law enforcement crews did likewise, gathering evidence.

Agitators worked the crowd like minarets, shifting, moving, and teasing the brainless beast. They had come to transform the harmless crowd into a statement of defiance—or was it just sport? One of the organizers sidled up to Andrew and said, "We need to storm the line." Before Andrew could respond with a rational objection, the man moved on to spread his message. Andrew knew he would remain in the background, critical of the effects of the carefully placed discontent.

The crowd shifted to the edge of the hotel. Andrew moved against the flow, trying unsuccessfully to push back. The batons and shields moved in unison, straining to push the ripple back as the empty space between the two groups decreased. Screams and blunt thuds pierced the night. The spin doctors sidled out the back to prepare a response to the thoughtless acts.

Despite the heightened security, several cracks developed in the line as riot police weaved in and out of the crowd. Andrew used the shadow of a riot van to slip past the undulating wave of police. Dressed in a tuxedo under his overcoat, the bowtie protruding out from the top, he looked like just another guest out for a breath of fresh air. The police on the steps—the last line of defense if the crowd stormed the hotel—ignored him as he passed. Behind him, the audible popping of tear gas canisters began to disperse the mob.

Andrew obviously didn't have an invitation. He hoped he would gain entry by acting like he belonged. Milling with the legitimate guests, he watched the melee outside before following a group back to the main salon where people were awaiting the arrival of the new President. Andrew breathed as sigh of relief as he passed the entrance guards. He felt his left breast pocket to make sure the letter was inside. The letter was the reason for this intrusion. Once safely inside, Andrew scanned the crowd, looking for the intended recipient. It took only a few minutes to spot van Holder on the dance floor. Making his way across the ballroom, Andrew was stopped a few feet from the dance floor. He turned to approach van Holder, his eyes locking with the architect of the Amsterdam Protocol. The steel, cold glare looked back and smiled, penetrating Andrew's resolve.

As he turned to leave, abandon his plan, a muscular secret service agent grabbed Andrew by the elbow and led him to a side door.

"Come with me, please." Andrew looked back as he was led away. Van Holder had already turned back to his partner.

"Where are you taking me?" Andrew demanded. The man said nothing as they approached the service elevator where two other agents stood like roman centurions, holding the door for their captive.

"What is the meaning of this?" Andrew demanded again. "I have rights." His bravado elicited no response.

On the top floor of the Four Seasons Hotel, six more agents patrolled the hall and guarded the exits. Andrew and his escort walked past the agents to a door at the end of the corridor. After a brief wait, the door was opened and the two of them led Andrew inside.

McDaniel looked up as they entered. He got up, walked around his desk and approached them. "Hello, Mr. Dalton. I'm President McDaniel." Nathan offered his outstretched hand.

Not knowing what else to do, Andrew accepted the gesture and stammered, "It's Andrew, sir, I mean Mr. President."

"Yes, I know," McDaniel replied. He turned to the secret service agents and signaled that he wanted to be left alone. This was their first day on the job and they were reluctant to leave. A gentle prod by the new President eased them out the door.

"Did you arrange the reception outside just to create a distraction?" McDaniel asked, smiling.

Andrew took the bait. "Just a few malcontents. It was easy," he replied stoically.

"There are no easy answers." McDaniel took a seat.

"So it seems. How did you know I was here?"

"The FBI located you this morning," McDaniel said. He was thankful for the quick response to his request the night before, and made a mental note to commend his former roommate.

"Getting in wasn't as easy as I thought," Andrew admitted.

"You managed to do that by yourself. Impressive. But if you hadn't, you would have been brought up."

"Thanks." Andrew wasn't sure he was.

"My man says you were about to leave just after you snuck in. Why the quick exit from the party?"

"Not my crowd. To stuffy."

"Trying to play the hero." McDaniel queried.

"Something like that." Andrew wasn't sure he liked where this conversation was going. It was time to get to the point. "Your benefactor is not a nice man."

"So your letter implies. What makes you think I have any personal connection to William van Holder? Your letter was very explicit."

"Montana," Andrew replied.

"It's a government facility. I chair the subcommittee responsible for its operation." McDaniel wasn't about to admit he believed the wild accusations about van Holder.

"Not everything is as it seems, Mr. President. My girlfriend was held against her will at your facility just three months ago. You were there at the time." Andrew liked the sound of 'my girlfriend' as it rolled off his lips.

"Are you saying van Holder kidnapped her and brought her to that bunker, and then used her to hatch some elaborate scheme to control the ebb and flow of global commerce?" McDaniel used the colloquial name to describe what he was now suspected wasn't the research arm he had thought it was.

"He also tried to kill me. Then, and on several other occasions," Andrew added.

"Why would he do that?" McDaniel asked.

Andrew stood up and paced the room, stopping near the window to admire the view of the city with the Washington monument backlit on the horizon. He wasn't sure how much information to divulge. What if McDaniel was just playing him for a patsy and using him to consolidate knowledge about his enigmatic supporter? None of it mattered if he could free Dana. "You tell me."

"Are you implying that I had knowledge of this?" McDaniel was getting nervous. He wanted more information from the author of the damaging letter. How much did this young man know about his dealings with van Holder, the campaign funding sources and the timely accidents of his opponents? Surely these events had not just occurred along the way. He thought about the timing and chose to dismiss the coincidences. What about Charlie Booker? That was his doing. He wondered if Dalton knew that.

"You were there. I saw you in the ranch house with van Holder. What was I supposed to think?"

"It was a routine visit. What were you doing on federal government property?" McDaniel took the offensive.

"Rescuing Dana. I already told you that."

"No other reason?"

"What other possible reason could there be?" Andrew held up his hands.

"Espionage." The word rolled off McDaniel's lips slowly and hung in the air between them like vapor. Their eyes locked. In that moment, Andrew felt he had an ally, a bond forged against a common foe.

"My crimes are mounting—fraud, embezzlement, murder and now spying. No wonder the titan of American business wants me dead." Andrew smiled smugly. "What will I think of next?"

"It seems you've run the gambit. I hadn't heard about the murder, though."

He started to relay the entire story, but a knock on the door interrupted him. Andrew recognized McDaniel's press secretary from the television coverage leading up to the election.

"Sorry to bother you, Mr. President, but it's time to go," the press agent intoned. He turned to Andrew. "Sorry for the interruption. You've already taken up too much of his time."

Before Andrew had risen from his chair, McDaniel stopped him. "I'd like to finish this conversation. Where are you staying so I can send a car to pick you up in the morning?" He looked up at his press agent. "Please arrange to have Mr. Dalton brought to the White House at whatever time is open tomorrow." With that, Nathan McDaniel left the room behind the entourage assembled in the hallway.

Andrew gave the secretary his information and followed her out of the room. She sprinted to catch up to the moving train of strategists filing into the elevator.

By the time Andrew made his way downstairs, the party had thinned. *How long had he been up there?* The remaining guests were sitting in cozy groups, speculating on the new President and his initial moves. Andrew heard one person mention Calico. He paused to listen.

"…hard to believe the bill was passed."

"Do you think it will come back to haunt him?" a second person chimed in.

"Not McDaniel. He has an uncanny ability to distance himself from his decisions," the third conspirator at the table suggested.

"He must have a Guardian Angel," the first one said.

"Someone that makes problems disappear. Remember that Senator who was running against him…what was his name?"

Andrew moved out of earshot. He remembered the Senator who dropped out of the race a few terms back for personal reasons. Was he one of those 'problems' van Holder had fixed? Before he could answer his own question, he rounded the corner outside the ballroom and ran into the presidential entourage. In the middle of the crowd was McDaniel in muted conversation with a very attentive van Holder. All the anxiety he had displayed in their conversation upstairs a few minutes earlier had disappeared. *Had their meeting been just an act,* Andrew wondered, *or was McDaniel acting now?*

He began walking toward the crowd, hoping to deliver his letter of ultimatum to van Holder. He made it halfway across the foyer when he stopped dead in his tracks. Turning to look his way, arm in arm with van Holder, was Marion Fletcher.

Chapter 39

Biting cold gusts of wind funneled underneath the bridge, freezing every drop of moisture in its path. In his panic to leave the hotel, Andrew forgot his overcoat. He now regretted the hasty departure, as the wind forced its way between the massive posts of the bridge's undercarriage and accompanied him through the darkness.

This was madness. They had baited me and he was ready to spill his guts. They obviously intended to pry as much information out of him as possible, find out what he knew, what made him dangerous. He was still reeling from the sight of Marion Fletcher hand-in-hand with van Holder. He and Dana had trusted her, confided in her. And what about the information they had gathered with the help of her satellite codes? Somewhere in the far reaches of his mind, there was a missing piece to the puzzle. Something else had to explain the connection between the three people in the lobby of the hotel, the ones he had just left in a panic. He was now further than ever from figuring out why they had taken Dana.

The wind had left debris scattered on the sidewalk. Andrew kicked a juice box as he contemplated the logical scenarios. He looked up as the box sailed toward the lamppost. This simple action saved him from the car that suddenly sped towards him. Throwing himself in a doorway, he barely escaped the oncoming car as its tires drove up onto the curb. A zigzag race up the street brought him close to the front door of his hotel. The late model Oldsmobile didn't even slow down as it pursued him. He instantly lost his dislike for revolving doors as they twisted him to the safety of the hotel lobby. Guests checking in, bellmen and the hotel manager all stared as he skidded to a stop, clutching his upper legs. He bent over to catch his breath as sweat poured from his brow onto the marble floor. In a daze, he watched as the Oldsmobile doors opened and two suited men got out.

Gulping down a mouthful of air, Andrew turned and ran toward the exit adjacent to the elevator. People started to scream, a child wailed, and a lady toppled over a chair, knocking over the flower display in the centre of the lobby. The two men entered the lobby through the revolving doors and spotted Andrew instantly.

"*Freeze! FBI!*" was all Andrew heard as the exit door slammed shut behind him.

In the back alley, Andrew kept running. He searched for others backing up his attackers as he entered a side street next to the hotel. Staying in the shadows, he ran to the next intersection, looking behind him for any signs of activity. Andrew was certain he had seen a glimmer of acceptance of his story in McDaniel's eyes, a sense of camaraderie between them that pitted both of their causes together. It must have been an act, otherwise why would they now be hunting him?

He took the cell phone out of his breast pocket and flipped it open. The new model Motorola fit comfortably in his hand, the casing warming his palm. He found a doorway out of the wind and dialed. The phone rang twice before he slammed the lid shut when it dawned on him that Marion Fletcher had given him the phone. It had worldwide access through her communication system—one that could track the precise location of the phone in the time it took the first digital words to reach his ear. The phone went back into his pocket, useless for now.

At the end of the block, the neon glow of an all-night diner inviting patrons to experience the Capitol's best coffee illuminated the darkness. The payphone was at the back of the building, crammed next to a stack of discarded newspapers. Fishing out the Motorola, Andrew pushed call history and redialed the number into the landline, feeding coins to pay the charges. Jeremy Plowstock answered groggily on the first ring. Andrew quickly summarized the events that had occurred since he left Bermuda. It was reassuring to talk to someone he trusted.

"The deals were all verified, the money flowed, the businesses acquired. Why would van Holder purposely let you eavesdrop on his computer system?" Jeremy wasn't convinced that Marion Fletcher had turned traitor on them.

"We need to check again," Andrew said

"All of them?" Jeremy asked.

"No, start with the Calico Pharmaceuticals deal."

"Give me ten minutes." Jeremy wrote down the number from the diner and hung up.

Andrew settled into a booth with a discarded newspaper and a freshly brewed cup of Columbian dark roast. It was warm in the small diner. The windows were coated with a hazy film of moisture—a suitable smokescreen should his pursuers still be hunting him.

The article was at the bottom of the fourth page of the Washington Post—insignificant coverage in the least-read page of the daily paper. The headline read: "Visitrack Stops Retail Flow." The four-inch article caught his eye. He read it and then sat back to contemplate the information. According to sources close to the company, the entire system had been shut down for eight hours due to unexplained complications. The paper was a few weeks old, dated two days before Dana was taken in Bermuda. He wondered if it had anything to do with Dana's forced recruitment.

The phone in the back of the diner rattled. Several late night patrons glanced in the direction of the phone, but didn't get up; probably some loser calling a wrong number graciously provided by a pretty face in a pickup bar. Andrew answered before the second ring. Curiosity forced several of the patrons to lend their ears to the ensuing conversation, but they soon turned their attention back to the weary but attractive waitress behind the counter when they couldn't hear the muted voice.

"The money was deposited in small sums, accumulated and then sent to an overseas bank the same day Calico was purchased," Jeremy reported. "Before I called back, I checked a few of the other deals. They were all the same."

Andrew repeated his story about seeing Marion Fletcher with van Holder. "She's the key. All the details from the mergers came from her satellite codes."

"Did she see you at the reception?" Jeremy asked.

"No. I panicked and left before she noticed me." Andrew realized that if he had stayed, she may have given him an indication of her intentions.

"What next?" Jeremy asked.

"Can you access the main trust account?"

"Sure." Jeremy punched in the code to the main account. He was seated at his desk, the computer screen providing most of the light in the early hours of the day. He stifled a yawn as the computer searched the database. "Here it is. What am I looking for?"

"Any change in activity."

Jeremy scanned the transaction log. "There are no more deposits coming in. They stopped a few weeks ago."

"When exactly?" After Jeremy confirmed that the timing corresponded to the downtime of the Visitrack system, Andrew continued. "Have they started back up again?"

"No."

"Any funds leave since then?" Andrew wondered aloud.

"A small wire transfer for just over ten million. It emptied the account," Jeremy said. "The money was sent to a small bank in the Caymans. Never heard of it."

"Who sent the instructions?"

Jeremy was silent for a few minutes before responding. "That's odd. There is no issuing bank on the order. The transfer was one-sided."

"We can't use it unless it ties into a specific transaction, and now all of that information is suspect." Andrew was beginning to sense all their work had been a waste of time.

The discernible click on the line made both of the men pause. Someone was listening in on Jeremy's private line. Andrew was about to ask him if he heard the same sound when the line went dead. *What the hell!* Fumbling for change, he plugged the phone and dialed the Bermudian's number from memory. No answer. After hanging up and trying again, he dialed the banker's cell phone. After a dozen rings, the phone sprang to life. It was Jeremy.

"Call my cell in an hour." The line went dead.

Shit! Now what was happening? Andrew wondered as he left the diner. His face caught a blast of cold air as the front door opened. Outside the metro station next to the Smithsonian was a bank of public phones lit by small, energy efficient fluorescent lights. The rain drizzled onto the globe-shaped encasements that were too small to provide protection for the callers. Andrew ducked his head as far into the round opening as he could. The electronic beep connecting to Bermuda Tel buzzed in his ear. Jeremy answered on the fourth ring. Dispensing with pleasantries, he told Andrew to recite the number of the public phone and promptly hung up. It took two minutes for the return call.

Jeremy was out of breath. "I think van Holder wants his bank back."

"What happened?"

"All the activity—the searches we did—must have been logged somewhere. ASC goons stormed the bank like a swarm of locusts. Everyone was rounded up and held in the boardroom."

"You got out?"

"Do you remember the executive washroom at the end of the hall near the back room…the one with the private files? I ducked in there and crawled out the window."

"And you fit?" Andrew smiled as he pictured the large Bermudian squeezing through the small window.

"Funny guy. There's more. They came with the police and an arrest warrant…for me." Jeremy said, although more annoyed than scared.

Andrew didn't know what to say. If they had never met, Jeremy would still be comfortably running one of the best banks in Bermuda and climbing the corporate ladder.

Jeremy broke the silence. "It's not your fault. Shit happens. Van Holder probably had me pegged as the scapegoat right from the beginning."

"But why raid the bank if the flow of funds has stopped?" Andrew wiped the rain from his forehead. The drizzle had turned into a downpour.

"He must not know why the money stopped. Maybe he thought we had something to do with it," Jeremy speculated.

"He could have just asked Dana." Andrew's heart lurched at the mention of her name. *Where was she?*

"Maybe the question was raised."

"Are you saying she would deliberately put your life at risk?" Andrew suddenly felt defensive.

Jeremy carefully worded his next thought. "Perhaps she found it the best alternative."

"I have to find her." Andrew's voice was strained as he held back his emotions.

"Count me in. I have no intention of letting them take my bank without a fight," Jeremy affirmed.

"You've already done enough."

"Bullshit. By the way, how cold is it where you are going?"

"Bring a sweater, maybe two."

Chapter 40

Dana stretched her weary arms and suppressed a yawn as she stared blankly at the computer screen. The past three days had drained the color from her face, leaving grey shadows under her eyes. She stifled another yawn as she waited for the computer to boot to up. She had no idea where she was and didn't care. Since her abduction from Bermuda, everything had been a blur. Despite her desperate pleas and refusals to cooperate, they were relentless in their demands. She had no choice. Either she cooperated or Andrew would be killed. They had Andrew. She wondered where they were keeping him and if they would both be let go once she finished her research. The security appeared to be non-existent. She could have walked out several times…but they had Andrew.

Whatever they needed had to be delivered at a feverish pace. Several times she insisted they produce Andrew and let them talk, but her demands fell on deaf ears. They might be bluffing, but she couldn't take the chance. Each day she sat at the terminal and applied her computer model to the mountain of folders at the edge of her desk.

"Everything set up okay?" She heard Bruce Peterson's voice over her left shoulder. He had been her shadow ever since they had brought her from Bermuda.

"I could use a double espresso," Dana replied.

"Yes, madam. A double espresso and Danish coming right up." Bruce said, dropping another folder on top of the pile. "New search. Priority,"

"Do something about the lighting," Dana ordered, ignoring the folder.

"Maybe if you're a good girl." Bruce pointed to the grey folder on the pile.

"Fine." Dana looked at the name on the folder. It wasn't an American company. So far, they had her concentrating exclusively on American-based contractors with significant influence in Washington. Foreign-owned companies had been ignored. *Something must be happening*, she thought.

Bruce interrupted her thoughts. "A full dress-up—management, ownership, long- term contracts, political ties. Don't leave anything out."

"Why do you work for van Holder?"

"ASC is a great company," Bruce quipped.

"So, you'd work for a crook as long as the pay was good." Dana realized most of the people around her believed they worked for a company with a vision. Like the others, she believed ASC was a legitimate company trying to compete in a global marketplace.

"This is corporate America, right? I just follow orders and collect my pay."

"And harbor people against their will," Dana added.

"You're free to go anytime," Bruce said, shrugging his shoulders. He turned and walked to the door.

"Don't forget the espresso," Dana called after him as she sauntered to the coffee pot to fill her mug.

By the time the sun had filtered though the skylight, Dana had what van Holder needed—and what she may also need. She scanned the computer sheets as they spewed out of the laser printer. The company was British-registered and widely held. One name caught her eye—Mikos Popokulas. She recognized the name from the list of Amsterdam attendees that Marion Fletcher had helped them compile. It didn't take much detective work to conclude that this company was about to bid on a U.S. government contract. It was everything van Holder wanted. His Amsterdam contacts must be lining up to reap the rewards of their new partnership.

Dana filtered the report, burying as many inaccuracies in the details as she dared. The small lies wouldn't be noticed unless the information was verified. Dana smiled with satisfaction as the runner took the report.

Alone at her desk, she typed a quick email, reread the dialogue for clues and clicked send. She was careful to not ask direct questions in her electronic correspondence. Access to the Internet wasn't restricted, but it was watched. On the second day in Montana, she had fired off a brief note to Marion Fletcher, probing for news about Andrew. That was how she had learned of Andrew's captivity. Her first meeting with Bruce Peterson had been because of the email. He had produced a copy of the electronic conversation. Despite the warning, she had continued to communicate with carefully worded missives. Marion Fletcher had responded each time, urging Dana to be careful and cooperate.

"It's the best alternative for now," Marion had assured her.

Chapter 41

The Montana wind swirled around the three riders, enveloping them like a silk blanket, as the Polaris 800 RMK sleds glided silently over the white powder at speeds once thought impossible. The sound of the engine was muffled with specially fitted exhaust cases. The lead rider reached the final marker and headed toward the main encampment, his white suit and sled blending into the snow-covered field. After coming to a quick stop outside the command tent, the rider removed his helmet and went inside.

"Sir, there are two men about four miles from the main gate," the scout reported.

The commander of the 4th Reconnaissance Battalion out of Billings was not happy. In twenty-five minutes all hell would break loose, and two yahoos had decided to wander into the middle of their party. "Can you get them out?"

"Not without compromising our position, sir."

"Who are they?"

"Infrared signatures have been taken and sent to Washington. A wasted effort, in my opinion, sir."

"Has the assault team been notified of their presence?" The commander queried the reconnaissance man.

"Not yet."

"Advise the commanding officer of the First Assault Division of their existence and location. Maybe he can modify his entry."

"Right away, sir." The rider saluted and left.

"Hope luck is on their side," the Colonel muttered as he studied the map of the sprawling Montana ranch they were about to invade. He called Washington to report the presence of the unexpected guests.

Dogged by the piercing wind, Andrew slowed the rental car down and turned out the lights. They traveled the final distance in darkness, with only the light from what appeared to be the main ranch house keeping them on course. Jeremy's dark skin was a stark contrast against the whites of his eyes as he stared out into the bleak, cold night.

"Why anyone would want to live in this Godforsaken land is beyond me." He smiled and looked at Andrew.

"Are you warm yet?" Andrew chided.

"Two sweaters. You must think the color of my skin provides a natural heat source." Jeremy replied, laughing. After he had landed at Ronald Reagan Airport, it took just thirty seconds outside in the frigid air of Washington to send him back into the terminal to do some shopping. The thermal underclothes and lined parka had finally brought his body temperature back into the nineties.

Stopping the car outside the main gate, Andrew turned off the ignition and got out of the vehicle. Jeremy reluctantly followed him into the freezing cold night.

"Doesn't look like much activity," Jeremy observed, looking at the house and buildings. There was no sign of life at all.

"Most of the work is underground. Let's go." Andrew opened the cattle gate at the end of the drive and headed to the main barn where he had previously descended into the Bunker.

"How many people work here?" Jeremy scanned the area as they ran towards the barn.

"I'm not exactly sure. Dana said hundreds, but who knows whether she ever saw the whole operation."

"And this is run by the American government." Jeremy whistled at the enormity of the secret facility.

"Apparently. My guess is van Holder was conducting some private research at the expense of the taxpayer, thanks to McDaniel."

A light glimmered over the horizon.

"What's that?"

They stopped and stared at the light as it ascended the trees and was soon joined by a symphony of beams. The distinct whopping of rotor blades filled the night air. The two of them twirled around to see another group of lights from the other direction.

"Helicopters," Jeremy said.

"And lots of them. Do you think they tracked our flights?"

"If they did, you have made some powerful enemies." Jeremy slapped his friend on the back. "Come on. Let's not wait around to find out."

They ran towards the rental but quickly abandoned that avenue of escape when the entire area around the still warm vehicle was caught in a spotlight. Heading east towards the hazy moonlight, they ran to a hidden outcropping of rocks and aspen a hundred yards from the main ranch house.

A dozen Hueys approached the sprawling complex from two sides. Marines disbursed from the ones that landed outside the main gates to secure the area. The rest of the helicopters emptied their cargo of men and equipment around the main house and barn. Within minutes, the entrance to the Bunker was stormed by a platoon of infantry men. Lights, noise and swirling snow filled the sky. Andrew and Jeremy could see only Marines exiting the facility. Something was wrong.

Focused on the orchestrated military exercise going on around them, Andrew and Jeremy paid no attention to their immediate surroundings. The beam caught them like deer in headlights. The sound of Marines circling the grove of trees suggested that no escape was possible. The two of them stood silently, hands behind their heads, and waited.

Colonel Briggs led the incursion on the federal facility, his smooth fatigues belying the rigors of the invasion. He rubbed his left bicep. There was a time when he would have enjoyed a thick Cuban, but he no longer indulged in such activities at the behest of his wife of thirty years. As a Marine, he had never attacked anyone on American soil, so this operation did not sit well with him. But the orders had come from the highest level, and he always followed orders—except when he didn't. Whoever wanted him to infiltrate and secure this secluded spot in the middle of the night had better have a pretty good reason. So far, it looked like a complete waste of time.

Briggs set up command inside the main house. The large dining table served as the commanding officer's desk. When Andrew followed Jeremy into the kitchen, the first thing he noticed was that the furniture was covered with sheets. The house had been closed up.

From the corner of his eye, he looked into the den. It was completely empty—no books, no pictures, nothing. Something was definitely wrong.

A Sergeant led them into the kitchen.

"Your names." Colonel Briggs looked up and addressed the two captives.

"I believe it's my right to remain silent until a lawyer is present," Andrew chimed.

"Son, I'm not a police officer. In case you haven't noticed, we are Marines. You have no rights. This is a secure military site and you are trespassing." Briggs sat back and stared at the insubordinate youth.

Andrew didn't look away. "Excuse me, sir, but we were outside the gates and not trespassing when your soldiers arrested us."

"You haven't been arrested," Briggs shot back.

"Detained, then," Andrew clarified.

"Why are you here in the middle of the night at precisely the same time as my operation?" Briggs continued his questioning, unabated.

"I could ask you the same question, except, of course, I have no soldiers," Andrew retorted, looking at Jeremy who was enjoying the little show.

"Son, are you planning on playing verbal Olympics with me all night long?"

Andrew anticipated the military man would appreciate a direct approach, so he decided to be candid. "Listen, I don't know why you're here, but I know why we came. My girlfriend was kidnapped during a recent vacation in Bermuda and I have a strong suspicion that she is being held captive at this ranch. They held her here before, in the summer, when I broke into the underground facility to rescue her. The place was full of equipment, people and most of all, decision makers. Whatever they were doing involved the government and a company called ASC."

Briggs took a few moments to absorb the protracted explanation. He had achieved his success in the Marines by listening instead of reacting. After a pause, his glare softened. His experience told him that young man's story was true. "Unfortunately, your current suspicions are incorrect. She's not here. In fact, there's nobody here."

"You're lying! You were sent by the White House to stop me," Andrew accused Briggs. "She has to be here, below ground, in what they called the Bunker."

"Calm down, son. And watch your tone with me. Few men have called me a liar without regret." Briggs saw the desperation in the young man and wanted to help.

"It's just that…"

"There's no one at this site," Briggs interjected. "Above or below ground. This entire facility has been abandoned. I have no idea why my superiors would send my men and me on a wild goose chase in the middle of winter to infiltrate an empty government research station."

Briggs stood up and indicated they should follow him. A few minutes later they were three stories below the howling Montana landscape. The Marines had turned on only the safety lights, so shadows followed the three men as they walked around the stadium-sized room, the main area of the Bunker.

"It's hard to believe this place was like the trading floor of the NYSE the last time I was here," Andrew said, shaking his head.

"By the looks of things, they left in a hurry." Briggs picked up one of the scattered cables lying on the ground.

"The question is…where did they go?" Jeremy asked. The comment lingered in the air.

They roamed the large room for several minutes looking for further evidence. Tucked into the edge of one of the abandoned cubicles they found a section of USA Today. It was only three days old.

"A rather hasty departure, indeed," Briggs intoned.

Back at the main house, Briggs sat across the massive kitchen table from Andrew and Jeremy and contemplated their fate. Technically, he was required to process their capture. The courts would decide whether they had broken any laws because they happened to be at the wrong place during a military operation, but that was cumbersome. The young accountant's story, although farfetched, seemed sincere. His knowledge of the infiltration site was certainly accurate.

Andrew interrupted the silence. "Are we free to go?"

"Not technically," Briggs said, articulating his thoughts, "but this futile exercise doesn't deserve any further complication."

"Thank you," Andrew and Jeremy replied in unison.

Briggs stood up and held out his hand. "Good luck."

Several hours later, as they sped towards the rising crest of the dawn sun, Andrew felt a wave of desperation sweep over him. After leaving the ranch, he and Jeremy had speculated about where the facility had been moved. The quick departure was no coincidence; the coordinators of the Bunker must have been tipped off. The search for Dana was stalled. Looking at the windswept snowdrifts, Andrew observed a solitary blue jay struggling in the stiff breeze, finally landing on a tree branch close to the trunk and out of the wind. *Survival tactics were well entrenched in nature*, he thought. He suddenly knew what he must do next.

The report filed by Colonel Briggs took three days to reach the Pentagon. A locator number on the top of the manila file indicated which department would review and analyze the operation. The clerk responsible for delivering the report ensured that a copy of the original document would arrive at the appropriate department first thing the next morning. Occasionally, a report was delivered outside the Pentagon—sometimes to Langley or Arlington—but this report was directed elsewhere. *Highly unusual,* the clerk thought, but after recognizing the recipient, she stuffed the copy into an envelope and sent for a courier.

Chapter 42

The ASC acquisition coordinators were speechless as they stared at their boss. Several uncomfortable moments later, one member of the group lowered his eyes, shut his portfolio and sat down.

Van Holder kept his gaze on them as he rubbed the stubble on his chin. Fatigue was apparent in the group; dinner had been brought in and cleared hours earlier. Fourteen of the company's brightest minds had been working overtime for weeks to close the deals on companies summarized on a hit list they received daily by email. They had no idea from where the information came, and didn't dare question the source. Packages would appear, instructions provided and the team would gear up. It was not very often they met as a group. Forty-eight hours earlier, each of the coordinators had been summoned to New York from their offices around the world. They had had little time to pack. They were told to bring their portfolios and little else. No return flights were booked. Each was provided a suite at the Manhattan Four Seasons. Their sparse luggage had sat unopened since their arrival.

Van Holder stared at the faces around the table. He was not about to let the European manager off the hook. Most deals had a purpose and were part of the grand design. He had plucked Dana McLeod from Bermuda so she could continue with the research model bearing her namesake. But the parameters would be altered. With his loosely held alliance, van Holder had initiated his grand design into the heart of commerce—government appropriations. It was time to control the hand of Midas.

Pete Moss, the European merger coordinator for ASC, had brought in a rogue deal with his portfolio. It was a good deal— probably a great deal—but not part of van Holder's vision.

"Where did the plan originate?" Van Holder finally asked.

Pete Moss looked up from his lap. "Greece."

"Who brought it to you?" Van Holder pressed.

"The information came directly from the office of the CEO. You were mentioned." Moss was reluctant to include the last statement.

"So it seems. What have you done so far?" Van Holder was amused. Since Amsterdam, Mikos Popokulas had proven to be a valuable ally, providing information and contacts on several occasions. Most of the information was benign, but the effort demonstrated his willingness to participate.

"Mikos Petroleum Ltd. receives preferential treatment from the EU," Pete Moss began. "I was able to confirm the memo through a contact in Brussels."

"And..." van Holder prodded.

"Mikos is set to receive a lucrative contract to supply oil to the U.S. He has already made arrangements to increase his supply chain by partnering with the Kuwaitis, despite his loathing for their business practices. In order to meet the obligation, he intends to contract with Thomson Liner Corp, a British-based, Liberian flag shipping line. TLC is a public company trading on both the London and New York exchanges.

"Timing."

"According to the handwritten note, the announcement comes in eight days," Moss concluded.

Moss had sent the information to van Holder's office earlier in the week to seek approval. The conversation between the two in the luxurious surroundings of the Four Seasons had been rehearsed. This was why the team had been assembled. The slush account generated by the Debitfund program had disappeared and ASC was running out of money. In order to stay in control of his Amsterdam Protocol—and feed his own ego—van Holder needed to push on. Financing would come too late; bankers had too many lawyers telling them what not to do. This was a chance to rebuild the war chest.

As a precaution, van Holder had run the McLeod model on TLC. Everything had checked out. Mikos had offered him an olive branch. In return, van Holder would extend the Greek a closer look at his vision and a share of the enormous profits. Absolute control needed dedicated participants.

"Any information on TLC that we need to know?" Jessica Hume asked, brushing a strand of hair from her face while taking notes on the discussion. Intensely driven since graduating at the top of her class at Harvard, she had joined ASC three years earlier as the European acquisition specialist.

"From what I can gather, they probably shipped wine to England for Henry VIII. Their pedigree is substantial, management sound, and they have about six hundred million in the bank," Moss recited from memory.

"Dollars." Jessica queried.

"Pounds," Moss replied to several soft whistles from his colleagues.

"What's the break-up value?" asked Matthew Yip, the Asian manager.

Merger and acquisition people rarely cared about the value of a company as a going concern or operating business; they were more interested in the asset break-up value. The higher the break-up value, the better the deal. ASC's splurge of new acquisitions had taken the team by surprise. Very few of the companies being sought had met their criteria for a good buy, and most of them weren't being dismantled. They knew something strange was happening.

"Let's not get too far on this one," van Holder interrupted. "Perhaps it's not even an acquisition target. I suggest we go in slowly until more research can be done. In the meantime, go have some fun. Time to stop for the night."

As the team filed out, van Holder asked Jessica to stay behind. The door closed behind the last of group with a comment that she would catch up with them later.

"Did you uncover any further details on the Amsterdam incident?" Van Holder chose his words carefully. Because she was based in the Dutch capital, he had asked this bright young associate for a favor after Catherine disappeared.

Rumors about the disappearance of his Russian assistant had spread though the company, and Jessica had heard them all. "I assigned one of the clerks in my office to check every Jane Doe admitted into the city hospitals. Nothing. Are you sure she disappeared in Amsterdam."

"She had some unfinished business after the conference. It was only supposed to take a few days."

"I'm sorry," Jessica replied, smoothing her silk blouse.

"Catherine is very resilient. I'm sure she'll show up. Thank you for trying." Van Holder smiled, stood up and extended a hand.

When Jessica took van Holder's hand, she felt the warmth of his grip. The hand lingered for a moment, presenting an invitation. The group would have to explore New York without her.

Loose ends bounced around van Holder's head as he lay in bed the next morning. With an army of security and special project personnel, the untidy edges of his deals were quickly being dispensed. But Dana McLeod would be a problem. While her ability to manipulate database information was invaluable, her willingness to cooperate wouldn't last. Up until now, they had used the constant threat of Andrew Dalton's death to motivate her. His recent appearance in Montana meant that Dana may have just become a loose end.

He turned his attention to the soft, warm curves next to him. He moved his hand over a breast and down further, massaging for a few moments. The satin sheet danced as the caress continued. Van Holder glanced at Jessica. To bad she didn't possess the same diverse talents of his head of security. He would like her close by. Ending the brief attention, he moved his hand away, got up and headed for the shower, suggesting she may want to get ready for the day's events before closing the bathroom door.

She lay in staring at the ceiling, waiting for the urge to subside. She was disgusted at what she had done, what she had now become. How could she have done this? She did not need this or him.

At 6:30 a.m. the next morning, the team assembled in the conference room on the mezzanine level of the hotel. Van Holder entered the room.

"People, I trust you had a good night's sleep. It's going to be a long day." His eyes rested briefly on Jessica. She turned away in embarrassment before his gaze continued around the table. "In three hours, the market opens. For the next forty-eight hours, each of you is to acquire, through the companies in your individual groups, stock of Thomson Liner Corp. After New York closes, you are to buy on the overnight market and continue when London opens at midnight, Eastern Standard Time." Van Holder cast his eyes around the room.

The energy in the room was palatable as the team realized they had just been given a blank check to trade. In the world of corporate takeovers, information is king, and their boss was going to ground on a handwritten note. Everyone spoke at once. How much could they get before the exchange put on the brakes? As the coffee pots were emptied and the Danish and bagels devoured, the strategy for the day emerged. Then Pete Moss mentioned Oceanic Transport Corp. As a rival of TLC, OTC was the quintessential oil tanker operator that controlled most of the oil shipments worldwide for OPEC and many of the smaller producer countries. The reason Mikos used OTC was because it annoyed the Middle East producers.

"If TLC gets this contract, what happens to OTC and its relationship with Mikos?" Jessica asked. She had articulated what everyone had been thinking.

"Sell short," someone said. Hedge fund managers employed the technique to minimize risk, but it was also a way to earn quick profits if someone had reason to believe a company's stock might suffer.

"Any harm in cross buying?" the UK manager asked. He was considering the idea of buying into the companies that supplied Thomson.

"What about funding?" Moss inquired.

Van Holder wondered why that question hadn't been asked earlier. "Use the available cash and margin where the lines are established. ASC has standing credit facilities of five billion. All of it will be available."

"Is there a maximum exposure?" Moss asked.

"Not unless the information changes," van Holder replied. Mikos would gain considerably by the acquisition. It was the basis of the Amsterdam Protocol, the driving force behind the partnership. ASC consolidates control while everyone in the pact gets rich.

9:15 a.m. Time to buy.

Van Holder set up a situation room in his suite. Much to her chagrin, Jessica was instructed to coordinate the group, back in his room. Each trade was electronically logged into a trading system. Jessica's computer consolidated the multitude of brokerage accounts into a master file. The total shares acquired were added up and their average price displayed on the screen. If the market started a rally to sell, the computer instructed several of the team members to follow suit and smooth out the bid price. Jessica spent the day staring at the screen, questioning her involvement with ASC. She had gone to school to help companies succeed, not to seek and destroy.

By the time the NYSE closed, sixteen percent of the company was owned by ASC and its affiliates at a cost of just over seven billion. The price of Thomson stock had increased by only seven percent. It had been a good day. If the stock rose by thirty percent on announcement, van Holder stood to make two billion dollars. A good start, but not enough. The system also watched the short selling team. They had a lot of takers. No one believed the stock price of Oceanic would drop any time soon.

The group shut down until the London market opened, when the process would begin all over again. Dinner was at Chez Michaels, an upscale eatery close to the hotel.

Stepping from the shower, Jessica studied her body in the soft haze of the foggy mirror. Cupping her breasts, she turned and looked at her profile, admiring the way they stood out, firm and healthy. She didn't need to worry. Men always did double takes to get a second glance. The rigors of her job meant that she didn't have enough personal time, but she persisted and kept in shape by running and lifting weights in a makeshift gym set up in the spare room of her small Amsterdam apartment.

Wrapping a terry cloth robe around her body, she left the bathroom to get changed. Van Holder was seated on the couch, sipping a martini. A second drink was sitting on the coffee table.

"Help yourself."

"How did you get in here?" Jessica was surprised, as she wrapped the robe tighter around her body.

Van Holder held up a key. "You left it in my room last night."

"Why didn't you give it back earlier?" Jessica asked.

"I assumed it was an invitation," Van Holder said. He stood up and handed the fresh martini to Jessica.

"You assumed wrong." She didn't accept the drink.

"I underestimated you." Van Holder put the frosted martini on a ledge by the fireplace.

"What we did today was not right," Jessica said, immediately regretting the inference to van Holder's business practices. She had heard stories about him.

"You didn't think it was such a bad idea last night." Van Holder moved closer.

"Last night was nothing special," Jessica intoned. The insult hit.

Rage welled up inside van Holder. Taking another step forward, he pulled Jessica's robe free and grabbed her left breast. Jessica backed away, clutching the robe. Van Holder squeezed harder. Blood drained from Jessica's face, leaving her lips red and trembling. She moved to release his grip. Van Holder shifted his weight to prevent an avenue of escape. Jessica's slap made van Holder smile at the challenge. He pushed Jessica onto the bed.

It might have been all right had the phone not rung. The sudden distraction caused van Holder to loosen his grip on Jessica as she lay exposed on the bed. Seizing the opportunity, she dug the nails of her free hand into the soft flesh under his eye. The reaction was immediate. In a swift karate move, van Holder came down hard with his open palm and caught Jessica on the chin, driving her head to the left. The snap echoed in the large suite and Jessica went limp, her neck broken.

Van Holder stood up and rubbed the tenderness under his eye. *A shame*, he thought as he turned to leave. As an afterthought, he grabbed the two martini glasses and left the room. Exiting the elevator on the mezzanine level, van Holder discarded the glasses and dialed a number on his cell phone. After brief instructions, he dialed a second number.

Later that night, a cube van pulled into the loading dock of the New York Four Seasons Hotel. Two men rolled a linen trolley onto the service elevator, picked the lock and headed up to the designated floor. Finding the plastic magnetized key on top of the fire extinguisher box as instructed, they entered the suite. The woman's cold body was pale blue and her head was tilted awkwardly to the right. Her eyes stared blankly at the men as they lifted her into the trolley. Any evidence of her stay at the hotel was quickly erased. The sanitized key card was tossed on the bedside table before they left.

At the United Airlines check-in counter, a woman handed over her passport to the agent. After answering the required security questions, she accepted her ticket and put it in her handbag. In keeping with the company's mandate regarding personalized service, the airline agent concluded the encounter by responding, "Have a nice flight back to Amsterdam, Ms. Hume."

Chapter 43

"**D**o you have any idea what kind of trouble you're in?" Josh Young cradled the phone between his ear and neck, stretching his stiff frame as he stared out the window of his office. "Hold on a sec." Andrew heard the door slam before Josh came back on the line. "Is everything okay?"

Andrew had called his former colleague for a favor. "You don't know the half of it."

"There's a warrant out for your arrest."

"I thought that was taken care of."

"Apparently something new has surfaced that puts you at the scene."

"At what scene?" Andrew wasn't sure they were talking about the same thing.

"The murder scene." Josh spoke slowly.

"Bob Craft." Andrew cited the name of the chief accountant he had met back in June. He hadn't told many people about his meeting with the SuperMart accountant.

"How did you know?" Josh was surprised.

"He was alive and well, sipping his glass of Merlot when I left his house."

"That's not what the paper is saying," Josh replied.

"You can't always believe what you read in the papers."

"So, you didn't do it?" Josh asked, feigning disbelief.

"I haven't seen the papers recently," Andrew admitted.

"Where are you now?" Josh asked.

Andrew looked around the room he temporarily called home. The old motel was off the main highway on the outskirts of a small town in upstate New York. The paint was cracked and peeling off the walls. "In the country," he replied. He quickly changed the subject. "What did Frank say?" asked, referring to his boss and mentor at the firm.

"There was a full-on staff meeting. Anyone who has contact with the alleged should suggest that he turn himself in...yada, yada, yada."

"Oh," Andrew replied.

"Don't worry. My lips are sealed. I just want a kickback on the movie rights." Josh replied.

"Sure thing. What else did the paper say?" Andrew asked, wondering what he was up against.

"Do you want a copy?" Josh asked.

"Email." He recited a hotmail account.

"Being sent as we speak." Josh attached the file to an outgoing message and pressed send. "So what can I do to help?"

Andrew summarized his request. "Tomorrow afternoon enough time?"

"Piece of cake. I'll fit it into my sixteen-hour day," Josh joked. His tone became more serious. "Make sure you read the article. And don't reply to my email. Most of our incoming mail is being logged." They agreed to talk in two days.

An audible click was missed as the two friends said goodbye. A third phone was put in its cradle a moment later.

The drab motel didn't have high-speed Internet, so Andrew connected through the landline. It took an eon for the two-day-old newspaper article to download.

City CPA Sought for Murder

AP San Francisco - Authorities confirmed today that new evidence has been made available in the brutal slaying of Bob Craft, a 49-year-old SuperMart accountant found dead in his apartment last June. Based on this recent evidence, a warrant has been issued for Andrew Dalton, a CPA formerly with Brooks & Steiner.

Mr. Dalton disappeared shortly after the killing and at the time was only someone of interest. He has not yet been questioned. The Assistant District Attorney stated that the evidence clearly shows that Mr. Dalton was at the home of the victim shortly before the death. "…. and clearly had a motive," the DA was quoted.

The motive may be linked to a prior charge of embezzlement at the grocery chain where Dalton was originally charged with orchestrating an elaborate computer fraud. Although these charges were later dropped, the DA indicated that investigation is being reopened.

Calls to Brooks & Steiner have not been returned. Sources close to the partners have stated that they are cooperating with the authorities and that Mr. Dalton is no longer employed with the Firm.

Andrew reread the article several times, looking for clues as to what new evidence had come to light. Then he remembered something important: During his meeting with McDaniel, he facetiously admitted to being a murderer. *Was this conversation recorded? Afterwards, did the President-elect make a public statement to create the uncertainty?*

Across the city, the waiting game was over. It was time to cash in on the tedious waiting. It was only a matter of time before the subject would seek help from his former office. Their informant had called in the information and they now had an address—a small motel north of the city.

Two cars were dispatched and positions were taken up around the hotel. The police were not alerted. Orders were followed. This was to be quiet and low-key. The subject was in a room on the second floor. They waited for the occupant to leave. When they were sure the room was empty, they crashed through the cheap pine door. Within minutes, the room was emptied, the men gone. They had no idea what information was on the computer. The rest of the booty would be tossed. To the occupant, it would look like a random theft.

Andrew drove his rented Toyota Camry along the expressway to his nightly spot outside van Holder's upstate New York mansion. As he waited, the cool night air condensed on the windshield. Every fifteen minutes, Andrew started the car and defrosted. The city lights took on a shadowy glow in the early evening hours before the sun went down. An orange hue cast sleepy shadows from the streetlights lining the driveway.

After a few hours, a black Lincoln finally emerged from the garage and sped past Andrew on its way to the expressway. *This is promising,* Andrew thought, tailing the vehicle at a safe distance. Twenty minutes later, the Lincoln stopped outside a large warehouse stuck off the expressway north of New York. Van Holder emerged from the passenger side of the car and went inside. The driver remained in the car.

As Andrew rolled the Camry into a side road, the pea pebbles crunched under the tires. He got out of the car and headed to the warehouse. Skirting the side of the building, he located an unlocked side door and entered. The creak echoed throughout the superstructure. Several heads turned to stare at Andrew before reverting back to their computer screens. As Andrew made his way to the front of the warehouse, it was obvious that the Montana Bunker had been reproduced in this new location. No one bothered to challenge him as he strode up the aisle between two rows of occupied workstations. *Why was the security so lax?* he wondered? *Why didn't anyone care that he was there?* This wasn't what he expected. *What was so different about this place that van Holder's private police force didn't have to protect its secrets?*

He was certain Dana was somewhere in the warehouse. *She had to be,* he thought.. As he made his way to the front, he thought he spotted her in the first row. Four desks from the front, Andrew froze when he saw van Holder leaning over her cubicle. When he looked up and saw Andrew, their eyes locked. Hatred penetrated Andrew's glare. Van Holder turned around and smiled. The woman at the desk peered around the cloth barrier. It wasn't Dana.

"You certainly are persistent." Van Holder's smile was still painted on his face.

"Where is she?" Andrew demanded.

The woman looked up at van Holder, who suggested she leave. "What do you think?"

"Here. I know she's here," Andrew spat.

"Why are you still alive?" van Holder quipped.

"What have I ever done to you?" Andrew shifted his weight onto his left foot and leaned against the edge of a desk.

"Come with me." Van Holder walked to a side hallway lined with doors. Andrew didn't follow.

"If you really want answers, come with me." Van Holder turned around and continued walking to an office at the end of the hallway. The room was furnished in expensive cherry and leather—misplaced opulence for a corrugated steel and cement slab warehouse. But van Holder didn't like to work in squalid surroundings.

Andrew entered and closed the door. "No hired mercenaries this time?"

"They're around." Van Holder grabbed two glasses. He filled them with scotch and handed one to Andrew.

"You knew I was coming."

"Eighteen-year-old single malt. One of my companies in Scotland sends over a case every month."

Andrew set down the glass without taking a sip. "Why are you destroying our lives?"

"If you're referring to Dana, she's perfectly safe. My opportunities required her services for a short period. She's been free to go, but has chosen to continue her research." Van Holder raised the glass, savoring the drink.

"Let me see her. She *will* leave with me."

"She thinks you're dead." Van Holder stood up to refill his glass.

Andrew looked around. The room was bathed in a soft glow from the overhead lights. "Am I?"

"With one phone call. Not dead, but most likely in prison for the rest of your life." Van Holder spoke as though he held all the cards.

"Why me?" Andrew asked, feeling defeated.

"Convenience. My programmer made a mistake and you were the fix. The rest just happened."

"He's dead, you know. So is the Russian."

Andrew's declaration appeared to have a strong effect on van Holder. His eyes narrowed, momentarily losing their focus. Perhaps she was his weakness. "What happened?"

"Where is Dana? She'll be happy to know I've been resurrected," Andrew said, feeling somewhat triumphant. He wasn't about to give this maniac the benefit of an explanation.

"Perhaps we could make a deal," van Holder offered.

"You said yourself that I'm a dead man...or close to it," Andrew stared at the man across the room.

"I want to know what you know…the information that was taken in Bermuda." Van Holder stated.

So they're afraid of what we discovered in Bermuda, Andrew thought. The satellite uplink from Fletcher had been effective after all. His small exhale was audible in the room. The two men, each wary of the other, stared across the silent void between them.

Van Holder suddenly held up his hands. "I have partners to protect," he said.

"Like McDaniel?" Andrew spit the words out.

Van Holder seemed anxious to end the conversation. "Bring me whatever information you have."

"No deal until Dana is safe with me. Then we talk." Andrew turned to walk out, but stopped cold at van Holder's reply.

"Give me everything you have within forty-eight hours…or Dana *will* be killed."

Chapter 44

Dana stared blankly at the wall of her tiny cubicle, drained of all energy. Tears streamed down her face, forming a pool on the desk. Andrew was alive and here with van Holder! She had seen him, signaled and called out his name. But he had walked out. They weren't keeping him like a caged animal. A rush of adrenaline clouded her thoughts. Then, as the fog lifted, she realized they hadn't been holding him at all. It was time for her to leave.

Making her way to the side door, she took one last look over her shoulder before pushing the door open. Out of the corner of her eye, she saw Bruce heading for her desk. He looked over and for a split second their eyes locked. Understanding registered on his face as the exit door closed behind her. Once outside, she heard him screaming orders. She ran alongside the building to the road beyond. The crash of the door behind her and the shouts of her pursuers only increased her resolve. Speeding up, she rounded the corner and made her away to the road, where she slipped on a patch of ice and fell. Within minutes, she was surrounded by four pairs of legs, lifted up forcefully and brought back inside.

Bandaged and dejected, Dana sat at her workstation and logged onto the computer. Hopefully, she could cause some damage to their network. She composed an email to Marion Fletcher, which she reread to herself twice before sending. She had held nothing back. She knew Andrew was alive and that was all that mattered. She prayed Marion could help. Attached to the email was a list of the numerous companies van Holder had asked her to research. She was convinced he was trying to control the appropriation process of the U.S. government. Somebody had to expose his plan.

Unfortunately, the email never left her computer. Before Dana had a chance to do further damage to the network, her computer screen went blank. The smile on Bruce Peterson's face as he came down the corridor said it all.

"I told van Holder not to take any chances," Bruce said.

"Well, you should be happy. A gold star on your performance report."

He handed Dana the email to Marion. "This didn't get sent, so don't have any false hopes," he said.

"You can't make me work, you know. Andrew's alive. I saw him." Dana replied, tears streaming down her face.

"It doesn't matter. Van Holder has decided to proceed without your services," Bruce stated flatly.

"I thought he couldn't live without me."

"Changes have been made. Information will be gathered differently."

"So, what happens now?" Dana wasn't feeling very confident. She had been safe as long as they needed her, as long as she thought they had Andrew. Her dash for freedom may have cost her everything. Bruce's attitude was sickening. *Did he know he worked for a cold-blooded killer? Probably.*

"Van Holder said to make you comfortable," Bruce said, smiling.

"No firing squad?"

"Not yet." His smile quickly disappeared when two security guards flanked Dana. She followed the two guards back to her room. She wanted to kick herself for trying to escape without a plan.

Ten thousand miles away on a different continent, two co-conspirators stared at each other across the table, the deal complete, signatures penned at the bottom of each page. The ink spread across the paper as the Greek signed his name. Putting the pen down, he looked past his guest to the ocean beyond. The plan had been superbly executed. Being a part of such a scheme made the Greek remember the days when he had been penniless but determined.

"It is a beautiful night," the woman said, gazing at the surf as it cascaded onto the shore.

"Such a wonderful island," the dealmaker intoned with a smile.

"Too bad I have to get back."

"My island is your home, always," the Greek affirmed.

No money would be made, but it was an agreement of a lifetime. The two of them sat back, content. Ouzo was ordered and they toasted their success.

Chapter 45

The mess in the motel room mattered little to Andrew, but they had stolen his computer containing the vital codes he needed to access the backup servers. At first he thought it had been a robbery—some punk lifting the laptop to pawn for a hundred bucks—but the timing and the delay with van Holder had been too coincidental. It was time to move.

By the time he packed up and checked out, it was past midnight. Andrew was tired, but time was critical. He prayed Josh would come through. A black, late model sedan cut him off as he exited the parking lot. A split second later, with little time to react, he rammed the rented Toyota into the side of the sedan. He jammed the gearshift into reverse. Spinning around towards the other exit, he was confronted by a duplicate of the damaged car he had left behind. The second car nudged into his bumper, pushing the Camry backwards and cutting off any chance of escape. A minute later, he was sitting in the back of the undamaged Lincoln.

No one spoke or even acknowledged Andrew's presence during the trip from the motel to the airport. After a thirty minute flight and an hour's drive, he stood in the foyer of a grand house on the outskirts of Washington. His escort looked at Andrew and mumbled the first words he'd heard since being apprehended. "Leave your coat on. You'll only be inside for a minute."

Andrew put on his coat. Only one man had enough interest in him to go to this much trouble. *But McDaniel wouldn't live here, he's comfortably settled into the Oval office*, he thought. It was a short walk to the small guest residence by the Hudson River. McDaniel did indeed greet Andrew at the door. The handshake and concern were unexpected.

"We found you." McDaniel said, sounding relieved.

"I didn't know I was lost," Andrew replied, puzzled. Glancing over the President's shoulder, he gaped in disbelief at the two women seated in the living room. One of them was Marion Fletcher.

"Sorry about the motel room, and the computer." McDaniel said apologetically.

"You took it? Why." Andrew asked.

"It's been sent to Langley. The CIA will analyze the information on the hard drive."

"And then you came back for me?"

"What happened the last time? We were supposed to meet."

"I saw you with van Holder...and her." Andrew said, pointing to Marion.

Marion walked over to Andrew and extended her hand. "Sorry Andrew. After you left Bermuda, I had to do something."

"Why?"

"Dana had contacted me by email."

Andrew heard the words, but their meaning didn't register. He no longer knew who to believe or trust. It had started out as self-preservation but had become a quest for revenge. Revenge for trying to kill him, revenge for thinking they could beat him, revenge for trying to ruin his life. At one time, he had thought McDaniel could be trusted. Maybe paranoia had changed his mind and desperation had changed it back.

"Van Holder threatened to kill Dana if I didn't cooperate," Andrew said finally.

"He abandoned the facility in Montana," McDaniel said.

"I was there. Colonel..."

"Briggs," McDaniel interrupted. "He sent me his report. Mentioned you were there. That was when I sent the secret service to find you."

"Everyone seems to be chasing me," Andrew said ruefully. How many other people wanted to find him...or kill him?

"You were wanted for questioning about a murder." The second woman, someone he did not recognize, intoned.

Andrew was taken aback. Had the President tracked him down just to ensure whatever he had going with his money tree didn't rub off? "It wasn't me. When I left the house, the man was alive...and quite amorous, I might add." Then he paused. "What do you mean...*were?*"

"The investigation has been called off. A matter of national security," McDaniel replied.

The second woman in the room approached the group that had congregated around the front door. "Hi, I'm Jessica Poole," she said warmly, extending her hand.

"My running mate, the Vice-President," McDaniel explained.

"Do you mind if I sit down?" Andrew asked. What little energy he had left was quickly waning.

The three people crowded around the door parted so Andrew could move inside. After he was settled on the couch, drinks and some food were brought in. While he devoured the plate of sandwiches, the others spoke quietly in the corner by the fireplace. They rejoined him as he was polishing off his second beer.

"Marion briefed us on what Dana has been able to convey from inside van Holder's facility," Jessica began.

"Is Dana alright?" Andrew asked, almost choking on his soda. He stood up. "I need to get back."

"As far as we know, she's fine. She's a brave girl to do what she did," Marion said.

"Why don't you sit down and relax, Andrew. We have a lot to go over and need your help," Jessica said.

Andrew accepted her comforting reassurance and sat back down. "Why were you with van Holder in Washington?" Andrew asked Marion.

"When Dana contacted me to tell me she was in Montana, I called van Holder to find out what was going on. He didn't divulge anything. So much for trust in partners."

"Marion called me when she arrived in Washington." Jessica Poole explained. "We've known each other since college. I invited her to the celebration dinner."

"So the information we collected in Bermuda is authentic," Andrew said.

"Yes, and it's quite important," McDaniel said. "It appears my naiveté and drive to win the election may have clouded my judgment."

Jessica spoke next, ignoring McDaniel's self-abasement. "From what we can gather, van Holder is gaining control of companies involved in government appropriations. We think he intends to put a stranglehold on the U.S. economy."

"The *world* economy," Andrew specified. He remembered reviewing the details with Jeremy when they thought the information was fabricated. "Every deal made by ASC links industries in most major countries," he explained. "As the deals continue, entire supply chains are linked to ASC and the other partners who attended the Amsterdam meeting." He turned to Marion. "How did you manage to avoid his reach?"

"I've cooperated with him. Van Holder thinks my communicating with Dana is on his behalf."

Andrew turned to McDaniel. "Why would van Holder spend all that money to get you elected, only to topple the government afterwards?"

"He expects abject loyalty. I'm sure he has a backup plan if my government doesn't cooperate," McDaniel said.

"That's his style," Andrew agreed. He looked at the three people staring at him in the great room of Jessica's home. Time was running out. In less than 36 hours, Dana would be killed if he didn't meet van Holder's demands.

"Can you explain the data you've accumulated?" Jessica asked.

"Once Dana is safe." Andrew replied.

"I understand."

Again, Andrew turned to McDaniel. "If you knew about van Holder, why didn't you storm his operation and shut him down?"

"He hasn't been caught breaking any laws yet."

And you want your Presidency scandal-free, Andrew thought to himself. "Hopefully not for long," he said.

Jessica stood up and walked to the bar to pour another round of drinks. "You know anything?" she asked Andrew.

Andrew looked up at the confident woman, who he believed would make a strong Vice-President. "It would probably be better if you didn't know."

She and McDaniel nodded silently. Marion smirked. "Is there anything we can do to help?" Jessica asked. Before leaving, Andrew summarized what he needed.

Chapter 46

Josh came through with flying colors. Andrew was pouring over the email in his new quarters at the Four Seasons in Washington. Bodyguards were stationed on either end of the hallway outside, courtesy of McDaniel. Now he was able to wander freely, without the fear of being arrested or killed.

The phone rang—his anticipated call from Jeremy. Hopefully, everything was complete.

"Do you know how beautiful it is over here?" was the first thing Jeremy asked.

"You already live in paradise. What could be better than a tropical island full of gardens and beautiful women?" Andrew replied, shaking his head at the Bermudian calling him from half way around the world.

"Full of American tourists and British snootiness. I'll take life on a Greek island any day. Mikos offered me a job."

Andrew paused to consider this latest development. Could they trust the Greek tycoon? Maybe he was working for van Holder and using the job offer to draw them in. Surely their request had been obtrusive enough. Jeremy was a talented financier…perhaps Mikos recognized a secondary benefit from their charade. "Are you going to accept?" he asked finally.

"Too early to tell," Jeremy responded without hesitation.

"Good idea to wait," Andrew replied. "Is everything set?"

"Couriered yesterday. The package should be at the hotel first thing tomorrow."

"Thanks, Jeremy." It would be a long night of worrying. He needed the signed agreement before he could meet with van Holder.

"So, everything is ready?" Jeremy asked.

"I've got the trading list. It's the last piece of the puzzle. Van Holder will jump at the chance to cooperate."

"See you in Washington."

Andrew knew the Bermudian had already done enough. "You don't need to come back."

"This isn't done yet. Dana isn't out of harm's way. I'll see you in twelve hours," Jeremy said before hanging up the phone.

Looking down at the list Josh had sent, it was clear van Holder had taken the bait. The only thing left to do now was drop the bomb. He smiled at the tidy folders on the coffee table. Gathering up the pile, he looked at his watch. When the documents from Jeremy arrived, he would be ready.

Thin clouds shrouded the pale moon as Andrew approached the front entrance of van Holder's building. Two burned-out streetlights on the road near the warehouse raised Andrew's suspicions, but the tagalong government team stayed well back. An emergency signal had been established. With his luck it would arrive after he was dead. Van Holder was expecting him to arrive with a crateful of research like an auditor going in for the kill. He didn't want to disappoint. He went inside, clutching the two cases. The important document was stowed safely in a small briefcase held tightly against his body. Within minutes, he was facing van Holder.

"Right on time." Van Holder gestured for Andrew to place the cases against the far wall.

Andrew put the two cases down, but kept the small briefcase by his side. "Time management is one of my virtues," he replied proudly.

"It looks like you've been busy."

"Thanks to you. I'd like to think of it as damage control," Andrew quipped.

"I suppose this isn't everything," van Holder remarked.

"Kitchen sink and all."

"Nothing held back for security?" Van Holder looked surprised.

"A deal is a deal. You have what you want. Now bring me Dana so we can leave." Andrew said impatiently.

Van Holder pressed his fingers against his chin. Andrew held his glare as they squared off like two lions over an evening kill. Andrew wondered whether his gamble would pay off. A slight pressure on the opening of his briefcase redirected van Holder's stare. The two of them locked eyes again. No verbal exchange was necessary. Van Holder smiled knowingly as he picked up the phone. A few moments later, someone came and removed the boxes. No instructions were relayed; they knew what had to be done to prove the authenticity of the data.

"Have a seat," van Holder said.

"Just bring Dana here and we'll leave." Andrew stayed satnding.

The information in the small folder at his side gave Andrew the confidence to speak strongly. Since the deadly encounter in Montana, he had been trying to avoid becoming one of van Holder's loose ends. He had no assurance that this would change anything. Van Holder only wanted the files so he could eliminate all the evidence.

"Did you have a pleasant visit with Senator McDaniel?" van Holder enquired casually, raising his eyebrows.

"You had me followed?"

"Of course."

"So he truly is a pawn."

"He tried to have you killed...in Boston."

Andrew flinched at the man's icy stare. Van Holder appeared to be enjoying the revelation. It didn't matter anymore who had set the target. It was clear that McDaniel was only trying to protect the office he would soon fill by tying up his own loose ends. Despite the shock of hearing that McDaniel had risked the presidency by trying to have him and Dana killed, it wouldn't matter after tonight. Now that McDaniel was in the White House, they were no longer a threat. With a calmness that belied his inward turmoil, Andrew extracted a single sheet of embossed paper from his folder. The paper contained two paragraphs of instruction. It was an original document, signed and sealed, the perforations of the seal creasing the corner. Andrew slid the paper across the desk. Then he sat back and waited.

At first, the head of ASC and architect of the Amsterdam Protocol glanced nonchalantly at the single sheet of paper lying in front of him. Andrew watched as the first few words began to register. Then the severity of what it contained hit him like an insect colliding with a speeding car. Its impact was unmistakable in van Holder's expression—anger, revulsion, confusion and then, finally, clarity.

Van Holder smiled wanly. "It was all a setup," he finally said.

"Everything but the short selling. That was just lucky." Andrew moved his chair away from the desk.

"Peter Moss?"

"He thought the world of you and ASC until he saw how easily you would destroy anyone who got in your way."

"And Mikos. Why him?"

"A friend of Marion Fletcher's. He was the one who thought up the scheme." Andrew had to give the man credit for rebounding so quickly.

"What makes you think this makes any difference to me?"

"You're out of money. You risked hundreds of millions in cash and credit to make this deal—more money than you could afford. The money you were funneling through Bermuda—stolen with the help of Debitfund—dried up and your grand plan to monopolize the U.S. government appropriations system is falling from your grasp."

"And I suppose you can make it all go away," van Holder sneered.

It was a gamble. He had compared the list of companies that were buying TLC shares with the list of companies generated through the McLeod model. Except for the obvious institutional buyers, they all matched. If the agreement Andrew had just presented to van Holder were in effect, TLC would fail to get the contract from Mikos and all existing contracts currently held with the shipping giant would be terminated. It would bankrupt TLC.

"Mikos doesn't really care who transports his oil. Since you now control over seventy percent of TLC, you stand to lose the most."

"I'm prepared to bet that he does care. What is your backup plan?" Van Holder was calm. To calm.

Before Andrew could answer, the door opened and two of van Holder's security men entered. Andrew recognized one of them from the chase in Montana. He was escorted to a small room at the back of the warehouse. The door was locked and the two men walked away. His gambit had failed, but Andrew figured he was safe as long as van Holder felt threatened by the damaging information they had amassed.

The empty room was meant for storage. Remnants of a broken water line lay in one corner. The previous occupants of the building hadn't maintained it very well. Sitting on the floor with his back against the wall, he removed the car keys from his pocket and pressed the red panic button on the fob. He wondered how long it would take...

He awakened with a start when a black glove was placed over his mouth. It was dark, except for the green glow emanating from the night vision goggles staring down at him. A shadowy figure placed a similar pair of goggles in his hands. Adjusting to the eerie light, Andrew stood up and followed the man as he gestured and moved out into the hall. A voice from a speaker attached to the goggles broke the silence.

"We didn't expect to hear from you." Timothy Smith worked for a private security firm, hired for the occasional freelance job. Jessica Poole had recruited him to track down Andrew and bring him to Washington.

Andrew was relieved. The plan in Washington had called for Timothy to become Andrew's backup plan. The key fob had been equipped with a GPS tracking signal, accurate to two feet. Andrew had activated the signal as instructed and was glad it had worked. "Did anyone see you?" he asked.

The man didn't respond. Andrew refrained from asking any other questions as Timothy motioned to his team. "Follow me." They headed to the other end of the building and out the back. "Your friend's in there," Timothy said, pointing to a small cluster of trailers similar to the ones used in the forestry camps where he had grown up.

Unless she isn't here at all, Andrew thought.

As though he had read Andrew's mind, Timothy spoke into the headset. "We'll have to neutralize the guards." He tapped Andrew on the shoulder. It was time to move.

Wooden walkways connected the individual trailer units that were arranged in a grid. Angular roof panels meant to keep the camp dry were positioned over the walkways. Security guards and cameras were clearly visible at both ends of the compound, where a set of stairs led into the grid. As Andrew watched the scene through his goggles, he observed several dark shapes approaching the security personnel. By the time they had reached the compound, the guards on both sides were unconscious.

It was time to get Dana.

Andrew was prepared to run through the maze of trailers shouting Dana's name, but Timothy's firm hand held him back. They had apparently done their homework. With two fingers, he motioned to the left. Timothy and one of his team members stopped four trailers away from the entrance and placed a small disc on the lock. A few seconds later, Andrew heard a fizzing sound. The sound stopped and the door swung open. Andrew went in first.

"Dana," he whispered in the dark room. "Are you there?" No Answer. "Dana?" he repeated.

"Andrew...oh, my God...how did you find me?" Dana's weak, sleepy voice came from the bed in the corner.

Instead of answering, he hugged her, finding her body shimmering through the green lens of the night vision goggles. "Come on, we have to go."

"I'm not dressed," Dana said. Andrew relished the warmth of her body as he held her.

Timothy entered the room and handed her a jacket from a pack he was carrying. *Their planning was complete, right down to the last detail,* Andrew thought. A moment later, a bullet lodged itself in the chest of the lookout positioned at the end of the portables. Andrew watched in horror as the bullet shredded the cloth. Silence followed, except for the thump as the man fell onto the aluminum gangway leading up to the trailers. A moment later, he somersaulted backwards to the safety of the trailers. Timothy caught up to the man, who had seemingly risen from the dead.

"State of the art biotech bullet-proof armor," he declared, looking down at the hole in his jacket.

Timothy appeared to be unfazed by the attack as the six of them huddled together by the entranceway. More gunfire punctured the thin aluminum walls around them as the lights of the camp came on. Several heads peered out of nearby trailers and then quickly disappeared. The men tore off their goggles to avoid blinding the innocent civilians.

"Now!" Timothy yelled as they exited the trailer compound. Three of his men surrounded Andrew and Dana. Men were running toward the trailer compound from the main warehouse, holding their weapons forward and taking aim at the fleeing group. Andrew found himself looking straight into the barrel of a machine pistol thirty feet away. His brain began calculating how long it would take for the bullet to arrive...

Suddenly, the attack force slowed their advance and then came to a halt. One by one, they dropped their weapons. Andrew turned to see the reason why.

Two dozen Humvees—warm, inviting and guarded by military personnel—were positioned away from the white van that had followed Andrew to the compound. The vehicles hadn't entered van Holder's property, staying instead on the main highway running past the warehouse and trailer compound. Casual but alert soldiers stood poised beside their vehicles. No guns were drawn and no positions were taken, but their presence caused van Holder's security people to rethink their strategy as the people they had been told to pursue quietly walked up to the waiting van, got in and left.

As their vehicle pulled away, Andrew spotted a soldier walking towards the group of Humvees from a building across the street. Strapped to his back was a rifle equipped with a large infrared night scope.

McDaniel had been true to his word.

Chapter 47

Andrew and Dana had no idea where they were being taken, but felt safe as the warehouse disappeared behind them. It was over. The fallout of the sting operation was no longer Andrew's concern; he had been assured that others would deal with it. He decided not to think about it. He cared only about Dana.

After thirty minutes, the two of them began to wonder where they were going. When Andrew questioned Timothy, he just smiled and said an explanation would be given shortly. *What exactly did that mean? Had they walked into a trap set by McDaniel?*

Several hours later, they turned off the main highway and drove down a small country road. A few minutes later, the van turned onto a hidden driveway that wound through rolling hills. Soon a house came into view, as did poorly concealed guards. Andrew correctly guessed they were in Virginia.

Timothy Smith, the leader of the force that had carried out the warehouse assault, confirmed they were at a safe house in rural Virginia that had previously been used to debrief turned Soviet agents. The house, which sat well back from the secondary road on the large property, was larger than it appeared from the quiet street. They were told they would reside there temporarily for their protection. Timothy rotated with the other guards and was apparently the only person authorized to speak with them. The others went about their business as unobtrusively as possible.

Andrew and Dana settled into their comfortable prison to await their fate. They had the privacy of one wing of the house and made good use of their time alone, gleaning what information they could from the television news. Timothy reassured them that once it was over and they were debriefed, they would be free to go. He never explained what "it" was.

Chapter 48

The demise of Thompson Container Lines left many of its long-time investors ecstatic. Except for a few stubborn institutional fund managers who refused to part with the darling of the shipping world, the bid prices offered were too good for most people to pass up. The un-materialized contract from Mikos Petroleum was only the beginning of the troubles. Within days, every major customer had bailed out. When ships reached port, unpaid crews abandoned their vessels, leaving them for salvage. As a result of the market devaluation of the TCL stock, shareholders lost over twenty billion when the bankruptcy was announced. Most of the loss was borne in one way or another by van Holder and his partners.

Van Holder stormed into President McDaniel's private office when he was finally granted an audience. When he had observed his two young adversaries leaving under the watchful eye of an army convoy, he knew McDaniel had betrayed him. He was used to having his authority followed with unquestioned obedience. The possible loss of his company didn't bother him as much as the loss of control.

Holding the single sheet of paper gingerly between his thumb and forefinger, van Holder waited anxiously for McDaniel to appear. Van Holder's body flinched as he watched the President enter and stride across the room, his hand extended as if to say hello to an old friend. Van Holder didn't rise.

"Why did you do it, Nathan? Together we could have controlled the world." Van Holder slid the paper across the desk—the cancellation of the Mikos oil supply contract, together with the shipping agreement made with Oceanic.

McDaniel grinned. He saw this as an opportunity to sever ties with his former benefactor. Although his office insulated him any threat from his former benefactor, he was surprised that it had taken so long for van Holder to arrange this meeting. He had been certain van Holder would barge into his office demanding reparations the day after Dalton and McLeod had been debriefed.

"It seems you don't get on well with partners," McDaniel replied.

"I could sink your Presidency."

"Of course. Your motives have always been transparent."

Van Holder glared at McDaniel. "Meaning…"

"Meaning that even you know having me here is better than the alternative." McDaniel knew about van Holder's complete dislike for his running mate, Jessica Poole. That was why he had chosen her; she was his ace in the hole.

"This doesn't change my plans. Within a few months, the structure will be back in place, despite the losses."

"It can't happen. The American people deserve more than to be pillaged by one man's greed and corruption." McDaniel commented.

"The American people have been rammed by so many titans of business over the past two hundred years. They wouldn't know what to do if it stopped."

McDaniel stood up. "No more lectures, William." He walked over to the large credenza near his desk and picked up a thin folder. He opened it to confirm its contents, placed the file on the desk next to van Holder and went to pour himself a drink.

"What's this?" van Holder asked without opening the file.

"Advance warning. Read it." McDaniel didn't offer the drowning man a drink.

Van Holder snatched the file impatiently. "What sort of game is this?" He tore open the file and glanced at the first page. The letterhead of the Securities and Exchange Commission said it all. Flipping to the second page, van Holder read the police report: "…positive match to DNA found on the dead girl, positively identified as Jessica Hume…"

Anger exploded inside him. "You bastard. The only reason you're sitting in that chair is because of me."

"But I am sitting in this chair," McDaniel replied, a grin spreading out across his face as he sat down.

It was too much for van Holder. As the rage exploded in his body, he jumped across the desk at McDaniel. The executive chair crashed backwards as the two men were thrown against the wall. Van Holder wrapped his hands around the soft flesh of McDaniel's neck and squeezed. McDaniel's bewildered eyes stared back at van Holder, the difference in strength of the two men dashing his chances of fighting back.

The crash and ensuing scuffle alerted the secret service men standing guard in the corridor. They made polite enquiries as to the noise and then abruptly forced their way into the room. Van Holder ignored their commands to stop and maintained a firm grip on the President's neck. Drawing their service revolvers and after ensuring they had a clear, safe shot, fired repeatedly at the madman attacking the President. Van Holder turned around when the first bullet entered his chest and stared blankly at the agents swarming him. As the bullets continued to pummel his body, he slowly closed his eyes and saw only blackness.

Chapter 49

Twenty-four hour coverage of the ensuing drama clogged the airways. Network programming went awry as newscasters found new angles to present viewers with the barrage of information that was being fed to the public. Andrew and Dana watched CNN with rapt attention at the unexpected turn of events.

The incapacity of the President was international news. The latest dialogue was somber as the world watched him being wheeled into Mount Sinai Hospital under the watchful eye of the Vice-President and an entourage of secret service agents. The White House announced that President McDaniel had suffered a stroke and would be under surveillance until a complete prognosis became available.

Reporters and camera crews vied for pavement outside the hospital as they waited for more information to broadcast around the world. McDaniel's wife and two adult children were inundated with requests for interviews, all politely declined. The networks quickly spun out documentaries detailing the President's career. William van Holder figured prominently during the rise of his political star, and was frequently mentioned in the hastily-put-together reports.

Savvy newsmen reported their ongoing frustration as repeated calls to ASC led nowhere. "Mr. van Holder is not available for interviews" or "Mr. van Holder is currently out of the country." Finally, they succumbed to the barrage of enquiries by acknowledging they had no idea of his whereabouts.

At the safe house, Andrew and Dana were glued to the television, channel surfing to follow the story as it bounced through the airwaves. Finally they settled on CNN and listened intently, arms around each other, as each polished anchor delivered fresh snippets of news. The day after McDaniel was hospitalized Jessica Poole arrived at the house, unannounced. Andrew was concerned about the President; he had seemed in such good shape when they met that night in Washington.

"How is President McDaniel?" Andrew asked after introductions were made.

Jessica Poole knew the American public would soon be told but wanted to tell the two of them personally. "He's dead," she said matter-of-factly.

"Oh, my God!" Stunned, Dana covered her mouth with her hand. Finally, she sat down and looked at the woman who was now effectively the President of the United States.

"The stroke was worse than they thought?" Andrew asked.

"The secret service men killed the President's visitor in error when he attempted to revive him after the stroke. Most of them will be reassigned. That is the official statement from the White House." Jessica replied as if she were reciting a well-rehearsed speech. She went on, "But the truth is, he was murdered."

"Murdered!" Dana exclaimed.

"Apparently, he was choked to death in the heat of an argument during a meeting at the White House."

"Who else knows?" Andrew asked.

"The information is classified. It will be sealed on grounds of National Security. I've granted the two of you special clearance. You had a right to know."

"Who killed him?" Dana asked, suddenly suspicious. She looked at Andrew. They suspected who it was, but wanted to hear it from her.

"Van Holder?" Andrew asked.

Jessica looked at the two of them eagerly waiting for her response. "Yes."

"What happened to *his* body?" asked Dana. "The news has been full of stories about the search for the man who supposedly 'created' the President."

"His body will turn up next week in Mexico—the victim of a random shooting." Jessica replied.

"So, it's over." Andrew went and sat with Dana, clutching her hand.

Jessica smiled. "I don't need to keep you here any longer."

Andrew looked at Jessica. As their eyes met, the revelation came. Andrew absorbed the stare, suddenly realizing the full impact of her comment.

"When was I set up?" he asked.

Dana stared at Andrew. "What are you talking about?"

Andrew looked at Jessica Poole, the woman who was about to become the next President and the first woman President of the United States.

"You tell her," he said.

"Amsterdam, when you first went to talk to Marion Fletcher. She called me." Jessica replied.

"You were college friends." Andrew remembered the introductions at her house in Washington. "At the time, I wondered why Marion was there, at your house. So, Marion must have set up the deal with Mikos. Jeremy was just the messenger."

"It all worked perfectly. I had to pull you in after you first contacted van Holder, to make sure the rest of the plan would go off without a hitch."

"How did you know van Holder would kill McDaniel?"

Jessica sat back in her chair and smiled. "I didn't. With the TCL trading—and the hotel murder details that just fell into my lap—I convinced Nathan to confront van Holder, draw him out to get the monkey off his back now that he was President."

"But you wanted to get rid of both of them. What about McDaniel?" Andrew realized that his quest to rescue Dana and clear his name now paled in comparison to the larger conspiracy he had been drawn into.

"His death was convenient. Once van Holder was ruined, information from you would have been used to have McDaniel removed from office."

"The Montana facility."

"Exactly."

"So you did this to become President." Dana said, bewildered.

"I did it because I love my country, as contrite as that sounds. I saw what van Holder was and how McDaniel was, and knew in my heart he couldn't lead the country. The country and the world are better off."

"You don't feel partly responsible for their deaths," Dana intoned.

"Of course I do, but what's done can't be changed. It's time to move forward. The country needs a leader not afraid to make tough decisions."

"Why not let the American people and the world know exactly how McDaniel died?" Dana asked.

"America is a strong country. Allowing the world to see our vulnerability would only hurt us. Nobody needs to know the truth. McDaniel will die a great statesman."

Andrew and Dana nodded silently. Their two deaths were nothing compared to the destruction that these men had wrought on the world.

Jessica stood up to leave. "So, now that this is all behind you, what are your plans?"

Dana looked at Andrew, her eyes beaming. "They're just beginning," she said, wrapping her arms around his neck.

"How do you end McDaniel's story?" Andrew asked between suffocating squeezes.

"The story has already been written. After a valiant battle, he will succumb tonight. I am heading back to Washington to be sworn in as President." She stood up and extended her hand.

"Good Luck, Madam President." Dana stood up and took her hand. Smiling confidently, Jessica Poole grasped Dana's hand like a seasoned politician and departed.

Afterwards, when they were alone again, Andrew recalled the meeting in Washington where Jessica had arranged Dana's rescue. He knew now that he had unwittingly created the scheme that put Jessica on top. Given the nightmare of what might have happened, he was only too happy to oblige.

Epilogue

The morning sun peeked over the horizon, creating a kaleidoscope of colors outside the hotel room window. It was five a.m. when Andrew flopped onto the bed, his bow tie loosened and cummerbund thrown to the side. He watched Dana in front of the window, staring out at the day, exhausted, exhilarated...beautiful. She undid the buckle on her shoes and with a gentle flick of her left foot, then her right, flung them to the corner of the room. Her body sparkled as the light reflected the thousands of tiny costume pearls that adorned her wedding dress. Andrew looked over at his new wife and smiled. The majestic sunrise paled next to her beauty.

"Have I told you how beautiful you are?"

"Only a million times. Help me with this dress, will you."

Andrew rolled off the bed and moved across the room, scooping the large dress into his hands so that he could roam underneath.

"The zipper, you jackass!" Dana slapped his hand. "Twelve hours in this straightjacket is enough, and you aren't making it any easier." She slapped the roaming hand again.

Andrew withdrew his hand, undid the clasp and rolled down the zipper, jumping back onto the bed to watch. Dana turned, curtsied, and retreated to the bathroom near the entrance to their suite to finish disrobing. Andrew doubted she would come out in anything but a fluffy terry towel robe, but waited anxiously just in case.

They were now husband and wife and holding onto the dreams they had shared every day since their departure from the safe house six months earlier. If it had been up to them, they would have had a quick wedding with the justice of the peace. Once they told their parents, however, they had ridden the matrimony freight train to this special day. Dana's Mom had taken it upon herself to organize the grand event. It had been worth the wait. Over four hundred people had attended to celebrate their special day. The contingent from the West Coast—Andrew's horde—had arrived in full force. They had decorated the main ballroom of the hotel in a winter motif, even though it was summer. If they couldn't have a quick, winter wedding, why not bring winter to the wedding? An eight-foot ice sculpture of two swans greeted the guests as they arrived at the reception. The happy couple received a two-week trip to the Caribbean as a wedding present. It was perfect.

Andrew had chatted with Jeremy until he was pulled away to perform other duties. Jeremy told him about his job with Mikos, which put his considerable talents to work. He said he wouldn't miss Bermuda, but Andrew wasn't convinced.

Jessica Poole's presence at the wedding was a surprise to most of the guests. The President had cancelled meetings at Camp David in order to attend. Only she and several close advisors knew about Andrew and Dana's courageous exploits and what they had meant to the American people. As gracious in person as she appeared on camera, Jessica was turning the office of the President into a campaign for world growth and universal freedom, even at the expense of American interests. Her calm approach to clarifying the long-term benefits made even the toughest critics stand down and take notice. Her approval rating was a staggering seventy percent. But on this fine day, Jessica directed the attention to where it belonged by toasting to Andrew and Dana's future.

Marion Fletcher also attended, although few knew about Andrew and Dana's relationship with the Australian businesswoman. She spent most of her time talking to Jessica about the sale of ASC and rounding up the Protocol participants. Only three other people in the room knew what they were talking about.

When van Holder's death was announced, it left ASC with no helmsman and no direction. More importantly, it left one of the largest privately held companies in the country without an owner. William van Holder, recently deceased, left no relatives, no heirs and no will; therefore, the assets of the companies reverted to the United States government. Every state in the union and numerous countries staked a claim for a share of the company. It might have ended up an international fiasco if Jessica Poole hadn't suggested the perfect solution— sell off the companies and assets and create a foundation to promote global commerce. Andrew and Dana were approached to head the foundation. They initially rejected the offer, but after several appeals from Jessica Poole and Marion Fletcher, finally relented. The papers were signed a few days before their wedding and the two of them embarked on a venture that would challenge and satisfy both their eager minds. Their future looked bright, the best part being that they could work together. The ambition that had torn them apart the first time would now work in their favor.

Dana returned from the bathroom, dressed as Andrew had predicted. "I love you," she said, lying down on the bed. She turned to blow a fish-lipped kiss across the bed.

"You're beautiful." Andrew smiled as he returned the gesture.

"Are you ready to leave?"

"I'll make a few phone calls on the way to the airport." He reached over to caress her shoulder underneath the terry robe. "What about you?"

"Same. By the time we get back, the Foundation should be in full swing. Don't stop, that feels nice."

"I wasn't planning on stopping," Andrew said as he continued down past her shoulder.

The pilot, who was sporting a weathered Boston Red Sox baseball cap, began to laugh when he heard where they were headed. "You're the first visitors to the island since I moved the owner to the site last fall." he said, as he stowed the bags in the small cargo hold of the plane. Andrew and Dana turned to each other with questioning looks. *Where exactly were they going?*

The isolated peninsula came into view thirty minutes later. On final approach, the two passengers arched forward to get a better look. It was definitely the private retreat described in the itinerary. The seaplane glided along the calm, green water of the lagoon. As soon as it touched the dock, a boy ran out of a small hut to tie up the plane.

An oasis surrounded by tropical blue waves dominated the landscape. Some small cabins dotted the beach, but it was the main house that drew attention away from the sand and surf. Built entirely of mahogany beams and glass in the shape of a dome, the structure seemed to emerge from the island, blending in as if it were part of the land. A lone man dressed in khakis and sneakers stood at the doorway; hands clasped behind his back.

Andrew and Dana approached the house, absorbed in each other and paying no attention to the man. At the foot of the stairs leading to the main building, they finally looked up. At first, neither of them spoke. They just stared, gaping at their host.

"Harry!" Dana spoke first, looking up at the smiling ghost.

"In the flesh," Harry said.

"We thought you were…"

"Dead. Me too. After I was shot, I drifted down the canal for a mile and apparently snagged onto a houseboat. The owner was home and pulled me out, she saved my life."

"But why didn't you contact us and join us in Bermuda?" Andrew asked, incredulous.

"It felt good to be considered dead." Harry looked at Dana. His eyes said it all.

"Thank you," she mouthed.

"Besides, by disappearing it was easier to help."

"Debitfund…you turned off the tap." Andrew smiled. "You started the game and ended it without ever playing."

"Seeing if it could be done was always the game."

"This is quite the home," Andrew said as he looked around the spacious foyer.

"My dad bought it years ago when the resort went into receivership. He turned it into a private retreat."

"Will you be staying here?" Dana asked.

"I have all the computer power I need," he said, pointing to a satellite dish hidden discreetly in the palms. "Enough of that. Come in…and congratulations. Sorry I couldn't make the wedding. Come, I want you to meet someone; my savior."

Dana looked at Harry and grinned.

"She's a goddess. Come in. She's dying to meet you."

Dana wrapped her arms around her husband and her friend, and the three of them walked into the house. The events that had brought them together were long forgotten, replaced with dreams for the future.

ISBN 1412076616-7